Bold, wanton thought!

This man was an archangel—St. Michael, perhaps. God's warrior.

He ambled closer and her heart began to pound. Though this meeting was really most improper, an unfamiliar excitement, potent and dangerous, skittered through her body as she envisioned…an embrace. A passionate kiss. Moans. Sighs. Her leg bared as his strong, lean hand lifted her skirt…

She flushed, hot with shame at her own vivid imaginings, while he continued to regard her steadily, not with arrogance or lust, but as if he could not look away.

"I beg you to tell me the name of the most beautiful woman at court," the stranger said, his voice soft and deep.

As his gaze seemed to intensify, not with lust or arrogant measure, but with attentive curiosity, Anne realized what she felt: desire. It spread over her like the rays of the sun when the clouds part…

**Praise for _USA TODAY_ bestselling author
MARGARET MOORE'S recent titles**

The Overlord's Bride
"Ms. Moore is a master of the medieval time period."
—_Romantic Times_

The Duke's Desire
"This novel is in true Moore style—
sweet, poignant and funny."
—_Halifax Chronicle-Herald_

A Warrior's Kiss
"Margaret Moore remains consistently innovative,
matching an ending of romantic perfection to the rest
of this highly entertaining read."
—_Romantic Times_

The Welshman's Bride
"This is an exceptional reading experience
for one and all. The Warrior Series will
touch your heart as few books will."
—_Rendezvous_

MARGARET MOORE

A WARRIOR'S LADY

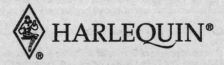

HARLEQUIN®

TORONTO • NEW YORK • LONDON
AMSTERDAM • PARIS • SYDNEY • HAMBURG
STOCKHOLM • ATHENS • TOKYO • MILAN • MADRID
PRAGUE • WARSAW • BUDAPEST • AUCKLAND

ISBN 0-373-29223-6

A WARRIOR'S LADY

Please address questions and book requests to:
Harlequin Reader Service
U.S.: 3010 Walden Ave., P.O. Box 1325, Buffalo, NY 14269
Canadian: P.O. Box 609, Fort Erie, Ont. L2A 5X3

It is both gratifying and humbling to know
that my work is read in so many countries.
This book is dedicated to all my readers
throughout the world, with thanks and affection.

Chapter One

In the great hall of the king's castle at Winchester, Lady Anne Delasaine delicately tore a piece of venison from the portion on the platter before her and held it out to the hound. His flanks aquiver with anticipation, the huge brown beast reached to take the tasty morsel from her fingers. He wolfed it down, then seemed to grin as he waited for more. She smiled in return and pulled off another piece.

The other courtiers supping there could be forgiven for assuming Lady Anne found assuaging the dog's appetite an amusing diversion that took all her feminine attention. In fact, however, she was listening to the conversation of her two dark-haired half brothers seated near her.

"I tell you, it is only a matter of time," the eldest, Damon, said firmly, his voice conspiratorially low. His brown eyes glittered beneath his heavy brows, which looked as if they had been parted by the sharp ridge of his prominent nose. "Henry must realize that he would be wise to listen to Eleanor and her kinsmen. We should be in their counsel.''

As Anne fed the hound another scrap, she kept her dismay and disgust at Damon's arrogant tone and vaulting ambition from her face. After all, he was not discussing a minor noble family—he was speaking of the king and queen of England.

Young Henry had recently wed Eleanor of France, a political match that had already created more tension than it relieved. Anne and her siblings were distantly—very distantly—related to Eleanor through their late father, and Damon had lost no time using that tenuous connection to full advantage. He had insinuated his way into Eleanor's entourage and Henry's court. Not only that, he had managed to include the rest of his family in that entourage, albeit for his own purposes.

"If they don't see that, we'll *make* them," the younger and brawnier Benedict muttered. Holding his knife in his thick fingers, he raised it and split the apple before him as if he were a headsman wielding an ax. "Everyone knows Englishmen are all fools."

"This isn't the place to make such a remark," Damon growled. "In case you haven't noticed, the hall is full of Normans more loyal to Henry than the king of France."

"I don't care what they think, and tomorrow on the tournament field, they'll find out we are the better men."

"Shut your mouth about the English," Damon or-

dered, effectively commanding his brother's silence and his obedience as he had since the death of their father three years ago.

Benedict, as usual, retreated into sulky silence and the matter was apparently closed. Her attention still supposedly on the dog, Anne did not have to see Damon's face to imagine his arrogant smirk. She had seen it often enough when he chastised his siblings, for since their father's death Damon had every right to rule the family, just as Rannulf Delasaine had, and with just as heavy a hand.

"Well, wait until I get a chance with my new tournament sword," Benedict mumbled after a moment. "Blunted it may be, but I'll have bashed a few English heads before I'm through."

"You'd better not ruin it on too many helmets. I'm not paying for a blacksmith to fix it," Damon replied. "You would have been smarter to get something less costly if that was your plan."

"Who was it had to have a new shield, eh, when there was nothing wrong with the old one?" Benedict charged.

Anne stopped listening as they began to quarrel about the new and expensive items they had purchased before traveling to Winchester, for this subject could have little bearing on her life at court and her possible future, which Damon would never discuss directly with her.

She clenched her jaw, knowing well his reason: she was but a woman, so she must do as he commanded.

Next year at this time, she might already be married off to some noble of his choosing, and with child. It would be a match made solely to increase Damon's power and influence, and it would be the fulfillment of what he considered the only thing she was good for. She had been unhappily awaiting that fate ever since she had reached her twelfth year and Damon realized his skinny, gawky half sister with the big eyes was going to be a beauty after all. Ever since, he had guarded her as fiercely as their other valuable possessions, and treated her exactly the same way—as if she had no will or mind or heart.

With a weary sigh she let her gaze rove over the huge hall magnificently decorated to commemorate Saint Edmond the Confessor, whom King Henry had made his patron saint. Henry always celebrated the saint's special day, October 13, with a feast and merrymaking.

The tables were set with fine white linens and silver plates. Torches burned in sconces in the walls, and the flickering flames of beeswax candles added to the illumination. Bright banners hung suspended overhead, and musicians in the gallery played softly, the music nearly drowned out by the conversation and laughter of Henry's guests.

She surveyed the well-dressed ladies in their fine gowns and headdresses, the smartly attired men in their satins and velvets and furs, and the richly colored tapestries. She set herself to enjoying the music of the minstrels and the exceptional food prepared in a variety of new and startling ways.

Across the hall, a boisterous group of young knights, merry and probably more than half in their cups, were clearly having a marvelous time eating the king's food, drinking the king's wine and enjoying the attention of young ladies who seemed utterly captivated by them.

That wasn't so surprising, for they were a good-looking bunch, well built and attractive. The two with curling black hair were the best-looking. They were probably brothers, judging by their coloring and their similar noses and mouths. The other three, who shared brown hair in shades varying from light brown to a rich chestnut, strong jaws and lean features, were also probably related. They were as broad shouldered and muscular as the other two, but not so conventionally handsome. The tallest of these looked to be the oldest, for there was something aloof and imposing in his manner that the others lacked. The youngest of the group appeared little older than her younger brother, Piers, and he was fourteen.

They all seemed very well pleased with themselves. No doubt that went hand in hand with being the spoiled sons of rich men.

A surge of bitterness welled up inside her breast. What would they know of deprivation or harsh punishments? Of being forced to fast, or beaten with a strip of willow for some minor infraction? Probably nothing, and neither would those silly, giggling girls so obviously trying to win their masculine attention.

The envy and bitterness slowly slipped away as she fed the hound again. Those giggling girls would surely be sold off in marriage just as she would be. Could she fault them, then, for having a little harmless flirtation when they had the chance? Wouldn't she, if she wasn't constantly watched over by her half brothers?

If she thought she could get away with it, she would probably be the most high-spirited one of all, knowing that she had but a short time to indulge in such levity.

"Have you gone deaf, Anne?" Damon demanded, his voice a harsh snarl in her ear.

She looked up to find him glaring at her, as he so often did.

She had long ago learned the best way to deal with her aggressive half siblings was to be as placid as possible—and pummel her pillow later. "What is it, Damon?"

"There is Lord Renfrew." Damon nodded at a stout, middle-aged man dressed in a long tunic of brilliant scarlet velvet that made him look like a fat red worm. "He's very rich, and his third wife died last Michaelmas. If he looks at you, smile. If he asks you to join him in the dancing, you will dance. Understand?"

"Yes, Damon, I understand."

His eyes narrowed as if he wasn't sure whether he believed her or not.

In truth, she had no intention of disobeying. If Lord

Renfrew looked at her, she would make a very cold, very unpleasant smile that would imply she would sooner eat dung than talk to him. If he asked her to dance, she would accept, and then she would step on his toes and ignore whatever he said. On the other hand, it might be better to avoid that situation entirely, in case the nobleman complained of her to Damon.

She rose and put her hand to her brow. "Unfortunately, Damon, I have a pain in my head. I think I had best retire."

Benedict joined Damon in his glowering.

"You do want me at my best, do you not?" she asked. "I will not be if I remain. Besides, don't you think a little air of mystery a good idea? I have appeared, potential suitors have seen me, so let me leave them wondering about me. You should stay here, of course. You may have another chance to remind Queen Eleanor that we are related to her."

She held back a relieved sigh as, after a moment's reflection, Damon nodded his permission. "Go straight to your chamber," he commanded with a scowl. "Don't talk to anyone."

"Not even Lord Renfrew?"

Damon gave her a disgruntled look. "If he addresses you, you may speak to him. Nobody else."

It was on the tip of her tongue to query him about the king, but she decided she would be wiser to get away before Damon and Benedict decided to accompany her, a prospect about as delightful as having a guard of sly and surly wolves.

After swiftly leaving the hall, she slowed her pace to stroll along the corridor lit by torches. Their smoke drifted out through long, narrow windows open to the air. She wrapped her arms about herself and shivered, in spite of the heavy velvet brocade gown she wore, for the October night was chill. She would be glad to get to her chamber, which would be warmed by a brazier full of glowing coals. There she could get into bed and let herself remember all that she had seen before she drifted off to sleep.

She would think of the beautiful gowns and rich fabrics. She would imagine that she was one of that giggly gaggle of girls, except that in her waking dream she would bandy such clever words with the young men, they would be agog.

She wondered who that particular group of young men were and where they came from. Were they English or French or some other nationality? Were they sons of great lords or minor nobility? Were any of them married? What of the one who seemed more mature than the others?

She heard a sound behind her and halted, turning to see what it was. A mouse, perhaps, or the wind.

A man stood in the shadows.

She stiffened, then reminded herself she was in the king's castle, and there were many soldiers on guard. She had but to scream, and she would be heard. As her half brothers knew, she could scream very loudly.

The man stepped out of the shadows into the flickering light of the torches. It was the eldest of that merry group in the hall, the one with chestnut-brown hair. The aloof, impressive one.

Standing up, he seemed even more splendid than when he had been sitting down, with long, lean legs she had no business staring at. His plain black tunic reached to mid-thigh and stretched across broad shoulders. The pristine white shirt beneath made his tanned face seem even more masculine.

Most intriguing and unusual, though, were his eyes. They were light-gray and rimmed with black, so startling a contrast to his dark complexion, they seemed to glow in the torchlight. His nose was particularly fine, and his lips were full and made her wonder what they would be like to kiss.

Bold, wanton thought!

Still, those others in the hall could not really compare, not now. The curly-haired young men could be cherubs, while this man was an archangel—Saint Michael, perhaps. God's warrior.

He ambled closer and her heart began to pound, the throbbing loud in her ears. This was a situation entirely new to her, and entirely exciting. But this meeting was really most improper.

Yet her half brothers were back there in the hall, no doubt quarreling about something. Piers was in his room, sulking because Damon had made him stay behind as punishment for not polishing his armor well enough. She was, in the only sense she ever was, free, if only for a little while.

An unfamiliar excitement, potent and dangerous, skittered through her body as she envisioned a clandestine rendezvous with this man. Her mind reeled as pictures of what might happen in a secluded corridor flashed unbidden into her imagination.

An embrace. A passionate kiss. Moans. Sighs. Her leg bared as his strong, lean hand lifted her skirt...

She flushed, hot with shame at her own vivid imaginings, while he continued to regard her steadily, not with arrogance or lust, but as if he could not look away.

No one had ever looked at her like that, and no gaze had ever made her feel so warm and yet so full of dread at the same time. It was not fear that he might hurt her, though, a fear she already knew too well. She could not yet name the powerful new feeling surging through her.

"Who are you?" she demanded, trying to sound calmer than she felt.

"I want to ask you the same question. I beg you to tell me the name of the most beautiful woman at court," the stranger said, his voice soft and deep and very different from her siblings' harsh tones. Damon and Benedict sounded like bears. This man sounded as she imagined a majestic stag would, if stags could speak.

As his gaze seemed to intensify with attentive curiosity, Anne realized what she felt: desire. It spread over her like the rays of the sun when the clouds part.

Her mind urged caution. No matter how thrilling she found him, or how outrageously flattered she was by his attention, she was a lady, not some simple peasant girl, or even one of those flighty creatures in the king's hall. This young man had no business following her or speaking to her, and he had to know that as well as she. If he thought she would not mind, or even welcomed his advances, what did that say of his opinion of her?

Maybe she should flee—except that would be the action of a coward, and she was not a coward. Instead Anne straightened her shoulders and haughtily said, ''Who are you, to follow me in this insolent manner and ask who I am?''

Oh, God, Reece thought as he felt his face warm with a blush. He wished he had stayed in the hall and ignored his impetuous, uncharacteristic impulse to follow the blond beauty. He should leave, but to back away now would be fleeing like a coward. While he was certainly shy around women, he was no coward.

Nevertheless he knew full well he didn't have the charm, the eloquence or the looks of his friends. He had always been content to wait patiently nearby, half-afraid to open his mouth in case he sounded like a fool.

Until tonight, when he had spotted the tranquil,

golden-haired woman across the hall wearing a green gown of shining samite that fairly sparkled in the candlelight. She had to be unmarried, for her long, golden hair was uncovered and done in two braids, the ends encased in bronze. Her hair had glowed in the light like a halo, and she had seemed as serenely different from the rest of the young women at the court as an angel would. So he had foolishly decided to follow her from the hall.

The die was cast, he decided, and he must see it through.

But please, God, he silently and fervently prayed, *do not let her see me blush like a lad!*

"Forgive me, lady," he said with a contrite bow. "I meant no insult."

To his surprise, she didn't immediately turn on her heel and march away. Instead, her full lips turned up in a little smile.

It was like thinking your lance was broken and discovering instead that it was whole.

"Although you seem an impertinent fellow," she said, "I was not insulted."

"Then will you tell me your name, despite my impertinence?"

Her shapely brow rose in query. "You wish to know my name and nothing more?"

In truth, he wanted to know everything about her, but he had achieved much already and did not dare to hope for more. "Perhaps that should be all, lest I discover you are wed or promised to another."

Her brows lowered as she studied him, and he cringed inwardly. Obviously, that had not been a wise thing to say.

"I am not, but this is hardly the time or place to make introductions, sir."

He moved closer, almost as if pulled to her by an invisible thread. Maybe there was such a thread, for that might explain the tightening sensation he felt in his chest.

As if by divine inspiration, he remembered something he had heard Blaidd Morgan say to a woman once. Blaidd attracted women like blossoms did a bee. "Please, won't you take pity on me and tell me your name? Otherwise, I may risk injury in the tournament tomorrow, being overtired because I could not sleep for wondering."

Her brows, a shade darker than her hair, rose yet farther, and her green eyes that already sparkled like emeralds in a rich man's ring seemed to glitter even more, and—he was very pleased to believe—with merriment. "So if I do not tell you my name, and you happen to be injured on the morrow, it will be my fault?"

To his dismay, her glittering gaze faltered, and a frown clouded her visage. "I do not want such a responsibility. I assure you, sir knight, I already have enough burdens to bear."

The note of sadness in her voice touched his heart. "Forgive me, my lady, if I add to your distress in any way. I do not seek to add to the troubles you may have."

Her beautiful eyes widened, as if she was taken aback by his response. "It is a rare man who cares for a stranger's woes."

Reece flushed again, for her tone was full of both wonder and praise.

Then that gloriously merry glimmer seemed to light her from within again. "Besides, you have not told me your name, either."

She straightened her shoulders and issued a charming challenge. "If you first tell me your name, humble petitioner, I shall tell you mine."

His heart started to pound as it did before a lance charge and new hope thundered into life with it. She must not think him a complete fool after all. "My name is Sir—"

"Anne!"

The man's bellowing voice echoed off the walls of the corridor and the unknown beauty tensed as if she had just been caught perpetrating a serious crime.

God save him, he had not considered how it would look to others if they were seen or found together. He had been too intent upon learning who she was. Before he could speak, she did.

"Go!" She ordered him as if he were a foot soldier.

She pointed down the corridor to the door at the opposite end. ''Leave me to deal with Damon.''

Who, in the name of the saints, was Damon, and what was he to her? Brother? Cousin? Betrothed?

Not the latter, he most fervently hoped.

Whoever he was, as the dark-haired man came charging toward them, another dark-haired, bigger man following right behind, it was obvious he could not leave this fascinating young woman to deal with them alone.

If there was fault here, it was not hers. She had not enticed him or led him there, and he would certainly make that very clear.

As the two men bore down upon them, he recognized them as the men who had been sitting beside her in the king's hall. Because she had been paying no heed to them, and she was fair while they were dark, he had assumed they were not relations or had any claim upon her.

Obviously he was wrong, and if he had not been distracted by Blaidd right before she left the hall, he might have seen her speak to them. Unfortunately, Blaidd had just chastised him for staring, then started to tease him. Reece had turned away to tell his Welsh friend that Blaidd had quite the history of being distracted by women himself, so he should keep his mouth shut. If she had talked to these fellows, he had missed it.

The woman—Anne, he now knew—shoved him in

a way no person ever had. "You may leave me to deal with them, sir knight."

"I will not," he said firmly. "The impropriety is mine, and mine alone."

Clearly enraged, the two men came to a panting halt in front of him, their wine-soaked breath disgusting him. Their extreme reaction to a minor impropriety was no doubt fueled by wine.

He took the offensive as they tried to catch their breath. "Who are you?"

"We're her brothers," the biggest one growled, his beefy hands bunching into fists. "Who the devil are you?"

"I know who he is," the taller one declared as his lip curled in a sneer. "It's that bastard's son. This lout accosting Anne is Reece Fitzroy."

A jolt of anger shot through Reece, even as the big lout's eyes widened and fear bloomed in his eyes. So, he had heard of Reece Fitzroy, or if not him, his father, the man reputed to be the finest trainer of knights in England, and who was indeed a bastard.

"*Sir* Reece Fitzroy," he corrected. He made no effort to keep the scorn from his voice. "To whom have I the *honor* of speaking?"

The tall one drew himself up. "I am Sir Damon Delasaine of Montbleu, this is my brother Benedict and this lady you are bothering is my sister."

Reece felt like a bellows with a slow leak. He had heard of the notorious Delasaines. They would be the first on a list of all the families in the world a man of honorable ambition should avoid. He could hardly believe that this beautiful, spirited woman, so different from any woman he had ever met, was their sister.

"*Half* sister," Anne declared, as if determined to have that difference noted at once. She then addressed Damon Delasaine. "He was not bothering me, Damon. We were merely talking."

"Shut up and go, Anne," he snarled in response, "before we decide to let you share the beating he has earned."

Another jolt of anger, mixed with indignation and scorn, energized Reece. He stepped forward, the action alone—and perhaps his fierce expression—forcing Damon back. "I have heard of the Delasaines, and all I have heard is obviously true," he growled. "You are a base coward, for only a coward would strike a woman."

As Damon stared with glowering disbelief, Reece turned to Anne. "Thank you, my lady, for defending me, but I will fight my own battles. Go, as he says, and leave me to do it."

"Yes, go," Benedict snarled, pushing her roughly away.

At that sight, Reece's self-control snapped. He grabbed Benedict's arm and yanked him back so hard, he nearly pulled the lout's arm from its socket. "Let her alone, or by God, you'll regret it!"

Benedict stumbled as Reece let him go, but he

quickly recovered, and his eyes gleamed with malice and glee, the look of a man who enjoyed brawling, or beating up women. "Think so?"

Reece nodded. "Oh, believe me, you will."

Benedict held out his arms and gestured for him to approach. "Come on and try it then, cur."

"Reece, behind you!" Anne screeched.

Before he could turn, Reece felt an unexpected, sharp pain in his side as Damon's dagger slid along his rib. He fell to his knees and Benedict's heavy fist struck his face as Anne let loose with a bloodcurdling scream.

Chapter Two

Voices. Whispering voices. Hushed words swirling about in the darkness.

Reece's head ached as if a twenty pound sack of grain pressed upon it and his side felt as if it was pierced with a hot iron.

What the devil had…

The memories returned, dim at first, then rapidly growing clearer.

Lady Anne. Her brothers. No, half brothers. The agonizing pain in his side. Although he had only spoken to Lady Anne, he had been most foully and cowardly attacked from behind by Damon Delasaine.

The man was going to pay for that, and if he had harmed his innocent sister, Delasaine would pay even more. He had to get up and find out what had happened, as well as where the devil he was.

His eyelids cracked open. The beamed ceiling looked familiar and the stone walls… He was in the chamber in the king's castle he was sharing with his brothers, and it was very dimly lit. His eyelids fluttered closed again.

"Reece?"

That was the voice of his brother, Gervais.

"He's awake."

That was his youngest brother, Trevelyan.

"No, he's not," Gervais said in what was supposed to pass for a whisper. "He just groaned in his sleep."

What time of day was it? Reece wondered as he tried to wet his dry lips to speak. He moved in preparation of sitting up, and the pain sliced through him, wrenching another groan from his desert-dry throat.

"I say he *is* awake and we should summon the infirmerer," Trev whispered, his voice strained from more than the effort of keeping his naturally loud voice soft. "He said we should fetch him when Reece awoke."

"We should wait until we're sure," the ever-cautious Gervais retorted. "I don't want you to go running all over the castle for no reason."

Reece opened his eyes again and put his hand on his side. He was bare chested, with a cloth wrapped about him. A bandage, obviously, and it was damp where the worst pain was. He looked down and saw the blood as he struggled to sit up.

Gervais gently pushed him down. "Keep still, brother," he commanded with no attempt at a muted tone, his voice as firm as a general's but with relief in it, too. "You've lost enough blood, and they punched you in the face, too, the louts."

Yes, he remembered that, as anger swept through him, albeit accompanied by humiliation. He should have been more careful of Damon Delasaine and able to triumph over both them. Two on one shouldn't have made a difference.

"Can you see?" Gervais asked.

Reece nodded and forced his thoughts away from his own anger and shame. "What happened to Lady Anne after they attacked me?"

Gervais didn't answer right away. He came around the bed, leaned forward and lightly covered Reece's left eye with the palm of his hand. "And now?"

"Yes. Lady Anne—?"

"Thank God!" Gervais said with a sigh as he moved back and sat on the cot. "We were afraid he'd blinded you in your right eye. How's your head?"

"It hurts." Reece reached out and grabbed Gervais's arm. The lunge made him cry out at the sudden jab of pain from his side, but he asked his question with stern authority. *"What of Lady Anne?"*

"Taken to her bed, or so her brothers claim," Trev said from the foot of the cot, reminding Reece he was there.

He didn't like the sound of that. Either she was avoiding people because she was embarrassed or ashamed, or she had another reason, such as a bruised body, to stay hidden away.

If her siblings had harmed her in any way, they would rue the day as soon as the wound in his side had healed enough for him to challenge them to combat, either singly or together. He would be more than prepared for their treachery now.

"Damn, Reece, let go! You're going to break my arm."

"Sorry," he muttered as he released Gervais and lay back down, panting as the pain ebbed. "How long?"

"How long since they attacked you?" Gervais asked.

He nodded.

"It's midmorning after."

"Those damn Delasaines stabbed you in the back," Trev said, his voice very loud in the quiet of the room.

Not exactly the back, Reece knew, although Damon's blow had been cowardly just the same.

"By the time the king's guards got there, you were out cold," Trev continued.

Gervais regarded Reece with woeful sympathy, as if he were a sick baby. "Thank God the dagger ran along a rib, so no serious harm done. All you need is rest and time to heal. Don't give the tournament another thought. There'll be others."

Reece stifled another groan, this time of disappointment and dismay. He had planned to distinguish himself at the king's tournament. No chance of that now, thanks to the Delasaines.

"What about you?" he asked Gervais, who was also to be a competitor.

His brother shrugged. "As I said, there will be

plenty of tournaments to come. I wanted to stay with you.''

So both of their chances for honor and glory had been taken away.

''And it was a good thing he did, to stave off the rumors those Delasaines started to spread this morning,'' Trev declared. ''You won't believe what they're saying, those no-good, disgusting—''

''Leave it, Trev, until he's more himself,'' Gervais ordered.

Reece wasn't in so much pain that he didn't see the concern flit across Gervais's face.

''What?'' he demanded, once more trying to sit up. ''What are they saying?''

''Don't worry yourself about anything except healing,'' Gervais commanded, again pushing him down, although not so gently this time. ''We'll deal with those blackguards.''

The Delasaines were his problem, not Gervais's and certainly not young Trevelyan's. ''Leave them alone.''

''But Reece—''

''Until I am better.''

A look of understanding appeared in Gervais's worried eyes. ''Ah. You'll have your own vengeance, is that it?''

Reece nodded, although vengeance was not precisely the term he would use for what he intended. A lesson was more like. The Delasaines' anger might have been justifiable, but not the attack, or its savagery. He would instruct them on the concept of a punishment appropriate to the crime, one at a time. And if they had harmed one hair on Lady Anne's head, they would learn another lesson.

Trev gasped. "By the saints, I should fetch the infirmerer!"

He didn't wait for his older brothers to concur; he dashed from the room like a startled rabbit.

Regardless of Gervais's attempts to hold him down, and despite the throbbing in his head, Reece finally managed to sit up. "Now, what exactly are the Delasaines saying?"

Gervais frowned, reminding Reece of their father when he was displeased. "I would rather we didn't talk about this until you're more yourself."

"Tell me."

"They're saying you were…threatening…their sister."

"Threatening?" That was bad enough. Unfortunately, he was certain, by Gervais's tone, that there was more—or worse.

Gervais shrugged, as if the exact wording wasn't important. "Attacking."

"Attacking?"

Reece's heart began to pound. That was a very serious charge indeed, yet one that would justify their "punishment," and so the safest one for them. No one could assault a knight and not have to give a good reason. A simple breech of propriety was not nearly good enough.

Gervais's expression held resignation, and a confirmation Reece did not really want to see. "Aye, that's what they're saying, to excuse what they did. Nobody believes—"

"The king?" Reece interjected, naming the one man whose opinion in this business truly mattered, the one man who had the power to reward or punish or accuse as he saw fit. "Surely Henry doesn't believe it."

"We haven't heard what Henry thinks." Gervais cleared his throat. "Unfortunately, the Delasaines are related to Eleanor. Distantly, but related."

That was not good news. She might back them simply for the sake of a family tie.

Reece leaned against the wall behind the cot and closed his eyes again. This was bad. Terrible. With one impulsive act he may have put his whole future in jeopardy.

All his life Reece had had one dream: to be in the king's retinue, his inner circle, one of his trusted advisors. He could represent the minor lords whose ancestors did not come from the noble families of Normandy but whose forebears had more humble origins, winning their titles by skill and intelligence rather than solely by their birth. Now, by making enemies of relatives of the queen, he might have destroyed his chances.

Worst of all, if he had troubled himself to find out who the beauty was beforehand, he would have known to steer very clear of her, and her vicious brutes of brothers.

"The French make no protest about the Delasaines' accusation, of course, because of their relationship to Eleanor. Everyone else refuses to believe them. There have been several arguments already, and I think Blaidd Morgan's been in three fist-fights."

"Oh, God."

"Aye, Reece, it's not good—but they started it."

"I started it," Reece muttered. "I shouldn't have followed her."

"Harmless, that was."

"Obviously, it was not."

Gervais studied him closely, as if trying to read his thoughts. "It's, um, not like you to talk to a woman you haven't been introduced to, or even one you have, Reece." He ran his hand through his shoulder-length hair. "God's wounds, brother, it's not like you to talk to a woman at all, especially one as beautiful as that. What got into you?"

"I wish I could say it was the king's wine," Reece muttered, feeling the heat of a blush and recalling Blaidd's teasing comments that made him want to squirm.

"I don't know," he said at last. He shrugged, then winced.

"You should have at least told us where you were going."

Reece quirked an eyebrow. "Oh, and you and the

others would not have joked and teased and made sport of me all the more?''

Gervais wisely did not even try to disagree.

''I shouldn't have gone in the first place.''

''Aye, but you cannot change it now. Still, Father isn't going to be happy, and Mother will have a fit when she sees your face and hears you've been stabbed.''

Gervais always was a master of understatement. His father was going to think he had taken leave of his senses and acted like a fool. As for his wounds, his mother would want to examine him and fuss over him and generally make him feel about six years old.

He gingerly touched his swollen cheek, wondering how he looked. ''Is it bad?''

''It'll take a while for the swelling to go down, and you've bled in your eye, so it's as red as a demon's. The infirmerer says you should regain your strength soon enough, since you are—'' Gervais assumed a learned, pompous air ''—a healthy young man in the prime of life.'' He resumed his normal manner. ''Mother and Father will both be glad you're not dead, of course, but I think maybe we should leave Anne Delasaine out of it when we tell them what happened.''

''How can we?''

''The important thing is that you were viciously attacked on a poor pretext.''

Reece shook his head. ''I made a mistake, and there's no point lying about it.''

"I'm not saying we should lie," Gervais retorted, mightily affronted. "I'm simply suggesting that we leave the lady out of it."

"What reason would you have me give for my beating? And unless you plan to muzzle everyone at court or swear them to secrecy, they will hear the truth eventually. It would be better if they heard it from me."

Gervais's brows lowered as he regarded his brother's resolute face. "You won't say you deserved it or some such nonsense?"

"The Delasaines were wrong to attack me as they did, but I was wrong to follow Lady Anne and speak to her alone. I will say that to anybody who asks or speaks of what happened."

"Damn your honorable hide," Gervais muttered as he plucked at Reece's blanket. "I should have known better than to suggest anything less than the full and complete truth to you. Well, Father will make them sorry, whatever they say."

Reece tensed. "This is for me to deal with, Gervais. My lesson to teach."

Gervais's brown eyes flared with bright understanding and a warrior's approval. "I should have known you were going to say that, too."

"Then you agree to let me deal with this matter as I see fit?"

Gervais got to his feet and bowed with a flourish. "As you command, my liege, thus it will be."

"Good," Reece mumbled, knowing he could trust

Gervais to keep his word, no matter how jestingly he spoke. "Make sure Trev understands this, too."

"I will, brother, I will."

Standing at the window of her chamber in the king's castle assigned to her use during her family's residence in Winchester, Anne watched the sun set. The rest of the night and a whole day had passed since she had encountered Sir Reece Fitzroy in the corridor.

Closing her eyes, she again saw Damon's vicious, dishonorable blow. She had grabbed his arm and pulled him back, but he had shaken her off the way a dog might shake a rabbit. Thank God the king's guards had arrived.

They had listened to Damon explain, aided by Benedict, as some of the other soldiers carried away an unconscious Sir Reece. Once she knew he was safe, and seeing her half brothers occupied, she had slipped away and fled to her chamber. She had not seen Damon or Benedict since, but someone had turned the key in the lock of the door to her chamber later that night, and she was imprisoned yet.

As the hours had slowly passed, she had hoped Sir Reece's injuries were not life threatening. He had lost blood, the damp stain on his tunic evidence of that, and a terrible bruise had been forming beneath his eye the last time she had seen him.

She had remembered other things, too—the excitement most of all. She had never felt that way in her life and probably never would again. She doubted any

of her brother's choices for a husband would be able
to create even an instant's desire or passion. Unfortunately, if Sir Reece survived—and please God, he
must!—she was sure he would never want to have
anything to do with her again.

How long Damon intended to keep her here without
food or water she could not guess, but this was the
king's castle, not Montbleu, so her continued absence
would be more difficult to explain. Surely they could
not keep her here without food or water for much
longer.

Anne started when she heard the key in the lock of
her bedchamber door, then steeled herself as Damon
sauntered inside. She had been right not to expect Lisette, a maidservant from the queen's household assigned to her upon their arrival, Damon being too par-
simonious to bring any servants from Montbleu. In
truth, however, she preferred the vivacious, merry Lisette to the dour, ancient maidservant who cared for
her at home.

Her half brother twirled a heavy iron key around
his finger as he surveyed the chamber. This room was
certainly much finer than the small bedchamber she
had at home, and better furnished. In addition to the
wide bed with feather tick, there was a dressing table
and stool, a chair and bright tapestries on the walls.
The coverlet on the bed was silk, and the candles on
the table were made of beeswax. In the corner stood
the large chest containing the new garments Damon
had purchased for her before they came here, fine

feathers to entrap a rich husband, which was why he had been so uncharacteristically generous.

"Hungry?" Damon asked as he sat in the chair, carelessly crushing a cushion. Still spinning the key around his finger, he threw one leg over the arm and rested his elbow on the other.

Hiding her relief, she kept her expression bland. "I assume from your casual manner that you did not kill Sir Reece, or surely you would be busily plotting your defense at the king's court."

Damon smiled his evil little smile. "Of course he did not die. I struck to wound, not to kill."

Damon no more had the finesse or skill to strike in such a calculated way than she did, but she hid her skepticism from him, along with her other emotions.

"Of course you are hungry," he answered for her as he tucked the key into the wide leather belt around his waist. "But you will have no food tonight, either. That will teach you to talk to an unworthy young man and interfere in his just punishment."

Even though righteous indignation at his vicious attack on Sir Reece, as well as her subsequent imprisonment, burned inside her, Anne regarded her half brother with a bland expression and stoic silence. He was an arrogant, ambitious fool who had no idea of the magnitude of the possible repercussions from his actions last night, results that had also haunted her thoughts and kept her from sleeping. He couldn't have, or he wouldn't be so smug.

She watched him steadily, and fought to keep the

full force of her ire from her voice. "For a man who
has been calculating my worth for so long, you seem
blind to the implications of your attack upon Sir
Reece. For one knight to attack another in such a way,
and in the king's own castle, bespeaks extreme provocation. So what will the courtiers believe actually
transpired between Sir Reece and me? What could
constitute such provocation? Not simply talk. They
will think he was doing considerably more—and what,
then, will happen to my value as a maiden bride?"

Damon didn't look at all upset. "We were completely justified based on the shocking sight of Fitzroy
insolently accosting you in the corridor. But have no
fear, Anne. I made you quite the martyr. Indeed, you
should be pleased and grateful for all that I have said
in your defense."

She could well imagine the lies he would spread,
falsehoods that would justify what they had done, and
no doubt portray her as a helpless victim. "I am to be
grateful that you have portrayed me as the meek little
lamb in the clutches of the ravening wolf?"

"Clever girl."

Yet he was not so clever. "Then what explanation
have you given for punishing me?" she asked as she
crossed her arms over her chest, as if she could keep
her temper in check that way. "I should know it,
should I not? Or do you intend to keep me imprisoned
until it is time to go back to Montbleu?"

Damon's smile grew and his eyes gleamed with evil
mischief. "I have told everyone that you are so upset

by Sir Reece's unwelcome attentions, you have taken to your bed.''

He was, regrettably, a very good liar and she didn't doubt that most people would believe that explanation.

Nevertheless, she dared to raise a skeptical brow. ''With no servants to tend to me?''

''No, for you see, you are a woman of such delicate sensibilities, you cannot bear to be seen by anyone after what happened last night, although you have done nothing wrong. You will speak only to me, and I am doing my best to persuade you to come out. Why, you are even too distraught to eat. I assure you, the women of the court, and all the men save Fitzroy's brothers and those Welsh friends of his, are most sympathetic.''

Damon was cruel, he was greedy, he was a bully, but she could not deny this explanation would probably sound plausible to those who did not know them. ''We did nothing wrong, Damon,'' she repeated.

''Fasting is good for the soul.''

And you never fast because you have no soul.

Damon put both feet on the ground and his hands on his knees. He leaned forward, watching her intently. ''What did that bastard's son say to you?''

''He only wanted to know my name. He knows it well enough now.''

Damon snorted, his good humor apparently restored, as he slumped back in the chair. ''I daresay he does, and I daresay he won't forget it.'' He gave her a sly, knowing look. ''Piers is most upset.''

At the mention of her beloved brother's name, she stiffened.

Damon and Benedict were the children of their father's first wife. Anne and Piers were born of his second, who had died giving Piers life when Anne was seven years old. Since then, Anne had stood in a mother's place for him, and her love for Piers was as intense as any mother's could be.

"I would have preferred to tell him what happened myself," she said, trying not to let Damon see how upset she was.

"I could not allow that," Damon said, his smile thin and smugly satisfied.

No, he would want to paint his own picture and put his despicable actions in an honorable light.

It was bad enough to imagine the rumors and gossip flying about the court; she could not bear to think of Piers being fed lies. "What exactly did you tell him?"

"The truth—that our family honor was sullied and we punished the man responsible."

"And me? What did you say of my part in it?"

"I said the same to him as I have said to everyone, that Sir Reece insolently accosted you. I told him, as I did all the other nobles, that you were quite innocently set upon."

Damon's expression darkened. "Do not even think of contradicting a word of what I have said to anybody when I let you out tomorrow—not even Piers—or you know what I shall do."

Yes, she did know. He had made the same threat

for years, ever since she had been old enough to marry off, or sent to a convent. If she did not do as he said, he would see to it that she never saw Piers again.

"Very well, Damon," she replied, her loathing increasing as it did every time he threatened her.

Steepling his fingers, Damon smiled. "You have not asked how we fared in the tournament."

"I do not have to." She could tell by the look of blatant triumph on his face. "You are obviously uninjured, so I assume you were victorious."

"I won a fine ransom that amounts to nearly what we spent on you."

Damon acted as if she had personally bankrupted the family, but considering how little they had spent on her before deciding it was time to display her at court, she did not think the sum could be so very great.

Damon slapped his hands upon the arms of the chair and heaved himself to his feet. "Tomorrow you may rejoin the court. I would not be so cruel as to prevent you from seeing your beloved Piers on the day of his first melee."

Her heart lifted. Although she had done her best to hide her fears from the rest of her family, she was worried about Piers's first tournament, when he would be competing with other knights' squires. Damon and Benedict had taught him what they knew, but they were not good teachers and their lessons were faulty. They depended upon brute strength to win, not wisdom or skill. She dreaded that Piers, thinner and less muscular than they, would discover the hard way that rushing in and striking as often as possible was not necessarily a winning method.

Damon reached out and grabbed her chin, squeezing it hard enough that it brought tears of pain to her eyes. "Make sure you smile at Lord Renfrew when next you see him, Anne. He is most concerned for your welfare and impressed by your maidenly dismay." Damon's expression hardened. "And remember this. You agree with everything we say about what happened last night, or you'll regret it, just as Reece Fitzroy does."

At the reminder of the cowardly way they had set upon Sir Reece, her temper flared once more.

"You're bruising the merchandise, Damon," she muttered despite the pressure of his hand.

He laughed as he let her go. "Merchandise. I like that," he remarked as he sauntered toward the door.

While she rubbed her aching jaw, he paused and looked back at her over his shoulder. "A commodity to be sold or traded—that's exactly what you are, and all you're good for. Never forget that, Anne, no matter how many young fools talk to you."

Chapter Three

"Oh, la, my lady!" Lisette cried as she tied the lacing at the back of Anne's bodice the next morning. "You have been the talk of the court."

Rejuvenated by the bread, cheese and ale Lisette had brought from the kitchen—"For your brother says you are still too distraught to attend mass and break the fast in the hall, my lady!"—Anne didn't bother to subdue a sigh. She would be the object of curiosity and speculation, and it was tempting to stay in her bedchamber of her own volition, except that for once Damon had kept his word and she wanted to be in the hall waiting for Piers when the squires' melee was over. She could not watch the actual tournament, for that was considered most improper for ladies. The sight of two groups of armed combatants clashing in battle, even with blunted weapons, was thought to be too upsetting for their delicate sensibilities.

"There is no need for sorrow, my lady," Lisette said, sympathy in her cheerful voice as she adjusted the shoulders of Anne's emerald-green overtunic. The gown beneath was a darker green, trimmed with gold embroidery. "No one blames you for what happened that night."

Anne went over to the dressing table and sat upon the stool so that Lisette could arrange her hair. She picked up her hand mirror, an expensive item that Damon had complained about but purchased anyway. She was sure he had done that only to impress the maidservant, who was sure to gossip with other ladies' servants, who would tell their mistresses. He wanted all the court to believe they were wealthier than they actually were.

Anne ostensibly examined her eyes, but she was really looking at Lisette, to gauge her reactions better. "What do they say of Sir Reece's part in it?"

The maid flushed as she reached for the comb made of ivory. "I do not know what they think."

Anne didn't believe that for a moment. "It will not upset me if you speak of him, Lisette."

Indeed, she felt nearly desperate to learn more about the only man who had ever come to her defense. Of course, he had been wrong to approach her, but she had forgiven him for that almost at once.

Lisette's hazel eyes got back their familiar sparkle. "They are saying it must be a misunderstanding, my lady, for he is an honorable man. But he is young and so perhaps..." Lisette hesitated a moment, obviously searching for the appropriate word. "He was over-eager, carried away by desire. There is no denying your beauty, my lady.''

"Does this often happen with Sir Reece? Has he been 'carried away' before?''

Lisette shook her head vigorously. "Oh, no, my lady. That is why all the other ladies' tongues are moving so quickly. Never before. Yet he is so handsome, so strong, so silent, so mysterious...there is probably not a one of the unmarried ladies who do not wish he had followed her instead.'' She smiled slyly. "I think more than one married lady wishes he had, too.''

Strong, silent and mysterious—exactly the words to describe him. He was not anxious to boast or brag of his accomplishments, or spout fulsome compliments on her looks. Yet those eyes of his, so serious, so intense...no man had ever made her feel so beautiful or desirable, and all before he had said a single word.

"As long as they did not have relatives quick to anger. What do they say about what my half brothers did?''

Lisette frowned. "That they, too, were impetuous, and overzealous in their protection of their sister.''

Anne could barely keep the scowl from her face.

Lisette's slender fingers moved swiftly and with great skill as she braided Anne's bountiful blond hair. "They are all young men of spirit, my lady. What can one do but excuse them?''

Anne was in no humor to excuse Damon and Benedict, but she had no wish to discuss them more. "Sir

Reece's name is vaguely familiar, yet I cannot remember how I may have heard it.''

"His father is Sir Urien Fitzroy, famous for training knights,'' Lisette replied. "He has taught many of the nobility's sons, so of course Sir Reece and his brothers are very welcome at court.''

"Oh, yes.'' Those two young men who resembled him must, she reasoned, be those brothers.

Anne thought of all that Damon had said when he confronted Sir Reece. "Sir Urien was not nobly born himself, was he?''

Lisette shook her head vigorously as she reached for a ribbon to hold the braids in place over Anne's ears. "He is a bastard, they say—but so was William the Conquerer.''

"I noticed that Sir Reece was with some other young men last night, in addition to his brothers. Were they trained by his father, too?''

Lisette giggled and blushed. "*Oui.* Those are the Morgans, from Wales. Their father is a great friend of Sir Urien, and so yes, they trained with him. They are very amusing and *very* charming, the oldest one in particular. Blaidd is his name. He told me it means *wolf* in Welsh, but he may only have been teasing me. Those eyes he has, so merry and yet—''

A loud knock sounded on the door, making both the women jump.

Maybe Piers was hurt and this was a summons to the tournament field!

Anne rushed to the door and threw it open to find

a male servant with iron-gray hair and wearing a rust-colored woolen tunic standing on the threshold. "Yes?" she demanded breathlessly.

"My lady, you are to come with me, if you please."

"Why?"

He blinked. "I have no idea, my lady. The king tells me to bring you to the hall, so I bring you to the hall."

"It's not my brother?"

The man was too well trained to show much of his confusion. "No, my lady."

Lisette tugged at the back of her gown. "The king! The hall! Oh, la, my lady, we must finish your *toilette!*"

The man frowned a little as Anne let herself be pulled back to the dressing table.

"King Henry said *at once,*" he noted.

"*Mon Dieu,* she cannot go with her hair in the nest of a rat!" Lisette exclaimed, grabbing the silken scarf that matched the green of Anne's gown.

Anne rose. "I should not keep the king waiting. Never mind the scarf, Lisette."

Lisette stared at Anne as if she had decided to approach the king wearing filthy, soiled rags, then began to urge her mistress to adjust her sleeves, wear the scarf and pinch her cheeks to give them color for she was too pale by far.

Her stomach a knot of dread, Anne ignored her maid's exclamations. She had no desire to emphasize her cursed beauty and she truly believed it would be folly to keep the king waiting.

As for what Henry wanted, that wasn't so hard to guess: he must have heard about what had happened with Sir Reece.

If only her brutal half brothers had let Sir Reece go with a warning! If only she had fled the moment Sir Reece spoke to her. If only he had stayed behind in the hall.

She told herself it would have been worse if the servant had brought the message she had feared—that Piers was hurt. Nevertheless, she couldn't calm the nervous flutter in her stomach, or quell her dread as the servant led her down the stairs and out into the courtyard.

It looked like rain, she vaguely noted, the scent fresh upon the wind and blessedly welcome after the stuffier confines of her chamber. A breeze tugged at her gown as if urging her to stay where she was.

A nice notion, and she would have preferred that course of action, but as the king summoned, so she must obey.

Soon enough they were at the entrance to the hall. The servant shoved open the ornately carved oaken doors and gestured for her to go in.

She hesitated on the threshold as the sound of hushed voices, some curious, some censorious, many wondering, washed over her like waves of water. The torches had been kindled, although it was still day, to light the hall that otherwise would be as dim as a

cathedral. They enabled her to see the assembled
crowd, which parted like the Red Sea before Moses
when they realized she was there. The whole court
was assembled and waiting, save for the squires who
must still be on the field.

Every feeling in her heart urged her to flee, save
one—pride. Pride demanded that she accept her half
brothers' taunts and punishments with silent endur-
ance. Pride told her she must never do anything to
shame Piers, or herself. Pride ordered her to act as if
nothing at all were amiss and she was summoned into
the king's presence every day.

Mustering all the dignity she could, yet with her
face burning because of the lie Damon had told and
expected her to repeat, she began to walk forward. A
smile of relief and joy leapt to her lips when she saw
Sir Reece, until she saw the terrible bruise on his
cheek and his bloodred eye and felt his searching scrutiny. Had he heard Damon's version of events? Did
he believe she was a willing participant in the lies
Damon had told? She wished she could take him aside
and explain!

She tore her gaze away and spotted Damon and
Benedict standing on the queen's left. Sir Reece and
his friends were on the king's right.

The hall was not that large, considering it was in
the king's castle, and yet the journey from the door to
the king enthroned on the dais at the opposite end, his
queen beside him, seemed miles long.

At last she reached the dais. She made her obeisance to the king and waited for him to speak.

Henry tilted his head to regard her. He appeared thoughtful and cunning, although the latter might be merely the effect of his drooping eyelid. As always, he was sumptuously attired, wearing a knee-length tunic of ivory samite, the sleeves slit to reveal a fine linen shirt. His breeches were faun colored, and his boots were gilded in a swirling pattern, as was his belt. His queen was likewise richly dressed, in a gown of beautiful sky blue damask.

"My lady," the king began, sounding very majestic despite his youth, "a most disturbing situation has been brought to my attention."

Shifting a little forward on the carved and cushioned wooden throne, he gestured at Sir Reece, who took a step toward her. "A very serious charge has been leveled against this young man, and we would have the truth of it."

"Sire, I have told you the truth," Damon declared, likewise stepping closer. However, he didn't look at the king, whom he supposedly addressed. He spoke to Eleanor, their very distant relative. "This man attacked her."

Scandalized whispers filled the hall and an angry murmur rose up from Sir Reece's companions. The man himself stayed silent, his expression as enigmatic as she hoped hers was.

"So you have said, Sir Damon," Henry replied,

sliding him an unexpectedly suspicious glance, as if he was not automatically disposed to believe him.

If Henry suspected that Damon was lying about what had happened, would she not be wiser to stick to the truth, as every honorable instinct in her urged? Should she not cast her lot with Henry and Sir Reece rather than Eleanor and her half brothers?

But what of Damon's threat? He had complete control over Piers's life, too, so he could easily ensure that she never saw her beloved brother again.

"Sir Reece has denied the accusation," the king continued. "So we have a stalemate. Therefore, it is time to hear Lady Anne's version of events."

"My liege, she is too upset to speak about what happened," Damon smoothly lied to his king. "She is but a frail woman, after all."

The *frail woman* felt the power of righteous indignation strengthen her resolve. He might lie to his sovereign lord, but she would not.

Yet because of Damon's power over her and Piers, she must tread carefully. She dare not call him a liar in so public a place or indeed, at all. She must excuse him by saying that he was hotheaded and overly upset by an incident that would best be forgotten.

The words would be hard to say, but to stay near Piers, she would get them out somehow.

Yet the thought of doing so before the court, and especially in front of Sir Reece, increased her rancor to an unbearable degree. She must try to get a more private audience with the king.

An idea came to her and she acted upon it immediately. Damon had said she was weak. Right now, she would take advantage of that.

Anne slowly and gracefully pretended to swoon.

Fortunately, someone caught her by the shoulders and gently lowered her to the ground, sparing her the indignity of actually falling. She opened her eyes a crack to see Sir Reece's handsome, bruised face looming above her, his firm lips and strong chin close enough to touch and an expression of concern wrinkling his brow.

Her breathing quickened, and she gave in to temptation. She allowed herself to be held safely in his powerful arms.

But that did not seem enough. She wanted to reach up and caress his cheek, to feel that roughness beneath her open palm. She wanted to explain that she had no idea Damon was going to make such a serious charge against him and that she had no part in it. She wanted to slip her hand behind his head and pull him down for a kiss.

Somebody else was rubbing her hand vigorously. The king called for a servant to fetch water, and a voice with a Welsh accent ordered people to "stop your crowding and make room."

After an appropriate length of time and when the worst of the ensuing cacophony had ceased, she fluttered her eyelids as if returning to consciousness.

"Take deep breaths, my lady," Sir Reece brusquely ordered. "No need to rub so hard, Gervais."

She glanced down to see one of the young men who must be Sir Reece's brother clutching her hand. He stopped rubbing and let it fall.

"What happened?" she murmured, looking back up at Sir Reece.

"You swooned."

Now he didn't look or sound concerned for her health. If anything, his unusual eyes studied her as if he were a judge and she had been caught with stolen goods in her hands.

"I am…better…now," she whispered, telling herself that was not quite a lie. She did feel better—much better—when he held her in his arms. "It is the crowd, the questions."

She realized the king was hovering on the other side of Reece's brother. Damon stood behind the king, his face settling into a familiar scowl.

"Forgive me, sire," she whispered.

"I should have considered that it might be difficult for you and asked my questions without such an audience," Henry said with an encouraging smile. "If you are up to it, my dear, we could retire to my solar to finish this conversation."

"I believe I can manage that, sire," she murmured, pleased that her plan had worked.

"Sir Gervais, Sir Blaidd, help her," the king commanded.

"Gladly, sire," two deep voices said in unison. One pair of strong hands with dark hairs on the back of the fingers took hold of her right arm; another pair of hands took hold of her left, and suddenly she was hoisted to her feet. Meanwhile, Sir Reece rose and straightened his plain dark tunic, wincing slightly.

She had momentarily forgotten the wound in his side. How it must have hurt him to catch her, and yet his face had betrayed nothing of that pain, until this small sign.

Damon and Benedict would have been whining and complaining for weeks, demanding to be waited on hand and foot, if such an injury had been done to them.

"You two stay here with the others," the king ordered. "I will escort Lady Anne, and you may lend your arm to your queen, Sir Reece. We need no one else."

Anne dearly wished she could see the look on her half brother's face as the king himself led her from the hall.

Well, she could imagine it, at any rate, and she had to fight hard to subdue a smug smirk that would have done credit to Damon himself.

With Eleanor and Sir Reece following, Henry led her to a thick door behind a tapestry that opened into a smaller chamber much more comfortable than the hall. The room even sported a hearth in the wall, a very modern innovation, where a cheery fire crackled and blazed. Chairs covered with bright silk cushions stood near it, and on a finely carved table rested a silver carafe and goblets. Two servants waited there, standing as straight as sentries. Ornate tapestries of unicorns and other fantastical beasts hung on the walls.

With a sigh, the king sat near the hearth. Eleanor did likewise, in the thronelike chair beside the one her husband had taken.

"Sit down, my dear," Henry said to Anne, gesturing at a chair opposite, "before you swoon again. Thomson, some wine for the lady."

Anne perched on the edge of the chair and accepted the wine, noting that Sir Reece remained standing, his feet planted and his hands behind his back, as if he were on sentry duty, too.

After a delicate sip, she handed the goblet back to the servant and made a tentative smile at the king. "I feel much better, sire. Thank you."

Henry nodded, then folded his arms across his chest. "Now then, Lady Anne, what happened the night Sir Reece was beaten?"

The queen laid her hand gently on her husband's arm.

"Or punished," Henry amended after a swift glance at Eleanor, "as we shall determine before there is any more acrimony in my court."

Anne licked her lips before replying. "Sire, exactly what charge has Damon made against Sir Reece?"

The king's eyes widened a bit. Her question obviously startled him. Or perhaps the king was not used to questions at all. "Sir Damon has accused Sir Reece of trying to rape you."

She bit back a curse that would have done Damon

proud, even as she wanted to scream with frustration. How could he have said such a thing? This charge would not only taint the innocent Sir Reece, but her, too. Even if the details were lost to the memory of those in the hall, her name would forever be linked with a rape, as would Sir Reece's.

Therefore, she must and would clear Sir Reece of that terrible crime—but delicately, for her own sake, so that she would not be separated from Piers.

She glanced at Sir Reece. His stoic face revealed nothing, yet he must be feeling something, and probably anger most of all.

"Sire," she said, deciding to address herself solely to the king because she was treading on treacherous ground here. If she paid too much attention to Sir Reece, the king and queen might think their meeting had not been innocent. They might well conclude that there had indeed been no rape, but for the wrong reason, and her honor would suffer a different slander. "My half brothers leapt to the wrong conclusions when they saw Sir Reece talking to me in the castle corridor. He was not attacking me. We were merely exchanging pleasantries. He did not even touch me. Unfortunately, in their righteous zeal, they didn't give either of us a chance to explain."

"Sir Reece did not try to force his attentions upon you in any way?"

"No, sire. He followed me from your hall and spoke to me when I was alone in the corridor, which was inappropriate, but there was nothing forceful about it."

Once more the queen laid a delicate hand upon her husband's arm. "But they did have some cause to be angry?" he asked.

"Yes," she admitted.

Henry leaned close to Eleanor and whispered. She frowned, then whispered back. They glanced at Sir Reece, then her.

Anne marshaled her patience and tried to be calm. She had told the truth, and spoken as carefully as she could. There was nothing more to be done except wait to hear what the king decided.

That did not stop her from wondering what Sir Reece was thinking. Did he appreciate her defense? Did he have any notion of the risk she was taking telling the truth, for when Damon learned she had not agreed with his tale completely, he would surely be enraged. Being locked away in her chamber for a day or two would be the least punishment she could expect.

When her patience was beginning to wear as thin as one of her silk scarves, the royal couple finally stopped whispering and looked at them.

"We are inclined to believe you, Lady Anne," Henry announced.

Anne let out a sigh, and she realized Sir Reece had done the same. She glanced at him then, but he was still staring stoically ahead, apparently as intently ignoring her as she had been ignoring him.

"However," the king continued, "it is clear that there was some just cause for anger on the part of the Delasaines."

Sir Reece stiffened, but he did not speak. That silence seemed worse than if he had started shouting. It was like being in the presence of a great force of water held back by a decrepit wooden dam.

"We believe you to be an honorable knight, Sir Reece, and as such, you are duty-bound to behave in an exemplary manner," King Henry said. "This was not an example of the chivalrous behavior we expect from one of the knights of our court and especially a son of Sir Urien Fitzroy. It was improper of you to approach Lady Anne when she was alone.

"On the other hand, it seems that the lady's relatives reacted with far more violence than the original situation warranted."

The king rose to his feet, looking less like a young man and more like the sovereign of England. "Mistakes have been made. Enmity between two noble houses has been created. A charge has been leveled that will stain the reputation of both of you. However, I perceive a means to bring about a reconciliation and prevent further animosity.

"Lady Anne, Sir Reece, you must marry."

Chapter Four

"Sire, I must protest. I do not know this woman beyond a single meeting," Reece said, fighting to keep his anger and dismay from showing on his face.

He had been full of concern over Lady Anne's fate, especially when Gervais reported that she had kept to her room all the day after their encounter, and was relieved to see her enter the hall.

Indeed, more than relieved. As she had approached the king's throne, so proud and confident, he had again felt that thrilling jolt of fascination the very first sight of her had engendered. And her eyes—how her spirit had flashed forth from those sparkling green orbs.

Yet whatever emotions had passed between them in the corridor before her half brothers had arrived, there could not, and must not, be anything more between them.

"Marriages between families is a time-honored way of settling dissension. Many a noble bride has never met her husband until the wedding day," Henry replied, glancing at his wife. "That need not be a hardship."

"Sire," Sir Reece began again, so determined to have the future he had planned he dared to talk back to the king, "Lady Anne has made it clear that I did not dishonor her. However, people might suppose we are being made to wed because I *did* attack her. We shall both be as tainted as if I had."

Queen Eleanor fixed her steely gaze upon him, reminding him why the men in Henry's council feared her and her influence upon the young king. "Did you not take advantage of her?" she demanded. "Did you not treat her as if she were a serving wench and not a noble lady of my court? You made a serious mistake, Sir Reece."

"I did, and for that I am truly sorry," he replied, his contrition sincere—but so was his need not to marry Lady Anne, who was sitting so still, she might be a corpse.

Except for her vibrant eyes. He could feel their gaze every time he spoke, and try as he might to focus only upon the royal couple and find a way out of this dilemma, an image persisted in dancing about the edges of his rational mind: Anne Delasaine in his bed, in his arms, her naked body clasped to him as they passionately made love.

"But Majesty," he continued, his voice steady despite the tumult of thoughts and images flashing through his head, "to make us marry will certainly cause some people to think that there must have been some truth to the Delasaines' charge.''

''So does the sight of your bruised face,'' Eleanor retorted. ''It looks as if they duly punished you for a base crime. Or do you accuse my kinsmen of being savages?''

Even Henry looked rather shocked at his wife's stern question before he again addressed Reece. ''I will not have the Fitzroys feuding with the Delasaines. However it came about, this is a dangerous situation, and I will have it remedied before it worsens to poison my court like a festering wound.

''Therefore, Sir Reece, you may decide. Marry this lady—and without a dowry—or face a charge of attempted rape in the king's court in London.''

Reece's heart seemed to stop, and he knew he was trapped. That the king would even consider such a threat proved how determined he was about this marriage.

Henry turned his gaze onto Anne. ''If you think to protest, my lady, know that I will also charge your brothers with attempted murder for their attack upon Sir Reece. They should be mollified by the lack of a dower payment.''

He regarded them both with all the majesty befitting a king and spoke with firm decision. ''Unlike my father, I will have peace in my court, one way or another.''

Out of the corner of his eye, Reece saw Lady Anne rise and approach the king, as serene and lovely as an

angel. Although he noted her apparently humble attitude, there was something about the tilt of her chin
suggestive of defiance—a defiance he felt but did not
dare to voice.

Not that he intended to accept the king's decree as
his unalterable fate. He could not marry any woman
related to the notoriously vicious, untrustworthy, ambitious Delasaines. Given his own ambitions, he must
not be tied to such men in any way.

As his father had taught him long ago, when the
first plan of attack seems impossible, figure out another. And another, if need be, until you come up with
one that works, and that was what he must do.

Anne knelt before Henry and bowed her head, as
humble now as she had been resolute only moments
ago. "Sire, naturally as I am your loyal subject, I must
and shall obey your command," she said. "However,
I have a request, or a wedding gift to beg, if you wish
to think of it that way."

Then she smiled, and her beauty simply dazzled.
There was no other word for it.

Not surprisingly, for Henry was a man, he returned
her smile and cocked an inquisitive brow. A swift
glance at Eleanor showed that she was not nearly as
impressed, yet she was equally curious to know what
Anne was going to say next.

"Well, Lady Anne, what would you have?" Henry
asked.

"Sir Reece's father is Sir Urien Fitzroy, is he not?"

As Henry inclined his head in agreement, Reece

tensed, confused as to what his father had to do with this. She did not look as if she was about to complain that she could not wed the son of a bastard, even one who had raised himself in the world by skill at arms.

"I would ask that my younger brother, Piers, be allowed to train with Sir Urien, who is noted for his abilities in that regard."

Reece relaxed, although he wondered if this other brother would be like the older ones. If so, he would rather invite a viper into his parents' home.

"A most excellent idea, Lady Anne, and another way to mend this most unfortunate rift."

The king sounded very pleased, so once again, Reece did not venture to voice any objection to this scheme, either.

Besides, surely one lone boy couldn't cause that much trouble. His father had dealt with recalcitrant lads before; his reputation also stemmed from the way he was able to train even the most incorrigible and spoiled of youths. Surely he could handle Piers Delasaine, if need be.

Better than his son had handled the other Delasaines.

Reece fought to ignore the chiding of his shame. Indeed, he should be trying to think of ways to avoid his forthcoming marriage.

The king rose and held out his hand to Eleanor. "I shall leave you two alone to discuss the nuptials tomorrow."

"Tomorrow?" Lady Anne gasped, as shocked as Reece.

"Tomorrow," the king confirmed. "I would have this business concluded with all haste, before relatives and friends try to delay it."

Or the bride or groom, Reece suspected.

"At noon, as is traditional. Since this is my command, we will provide the wedding feast, of course."

If it truly comes to pass, Reece thought as he made his obeisance, for he was not yet willing to concede that the marriage was inevitable.

Henry and Eleanor departed, leaving him alone with his bride-to-be.

He had a hundred things to say to her, but he hardly knew where to begin, until he faced her and saw how pale she was.

"Are you ill?" he asked, as worried again as when she had fainted, and instantly recalling the sensation of her body in his arms.

She shook her head. "No. I did not really swoon. I wanted to speak to the king without the entire court listening."

She had tricked the king? God's wounds, she was an astonishing woman.

"I confess I was very relieved that my ruse worked." She made a little smile. "Thank you for cushioning my fall. I could have injured myself had you not caught me."

And held her in his arms, her body warm against his.

He fought the urge to clear his throat, for it seemed a lump had settled there. "And your brothers? Did they punish you?"

She shrugged her shoulders, and even that gesture was graceful. "I went a day and a night without food. It was no great hardship. I have fasted thus many times before."

She apparently thought little of it, but he would add this to the Delasaines' list of crimes and mete out a suitable punishment when the time came.

"It is good of you to be so concerned, Sir Reece." Again she smiled, and again, he felt dazzled, or as bashful as a lad trying to steal his first kiss.

But he had even been too bashful for that, afraid any of the village girls or serving wenches or young ladies who came to visit his home would laugh in his face if he tried. He was not like Blaidd and Kynan, who would probably laugh with them. He would have wanted to die from shame.

He hadn't kissed a woman until the Earl of Beaumonte's daughter had backed him into a dark corner one Christmastide. She had done more there, too.

Then a plan came to him, one that did not depend on delaying the marriage Henry was so keen on. It was not an easy solution, but given how little time they had before the wedding, it might be the only one that had any chance of succeeding.

He drew himself up, like a guard on the gate, and commanded himself to concentrate on what must be done to get out of this predicament.

And it *was* a predicament, no matter how attractive he found Anne, or how he hated to think of her with such brutes for brothers.

"Lady Anne, I deeply regret following you and speaking to you," he said, stiff and formal and very proper. "I did not foresee this most unfortunate consequence."

She cocked her head to regard him and he realized how very green her eyes were, like a tree coming into bud, or the grass of a meadow in springtime. "I'm sorry my half brothers hurt you."

He stiffened. He didn't want her pity, or a reminder that he had been ignominiously beaten.

She reached up and touched his shoulder. It was a simple act, and he had been touched in a hundred more intimate ways by other women after Claire, but never had the simple pressure of a hand upon his shoulder hit him with such force. Heat, tingling and exciting, spread outward from her hand, all the way below his sword belt.

No, his plan was not without some serious faults, if he ever forgot his ultimate goal and gave himself over to the desire coursing through him even now.

"Sir Reece, my half brothers are as responsible for this as you are," she said, the gentle words issuing from her full, soft lips. "If they had behaved as knights should, following me would have been nothing more than a charming encounter after a feast."

Charming? She found him charming, as women found Blaidd and Kynan Morgan charming?

He had feared his feelings alone could jeopardize his plan. Perhaps he should come up with another…if he had more time, and the king had not made such a terrible threat, and she was not looking at him with those brilliant green eyes.

"Regrettably, Damon will not see it that way," she continued. "He will be angry and blame you."

She spoke as if he must be afraid of Damon, or fear his wrath. "I am not afraid of him, or any man."

Yet what did her opinion of him matter, after all? He simply could not be married to a Delasaine for the rest of his life.

"My lady, since neither of us desire this marriage, I have a plan to free us from it."

She remained enigmatically silent and slowly crossed her arms. Her action drew attention to her shapely breasts beneath her lovely green gown. Desire—unbidden, yet strong as a mighty blow—threatened to rob him of rational thought, and never had there been a time he more needed to be rational.

He walked toward the king's chair, away from her and her shining eyes and luscious body. When he was sure his passing excitement had been conquered, he faced her again.

"Given the king's insistence, we must go through with the ceremony," he began as calmly as he could.

"Yes."

She sounded as composed as he wanted to be.

"However, there is no need to *stay* married."

Her shrewd, intelligent eyes remained fixed upon him as she patiently waited for him to explain.

This was torture, but he had to speak if he wanted to reveal his plan. He would not think of her as a beautiful woman, but one of the soldiers under his command.

Might as well try to believe he was the king of France.

"After a time," he said, not meeting her gaze, "when tempers have had a chance to cool, especially the king's, we can seek an annulment."

"How? On what grounds?" she asked, the only indication of surprise the slight rise of her shapely brows—or perhaps she was hopeful that he had found a solution to their mutual problem. Or was her tranquillity as shallow as his, a mere gloss upon more turbulent waters? "Will you bribe some clergyman to discover that we are, in fact, related and thus the marriage forbidden by consanguinity?"

What she felt, or did not feel, was unimportant, so long as she agreed to his plan. "I would have no relationship between our families of any kind, real or false, so the dissolution must be for another reason."

Her expression darkened. "What other reason?"

"Nonconsummation."

This time he was sure it was surprise that flashed across her face. "So we must marry but not make love?"

Resolutely determined, he nodded.

"You think the church will grant an annulment although we wed at the king's behest?"

"I see no reason they should not."

"Except that the king may not wish it."

"Yes, that is the greatest hurdle," he replied. "However, while my father may lack power and influence at court, he has powerful and influential friends. I'm sure Henry can be brought to realize that it would not be good to have them upset with one of his decisions. That may persuade the king to see that this was not his wisest idea. I'm sure your half brothers will agree. They're probably as angry about this marriage as we are, even if they don't have to provide a dowry. Therefore, Henry may not be spared the conflict he so evidently wishes to avoid. He should come to understand that it would be best if our marriage was dissolved. In the meantime, all we need do is obey his command, and have patience."

"And not make love."

"Yes."

"A clever plan."

Clever or not, it was the one he had come up with.

"For how long must we resist temptation?" she asked softly.

"For as long as we must," he answered. "I think it would be best if we leave for Bridgeford Wells at dawn the day after we are wed."

"Bridgeford Wells?"

"My family's home."

"Ah. Of course."

"We should not stay at court, under Henry's watchful eye, or those of prying courtiers, either."

"Very well, Sir Reece," she murmured, lightly laying her hand on his forearm. "I shall tell my brother to be ready, too."

He had forgotten about Piers Delasaine, and something of his curiosity about her petition regarding him must have shown on Reece's face, for she said, "I care a great deal for my brother, Sir Reece. I've been a mother to him since our own died giving birth to him. I want only the best for Piers. That's why I asked the king to let him come with us. Damon and the others are no fit teachers or examples for him. I would have him learn from the best of men, not the worst."

Pleased by her compliment to his father, he covered her slender hand, so light upon him, with his own. He owed it to her to have her sure of the truth. "Yet what your brother said was true, my lady. My father was born a bastard. I am but one generation removed from the gutter."

Her eyes flared, the sudden fierceness catching him off guard. "I am not a fool to judge by birth, Sir Reece. If noble birth was all it took to be chivalrous, my half brothers would be paragons, but most peasants are more chivalrous than they."

As her eyes blazed with spirit and fire, all the trouble that had brought them together drifted away. He became a man looking at a lovely woman of intelligence and compassion, remarkably free from the prejudice that tainted many a noblewoman.

He wanted to tell her so, or say something of how she impressed him, but the words would not come.

She pulled her hand free and glided to a door that, he realized, could not lead back into the hall where his brothers, his friends and her half brothers would be waiting, no doubt informed of the king's decision by Henry himself. They would surely all be anxious to speak of it and offer their advice, welcome or not.

He couldn't blame Anne for leaving by another exit, and he decided to follow her example.

After she was well away.

Gervais stared at his injured brother as if Reece had suddenly declared he was entering the priesthood. "You gave up? You agreed? You will wed that woman?"

Reece's gaze swept over the others assembled in their chamber after they had returned from the king's hall. Blaidd Morgan leaned on the windowsill, arms and ankles crossed with deceptive nonchalance. Blaidd's brother Kynan sat on one of the cots, his elbows on his knees and fingers laced, also deceptively calm, and Trev was seated on the floor, his legs folded like a nesting bird. Trev's expression, like Gervais's, spoke plainly of what he was thinking: that his elder brother must have been temporarily deranged to agree to marry Lady Anne Delasaine. Reece didn't doubt the Morgans thought so, too. They were merely better at keeping their opinions from their faces.

"I had no choice," he answered. "Henry was adamant, and he *is* the king."

The others exchanged glances.

"What, you all would have argued with him?"

He had them there.

"I did protest," he continued, "but Henry was in no mood for dissent, and I thought it wiser to agree to do as he ordered."

"You could have said you could not wed without your father's approval," Blaidd remarked.

"As though I am Trev's age? I think not." Reece crossed his arms over his broad chest. "I never said I was pleased with the situation."

"Glad I am to hear it!" Kynan cried with a Welsh lilt as his face lit with a grin. There was undeniable relief in his brown eyes, too. "Worried I've been about you, boy, that you had fallen under the woman's spell. First you follow a woman you don't know from the feast like you were Trev's age—" he ignored Trev's muttered protest "—then you let yourself get knocked to the ground and *then* you get yourself betrothed to a Delasaine."

"I made a mistake, I grant you."

"A *mistake?*" Gervais cried. "That's a mild word for it."

"And *I* am paying for it, not you."

"If you marry a Delasaine, we'll be tied to those louts," Gervais pointed out.

"Don't you think I know that?" Reece demanded, his hands balling into fists as he tried to keep hold of his temper. Gervais, younger than he, was making it sound as if Reece must not have realized all the ramifications of his betrothal.

As if Gervais thought, like Kynan, that he had weakly fallen under a woman's spell. "However, I will not *stay* married. I will have the marriage annulled as soon as possible."

The others, not surprisingly, looked stunned.

Trev was the first to give voice to his bafflement. "Annulled?"

"Legally ended. Dissolved," Reece clarified.

"So you'll marry her and then have it annulled?" Blaidd repeated, as if still trying to comprehend the plan.

"That's what I said, yes."

"How?"

"Not consanguinity, that's for certain," Reece answered.

"What's that?" Trev demanded from his place on the floor.

"In the church's eyes, a marriage between people related to a certain degree is illegal."

"But we're not related to the Delasaines, are we?"

"No, thank God," Reece replied. He darted a stern glance at Gervais. "And I don't want to be in any way, so that is not the reason I shall give."

"What else—?" Gervais began. He fell silent and his eyes widened like roses blooming. "You're not going to...?"

"No."

Blaidd and Kynan looked equally incredulous as the full import of his scheme sank in.

"Are you made of stone, boy?" Blaidd demanded after a long and dumbfounded silence.

"No, I'm determined. After Henry has calmed down, and if Father and our friends impress upon him the reasons we should not be married, I think Henry can be persuaded to allow an annulment. He only wants peace in his court, and I do not think the Delasaines look with favor on this marriage, either, so he will not have peace this way."

"No, they don't like it," Gervais agreed. "Looked at the king as if he was proposing to do away with their estate even though…is it true there's to be no dowry?"

Reece nodded, and Gervais whistled.

"Rumor has it they wanted to marry their sister off to Lord Renfrew," Blaidd said.

Reece hadn't heard this before, and he wasn't happy to hear it now. Lord Renfrew was too old, too fat and far too debauched—if only half of what was said about him was true—for Lady Anne. For any lady.

Perhaps he could speak to Henry and suggest he find her a good husband, a man who was worthy of her, who would love and cherish her, and recognize her merits.

A man a part of him would always envy.

"Then they will want the annulment, too," he said. "If Henry truly seeks peace, he should agree to grant it. Now his temper is too high, and he is too certain of his decision. Given time and a cooler head, he will surely see that this order was a mistake."

"I still don't understand," Trev said, scratching his chin. "What aren't you going to do?"

"Make the marriage fully legal," Reece answered. Despite the practical and necessary nature of his plan and his resolve, he felt as warm with embarrassment as if he were seated on a brazier of glowing goals.

"How…?"

"He's not going to love his wife," Gervais explained.

"Well, of course not. He never met her until yesterday. How could he be in love with her already?"

Blaidd looked at Kynan with a dramatically woeful expression. "I think somebody's education has been sorely neglected."

"We're not Welsh," Gervais retorted. "We're a little more…circumspect…about certain things."

Blaidd grinned, the very picture of merry devilment. "Obviously."

Annoyed, Trev scrambled to his feet. "What don't I know?"

Reece sighed and decided he had better explain, or Trev would pester him with questions until he did. "What I mean is, I'm not going to make love with Lady Anne and consummate the marriage. It won't be fully legal until I do and if not, I can have it annulled."

Trev blushed and looked very young. "Oh."

"Trev, my lad, I don't know about your brothers,

but I could use some wine," Kynan said. "Would you mind fetching a carafe?"

"All right." Trev hurried from the room, apparently eager to leave them and the discussion.

"God help me, I thought they'd hurt your head for sure, you seemed so meek and mild when we first got here," Gervais said with a chuckle as the door closed. "I was expecting you to be so angry you'd be chewing the leg of that chair."

"Meek and mild?" Reece repeated, insulted. "I am not meek and mild."

"You'd better pray you can be, boy," Blaidd noted, "with a wife like that you're swearing not to touch."

Kynan nodded, his expression grave. "Are you sure this will work, Reece?"

"Yes," he said, not admitting any doubt even to himself. "Henry's a capricious man, and I think he's more angry than anything else. Once his anger has fled, I'm sure he'll be more reasonable."

"If Eleanor also agrees," Kynan muttered darkly.

"Henry is the king, not her," Reece declared, even as he recalled the way Eleanor seemed to have Henry under control.

If that were so, his presence at court as one of Henry's loyal vassals could be even more important.

"Lady Anne's a beautiful woman," Blaidd noted.

"Very beautiful," Gervais added, doubts about Reece's plan obviously occurring to him, too.

They all thought he was that weak willed? Or prey

to desire? He, who had never been seriously tempted by a woman in his life?

Until now, a shrewd little voice whispered in his head.

He subdued any qualms, for there was simply too much at stake to give in to the desire Anne undoubtedly aroused. "I assure you, I can and I will keep my distance from her when the alternative is a union between our family and hers."

"You certainly sound determined," Blaidd remarked, sitting on the edge of the bed.

"I certainly am."

The other three exchanged dubious looks.

"You think I am that weak?" he demanded, wishing the Welshmen had gone back to their enigmatic ways, for once.

"She's got blond hair," Gervais offered, leaning against the wall. "It was her blond hair got you in trouble in the first place, wasn't it?"

Reece wasn't about to confess that Lady Anne's blond hair had indeed been the first thing he had noticed. "You said it before. She's beautiful."

"Well, then, you see? We're right to be worried!" Kynan cried. "And she's going to be in your bed every night, man! It would take a saint to keep from touching a beauty like that with her lying right beside you."

Kynan's words brought a vision of such astonishing clarity to Reece that his body responded as if Anne were naked in bed beside him at that very moment.

''I may not be a saint,'' he said, crossing his legs, ''but I can control myself.''

''Like you're doing right now, I suppose?'' Blaidd countered.

Reece blushed like a boy finally realizing what that change to his body meant, and the Welshman's expression grew sympathetic. ''Look, Reece, if anybody can do it, it would be you, but you've set yourself a difficult task.''

Because his friend was truly concerned, Reece's ire lessened. ''Or perhaps I have set myself a fitting punishment for causing this mess in the first place. If I had been more restrained, I wouldn't be in this predicament at all.'' He voiced another source of disappointment and frustration. ''It also means you get to stay at court, Gervais, not me, to speak up for our interests. Lady Anne and I should be away from court and curious, gossiping courtiers.''

Gervais manfully did his best to look disappointed, but without much success.

''Well,'' Kynan observed with the air of a philosopher pondering the mysteries of the universe, ''only human, aren't you? I mean, if we were all forced to marry girls we followed at one time or another, or made inappropriate remarks to in the heat of the moment, we'd all have been married long ago. You didn't kill anybody or do anything really serious, Reece. Her brothers are more to blame than you for the trouble.''

''Half brothers,'' Reece automatically amended. The moment the correction slipped from his lips, he wondered what had brought him to say that. The need to have even that little distance between his bride and her family, perhaps.

"Whatever," Kynan replied with a dismissive wave. "We all understand that this order is too severe for what you did, and so should Henry, eventually."

"I only hope my father does," Reece said, looking at Gervais. Their father did not possess a fiery temper, but his displeasure was something to be avoided, in part because his cold disapproval made it all the worse.

"I'm sure he will," his brother answered, trying to look as if he believed it. "Mother will be pleased, at any rate, to see Trev home from his first melee safe and sound."

"Yes, she will," Kynan confirmed. "Our mother fell on Blaidd's neck weeping after he returned from his first tournament."

"She did not!"

"She did, too. I remember distinctly."

Ignoring the Welshmen, Gervais clapped his hand on Reece's shoulder. "This trouble will soon be remedied. I'm sure of it."

Reece nodded and smiled, and told himself it would be so.

Now if only he could get the vision of Anne naked in his bed out of his mind.

Chapter Five

Anne stood at the window of her chamber, absently toying with a bit of broken stone as she stared unseeing over the courtyard below. For a mercy, Lisette had not been here when she returned from her meeting with the king. It had been bad enough hurrying past the little knots of inquisitive courtiers who were not in the hall.

So much had happened in so short a time she could scarcely comprehend it all. She was to be married, to the virile, enigmatic Sir Reece Fitzroy, who most certainly did not want her.

That meeting in the corridor had been but a harmless flirtation to him. She should have followed the urgings of her rational mind and left him the moment he came out of the shadows, but she hadn't. His sudden appearance, the mysterious man himself—it had simply been the most exciting, thrilling thing that had ever happened to her.

But then, disaster.

She flicked the stone out the window as her anger surged again. Damon and Benedict were vicious fools who had not foreseen the consequences of their cowardly attack on a knight of the realm. Instead, they had made what should have been only a cause for mild rebuke into a political problem, with her and Sir Reece to bear the punishment.

Well, at least Sir Reece considered it a punishment to be forced to marry. That is what Damon had planned for her anyway—a marriage to some man of his choosing, not hers. Likely Damon would pick a rich, influential man like Lord Renfrew or, even worse, a rich old lecher who would paw her body and demand a son.

Sir Reece was young, he was good-looking, he was virile and, while he had been impertinent by following her, he had not been lecherous. His gaze and his touch did not make her feel soiled, as others did.

It was so easy to envision sharing Sir Reece's bed. Warmth flowed through her as she thought of being in Sir Reece's strong arms, held in his powerful embrace, his lips hot and soft against hers.

Yet what else did she know of him? He had insolently followed her from the hall and spoken to her, although he had not been overtly lascivious. If anything, he had been deferential and apologetic.

But maybe she should remember the act more than the manner of his speech. Perhaps that was the true indication of the man's character.

And surely this marriage would only make matters

worse. Damon would be furious at the destruction of his plans. Although his brutality was partly to blame, he would never concede that. He would blame Sir Reece, her, even Henry, and seek to have his vengeance, one way or another.

Yet if the marriage was annulled, she would have to return to Montbleu, and her half brothers would again be able to marry her off to someone of their choosing.

No matter what the future held for her, though, she had achieved one good thing: she had been able to remove Piers from Damon and Benedict's influence. As she had said to Sir Reece, she would have Piers learn from good men, not bad.

The latch of the door moved. Perhaps the squires' melee had ended and Piers was finally come.

Once again, Damon strode inside, and she saw that even being spared paying her the dowry had not mollified him, as the king believed it would.

She leaned back against the sill, trying to put as much distance between them as possible, while he crossed the room in two strides. He raised his fist and struck her shoulder so hard the blow sent her stumbling sideways.

"What the devil are you playing at, Anne?" he demanded.

"I don't know what you mean," she said as she righted herself, her hand to her shoulder. "I'm not *playing* at anything."

He cursed her, the words crude and ugly. Then he cursed Sir Reece in terms even worse.

"I have no choice but to marry Sir Reece, Damon," she said, struggling to hide her rage at his words and his treatment of her. "I could not refuse the king's command, could I? Besides, when he said there would be no dowry, I thought you would be pleased."

"To have my sister wed to a Fitzroy? They should be paying *us* for the privilege!"

"Not when you told everyone Sir Reece was trying to rape me. The way you attacked him might lead them to believe he succeeded. It could be that no one you consider suitable will want me now—or had you not considered that?"

She watched her words sink in. By attacking Sir Reece, Damon was as responsible for all that had come after, and she would have him realize that. Hopefully it might make him think twice before he resorted to brute force again.

He did not look the least bit contrite as he circled around her, his steps slow and measured. "That does not explain why Piers is to go with you."

"I asked it of the king."

Damon's brows lowered ominously.

"You yourself have called him a nuisance so many times—"

"You had no right to ask that," Damon said, grabbing her by the shoulders. "I decide where Piers goes and with whom."

Anne twisted out of his grasp. "Do you intend to say that to the king?"

Damon did not answer as his scowl deepened.

"It is well-known that Sir Urien Fitzroy excels at the training of knights. Why not allow Piers the opportunity to learn from such a man and be in the company of youths from some of the most important families in England?" she continued, giving reasons Damon would surely agree with.

"Very well. I shall let the brat go."

Relief tumbled through her, until she noticed the sly, calculating look that had come to Damon's dark, beady eyes. "Perhaps your marriage to Fitzroy need not be a complete disaster," he said. "You are right. Fitzroy has trained many sons of the nobility, men who wield great power and influence at court—men who are his friends. When you are in his household, you can find out all about these men. If they meet and when and where. With whom they are allied, and who they perceive to be enemies. How they feel about the king and his queen, that sort of thing."

Dismay and the sickening sensation of defeat settled upon her. She should have held her tongue. She did not want to spy for Damon, or help him in his ruthless, ambitious climb to power. Perspiration began to trickle down her back beneath her silken gown. "And if I do not?" she queried.

"We will take Piers away and you will never see him again."

"The king himself said Piers is to train with Urien Fitzroy."

"The king doesn't give a tinker's dam about some boy," Damon retorted, his lip curling with scorn and complete confidence in his reasoning. "Especially if we say we would rather he learn in France, his family's home. Eleanor will agree with us, and so I doubt Henry would protest. He won't want a conflict with his bride because of a boy like Piers."

He was probably right about that. She had seen the way Henry looked at Eleanor; he would not wish to make trouble with his wife over a youth.

"Life at court is fraught with dangers, if one is ignorant of friendships and alliances," Damon said with a cold little smile. "You want us to be safe, don't you?"

Safe from the detection of whatever evil schemes they were hatching, he meant.

There must be some way she could avoid involvement in Damon's disgusting, dishonorable scheme. "I cannot write. You would not permit me to learn. How am I to get the information to you?"

Damon mused a moment, and Anne began to hope that she had found the flaw in his plan. But all too soon that scheming glow returned to Damon's dark eyes. "Benedict can follow you to Bridgeford Wells. You can tell him all you learn."

"You expect him to be welcomed into Sir Reece's home after what you have done?"

"Of course not."

"Then where am I to meet with him, or find out when?"

"He will await you in the village, claiming to be…a soldier headed home. You can find some pretext to go there. You will look for him, and he will be looking for you. You're a clever girl, Anne. You'll find him one way or another, because you know the penalty if you don't."

It was a vague scheme, one that could easily go wrong. And if it did, it would not be Damon who would suffer the most. "What if I am discovered? Or Benedict is?"

Damon shrugged.

"There is nothing wrong with a brother following to make sure his sister is being well taken care of, especially under such circumstances."

Anne could not keep the scorn from her voice. "Anyone who knows Benedict will know that is a lie."

"Lie or not, they cannot disprove it—unless you tell them of this conversation which, of course, you will not do, for then they will know you are a treacherous spy. For a wife to conspire against her husband is a serious offense. You would be imprisoned, at the very least."

He was right, and she wanted to scream as the trap closed around her.

Damon got to his feet and once more his hateful, cruel smile curled his lips as he ran his serpent's gaze over her. "There is no need to look so distraught,

Anne. All you have to do is seduce him and get with his child. That should protect you from your husband's wrath. And if you get him to love you, he will confide in you all the more. You are a beautiful woman. You should have no trouble there.''

He grabbed her gown and pulled her close, his breath hot on her face, his eyes fierce as a ravening wolf. "Only one thing matters, and that is that you do as I tell you or I will insure that you never see your beloved, darling brother again. How you find out what I want to know, or how you protect yourself against your husband's wrath, I leave up to you.''

He let go of her and she stumbled back. He chuckled, the sound low and without mirth. "By God, Henry may have helped us more than he knows.''

With that, he strode to the door, then slammed it shut behind him.

Anne slumped onto the bed. To think that marriage to Sir Reece had seemed a chance for a sort of liberty when the king had first proposed it, or at least certainly a far better fate than the one Damon had laid out for her. But now it seemed a terrible prison that would rob her of her honor and possibly cost her the only loving relationship she had in her life.

As for seducing her husband as Damon suggested… In one way, it was very tempting, but if Sir Reece discovered what she was doing, he would no doubt be furiously angry that she was attempting to foil his plan for an annulment. She knew enough of men's ire to realize that was something to be avoided.

God help her, what was she going to do?

The door to her chamber burst open again with so much force, it banged against the wall. She started and looked up, expecting Damon with some new aspect to his hateful scheme.

Instead Piers stood there, clad in chain mail that was too big because it had been Benedict's, and with a fiercely indignant look on his young face. Although he was but fourteen, he was already taller than she. His face was still more boy than man, however, and his body was thin as a sapling. His coloring was dark like Damon and Benedict's, and his glower made it seem darker still.

"Is it true, what I heard after the melee?" he demanded, his deep voice the one thing besides his height that reminded her he was growing up. "You are to be married to Reece Fitzroy?"

She had underestimated the speed of gossip. "Come inside and I will explain."

Her gaze scanning him for signs of blood or bruises, she saw no evidence that he had been hurt in any way as he marched into the chamber, and she breathed a little easier.

She wondered how much to tell him, until he fixed his vivid blue eyes on her. He was still too young to understand how marriage and family relationships could be made a weapon. She would not burden him with schemes and plans and politics. Not yet.

"I couldn't find Trevelyan Fitzroy in the melee," Piers began, "and when I said as much to the groom at the stable afterward, he told me Trevelyan had been summoned from the tournament on a family matter. Then I discovered you and my brothers had also been called to the king's presence. I guessed why. It was about what happened with Sir Reece, wasn't it?''

She nodded.

"I am your brother, too. Why wasn't *I* summoned?"

"I don't know," she answered honestly. "Perhaps Damon thought it better for you to remain in the melee."

"Or he wanted to have me out of the way. They all treat me like a useless infant."

She couldn't deny that, and they treated her no better. "The king has decided that the best way to deal with the animosity between our half brothers and Reece Fitzroy is for me to be married to him," she explained.

Piers ground his fist into his palm. "You can't. Unless he...?" He blushed from his neck to the roots of his hair.

"No, he did not."

"Thank God!" Piers's expression hardened. "But this order to wed makes it sound as if he did."

"I know, and neither Sir Reece nor I are pleased." Anne gestured at the stool and waited for him to sit. "There's no denying that what Sir Reece did has had unforeseen and serious consequences, but in and of itself, following me was no great crime. If Damon and Benedict had let Sir Reece go on his way with a rebuke instead of setting upon him and injuring him, that would have been the end of it. But now the king is adamant that we wed to insure peace between our two families, so we have no choice. I ask you, who is more to blame for the king's decision, Sir Reece or our relatives? Unfortunately, as a woman I have no say in this. I must marry because the king commands it.

"However, Sir Reece has a plan to have the marriage annulled. We are not going to consummate the marriage."

Piers's eyes flared with surprise. "He is willing to leave you alone?"

"Yes. As I said, it was his idea."

She hurried on, not willing to tell Piers all the reasons Sir Reece objected to the marriage, lest his pride be wounded. "The king has agreed that you can come with me to Sir Reece's home, to be trained by his father. Everyone in England has heard of Sir Urien Fitzroy and his talent for training knights. If benefit to you can come of this situation, I'm pleased."

"I'm not. This is terrible, Anne. The man's father is nothing but some peasant's bastard—"

"Whatever Sir Urien's parentage, he is a respected knight of the realm, and that is all the more impressive because he earned both the rank and the respect. You should share that respect, and appreciate this opportunity the king grants you. A wise man uses his chances as best he can."

Piers stared at his boots.

Seeking to lessen his dismay, Anne reached out and chucked his chin in a playful, maternal gesture. "Now you must away and pack your baggage, for the wedding is to be at the noon tomorrow, followed by a wedding feast that the king is providing. We shall be leaving for Bridgeford Wells, where Sir Reece lives, at dawn the next day."

Piers raised his eyes to her, and her heart ached at the hunger she saw there. "Damon agreed to let me go?"

Damon was no fit man for Piers to look up to, but Piers was still too young to see it, and he was blinded with admiration for an older sibling who, it could not be denied, usually won his fights.

Fighting was the one thing at which her half brothers did excel. In all else that made a chivalrous knight, they were woefully deficient. Yet she would not hurt Piers by revealing just how little thought they gave to his fate.

"We are all subject to the king's commands," she said, not lying, but leaving him free to interpret her words as he would.

Piers got to his feet. "When I am a knight, Anne, I will look after you, and I promise that you will not have to do anything you do not wish to."

Her heart full of love for him, she rose and briefly embraced him. "Cheer up, Piers. It could be worse, as we both know. Damon could be making me marry that fat sot Lord Renfrew."

Her brother's eyes narrowed. "You sound pleased to be marrying Fitzroy."

"I am making the best of it, Piers," she replied, "as you must make the best of going to Bridgeford Wells. Plenty of young nobles your age would sell their armor for this chance."

"I suppose."

She recalled something else. "You said you noticed that Trevelyan Fitzroy was not in the melee. Were you looking for him in particular?"

He turned away. "As you say, Anne, I have things to do—"

She put her hand on his shoulder to hold him back, then circled so that she could see his face as she questioned him. "What were you planning on doing, Piers, if you found him?"

Her brother's face flushed and he did not meet her gaze.

"Damon and Benedict have already meted out punishment, and more than Sir Reece deserved," she said sternly. "Henry threatened to charge them with attempted murder if they refused to allow the marriage. There was—and is—no need for you to involve yourself with the Fitzroys, beyond learning everything Sir Urien can teach you. Do you hear me, Piers?"

He nodded, looking very much like the little boy she had mothered for so long, his bright blue eyes full of love and devotion—an ample reward for any sacrifice she made for him.

*   *   *

Later than night, Damon marched into a tavern in the town of Winchester, grabbed Benedict by the neck of his wine-stained tunic and hauled him to his feet. The table rocked, sending coins wagered on the dice game sliding into the ale-soaked rushes on the floor.

"Wha' the devil?" Benedict cried as the other men seated at the battered table scrambled for the coins. "Let me go! I'm winning!"

Damon ignored Benedict as he all but dragged him from the smoky, stuffy building that stank of spilled ale and beef gravy.

Damon shoved his brother against the wall outside so hard, Benedict nearly fell. Righting himself, the brawny man glared at his thinner older brother with bloodshot eyes. "What's the matter with you?" he snarled, his words slurred with drink.

Damon glared at him, arms akimbo. "How much did you lose this time, fool?"

"I told you, I was winning!"

"How much have you lost today?"

Benedict didn't answer.

"All I gave you?"

Benedict shrugged.

His face full of rage, Damon raised his hand to strike, but instead shoved his brother along the street. "If I catch you gambling again, I swear I'll take what you owe me out of your hide!"

"The estate income is my money, too," Benedict whined. "You treat me like a child."

"Because you damn well act like one!" They

reached another tavern, one Damon favored, and he pushed Benedict through the door.

When Benedict realized where they were, he stopped sulking and grinned. "I'll have an ale."

"The hell you will. You've had enough." Damon sat on a bench in the corner and pulled his brother down beside him. Ignoring the rough-looking customers, he gestured for the broad-hipped serving wench, a middle-aged woman with few teeth and as tough as any seaman on the docks at Dover.

"Wine for me, Mary," he ordered, "and none of that watered-down vinegar you try to pass off as wine." He glanced at his brother. "Nothing for him."

Benedict scowled and reached for his nearly empty leather pouch tucked inside his tunic. "I can pay—"

"Shut your mouth and listen," Damon snapped, waving Mary away. When she was out of earshot, he leaned forward, speaking just loud enough for Benedict to hear. "And listen well, you sot! It's about Fitzroy."

"That piece of—"

"That son of a man with important friends, you dolt."

Benedict's mouth fell open as he regarded his wiser older brother.

"Yes, we were wrong to be angered by Henry's decision. Our illustrious sovereign has done something that may prove very helpful."

Benedict blinked, his duller wits obviously trying to comprehend.

Damon sighed with frustration, then explained. "Anne's going to be married to the son of a man with important, influential friends at court. She can find out who they are, and what they're up to. We can use that information, either to their detriment or our advantage. We'll know who to watch, who to avoid, who to be friendly to, that sort of thing."

Benedict's bleary eyes narrowed. "You hate Reece Fitzroy. His father was nothing but a lowborn bastard."

Damon made a false smile. "Well, no matter now. It's much better to have Anne married into a household where she can provide us with all sorts of information—and not only that, we are rid of her without having to pay a dowry."

Mary returned with the wine. Damon tossed a coin in her direction, a fiendish little smile on his face when she had to bend and retrieve it from the rushes.

Benedict eyed the wine hungrily and licked his lips as Damon gulped from the clay cup.

When he realized Damon did not intend to share, as he knew he wouldn't but hoped nonetheless, Benedict shifted conspiratorially closer. "What of Anne? Is she agreeable?"

"Would it matter if she wasn't?"

Benedict chuckled, a low, cruel sound. "'Spose not."

"Exactly." Damon set down his wine and wiped his thin lips with the back of his hand. "So here is your part in this. You are to follow Anne to Bridgeford Wells, where she will tell you what she learns.''

''Bridgeford Wells?''

Damon grimaced as his brother's question. ''Where the Fitzroys live. You know, in Castle Gervais?''

''Oh, aye, right.''

''Oh, aye, right, indeed! Nobody must know you are her brother. Tell people you are a soldier headed home. She will find you there when she comes to the market, or a fair. She will tell you what she learns, then you will come back to court and tell me.''

Benedict grinned.

''Yes, you get to travel and stay at inns and flirt with the wenches,'' Damon said sarcastically. ''But if you gamble away the money I'm giving you for the journey, you'll be on your own.''

''Why don't *you* go, then?'' Benedict asked, sulking again.

''Because I must stay at court.''

''What the hell for?''

''Because I have plans, brother, that require me to do so.''

''What plans?''

''*My* plans.'' Damon's eyes took on a superior gleam. ''No need for you to concern yourself with them yet. You do think you can do as I ask, don't you? You can remember what Anne tells you—or do I have to hire somebody else?''

''I can do it!''

Damon smiled. ''I thought so. I would keep this in

the family, if I could.'' He held out his wine. ''Here. Finish it.''

Benedict snatched the cup from his brother and gulped it down. When he was finished and slammed the cup down on the table, he saw Damon regarding him with cold, hard eyes.

''But if you fail me in this, Benedict,'' Damon said in a stern whisper, ''if you are caught or cannot remember what she tells you, I will cut you adrift. No more money, no more help when you get yourself in trouble.'' He leaned close again. ''No more dumping bodies of the men you've beaten to death in the river for you, or paying off women you've raped so you're not hauled off to prison like a common outlaw. Do you understand me?''

Benedict paled, for he knew that tone of voice and gleam of eye well. Damon meant these words and he would be absolutely ruthless if he decided to act upon them. ''Aye, brother, I understand.''

Chapter Six

Dressed in her finest gown, a deep blue velvet over-tunic with long sleeve slits that revealed a lighter, pale blue silken gown beneath, her blond hair enclosed in a netted cloth called a crispinette, Anne stood beside Sir Reece in front of the royal chapel while the priest—an ancient fellow who wheezed—blessed their union. She stared straight ahead, all her attention seemingly upon the elderly man. In reality, she was very aware of Sir Reece and his lean, hard muscular body but a hand's breadth away.

The tall, broad-shouldered groom was likewise well dressed in a black tunic embroidered with gold, dark breeches and black boots. She could smell the highly polished leather of his boots and the sword belt slung low around his narrow hips. His eye was still a bloody scarlet and his bruise a mottled purple, red and yellow.

The king, queen and the entire court, the Fitzroys, Piers and her half brothers were all in attendance. She wondered what everyone was thinking, although that concern was soon subverted. In another few moments, when the priest stopped muttering in Latin and ended the ceremony, Sir Reece would have to kiss her to seal their vows.

The priest fell silent, and she held her breath in anticipation. Sir Reece reached for her left hand. The ring, of course. That would come before the kiss.

She couldn't help trembling, any more than she could stop herself from looking up at his bruised face and red eye as he put a plain gold ring on her finger. She watched as his long, slender and yet strong fingers caressed the ring into place while the priest intoned the final blessing that would make them husband and wife.

It was done. They were wed, at least in name. And now it was time for the kiss.

Sir Reece took her by the shoulders and her body quivered at the contact. She tilted her head back and looked up into his eyes to see…what?

Calm acceptance of a duty done? A knight's obedience to his sovereign? The fire of desire, banked yet present nonetheless?

She honestly couldn't tell what emotion lay behind those intriguing light-gray eyes.

And then his lips brushed gently over hers, as soft and gentle as a spring mist.

At first. For an instant.

Then his hold tightened and his lips returned, more urgent this time. His mouth covered hers firmly, kissing her properly.

Completely. Wonderfully—so wonderfully, her whole body seemed alive from the touch.

Closer he held her, and the kiss deepened, taking her to different awareness of his body against hers, the strength of him, the power. The desire coursing through her, a feeling totally new to her. A carnal pleasure such as she had never known or imagined.

Suddenly, for the first time, she understood why a woman would break the laws of God and society to be with a man.

Reece ended the kiss abruptly and stepped back. His chest rose and fell as rapidly as hers, making her wonder if he felt as overwhelmed by that kiss as she did.

She could still read nothing in his enigmatic expression.

The king, however, seemed very well pleased, for he applauded. "Let us adjourn to the wedding feast," he cried, taking his wife's arm to lead the way.

Anne did not think she could eat a morsel.

"Shall we, Anne?" Reece said as he tucked her arm in his to lead her to the wedding feast, his hard muscle beneath her hand while they followed the royal couple into the hall.

Anne. He called her Anne. Her name sounded wonderful when spoken in his rich deep voice.

Oh, would that Damon had not come up with his disgusting plan! If only he did not control Piers's life the way he did hers! If only she could be truly married to this man and both she and Piers free of Damon forever!

Yet they were not free, and until that day, she must do as Damon commanded.

She forced herself to act as if all were well, or at least as if she were not distraught and angry. She would display nothing of her feelings, just like Reece.

So she tried to concentrate on the fine feast, even though she knew the bountiful largesse was more to appease the king's need for display than generosity toward the couple he was forcing into matrimony.

Mercifully Damon and Benedict were not at the high table, nor were any of Sir Reece's relatives and friends. Piers was seated between Damon and Benedict, but for once, that did not disturb her. Soon, he would be away from them, and in better company.

Despite the magnificent array of dishes—had there ever been so many sauces or roasted fowl at a meal?—she really could not eat.

Instead she surreptitiously watched the groom. His long, slender fingers curled around his goblet and lifted it to his incredible lips. There was a fluidity to his every movement that she found fascinating. He did not wolf down his food like Benedict, or pick at it like Damon.

When Reece reached for a small loaf of fine white bread set before him, he slowly began to tear it into smaller pieces, every action deliberate, and with a sort of masculine grace.

She began to imagine those hands on her body. Touching. Caressing. Exploring. Arousing…

"Anne!"

She started and found Reece giving her a puzzled look. "The queen is talking to you, Anne," he said quietly.

"Oh."

Very good, Anne, she inwardly chided. She sounded like a fool. And once she had dared to imagine herself the queen of clever banter!

Eleanor regarded her with an indulgent expression, as if Anne were a child. "I was saying, my dear, that you must take Lisette with you to your new home."

Anne forgot her annoyance. "Majesty?"

"She is quite attached to you. I think it would be a great pity not to take her with you. You have no objections, I trust, Sir Reece?"

Her husband's face was stoic in the extreme as he shook his head. "Of course not, Your Majesty."

Eleanor leaned back. "I thought not."

Anne glanced at Reece uneasily. Forced to marry, forced to accept her brother into his household, now forced to have a servant he probably didn't need. What was the queen doing? Trying to enrage him? To make their married life even more difficult? Or did she think she was doing Anne a favor? To be sure, she liked Lisette, and could find no fault with the girl's work, and yet Anne found it easy to think Eleanor had an ulterior motive. She had seen the way the queen seemed to dominate Henry.

Perhaps she enjoyed exerting control over people's lives. Perhaps it suited Eleanor to see an English noble miserably wed. Perhaps it even amused her.

Anne bristled anew at that thought. It was one thing to be made to do something by an overpowering brother or a king for political reasons; it was quite another to be forced to do something for another person's amusement.

She waited until the queen was talking to the king, then she leaned closer to Reece. "I like Lisette," she whispered, "but if you do not wish to have her in your household—"

He regarded her steadily with his cool gray eyes. "I have no more choice in this than I do in my bride. As the queen commands, so will Henry, and so I must obey."

He did not sound angry, and she took some comfort from that. Indeed, the prospect of having the cheerful Lisette for a companion was growing more appealing by the moment, now she knew that didn't upset Reece.

The servants arrived to clear away what remained of the food, and the minstrels struck up a louder, brighter tune for dancing.

"Sir Reece, you and your bride must join us in a dance," the king declared as he got to his feet and held out his hand to Eleanor.

Reece clenched his jaw, then forced a companionable smile onto his face. As the king commanded in this, so, too, they must do, yet he would truly rather face a screaming horde of Saracens than touch Anne again.

When they were formally joined in matrimony and he had merely brushed his lips across hers to seal the joining, he had felt a jolt of raw desire so strong, he had nearly lost himself, powerless to stop.

Indeed, the moment his lips met hers, if was as if his mind and body were taken over by the very spirit of desire and need. He forgot that she was a Delasaine and their marriage forced; he forgot about the necessary annulment and his vow not to make love with her.

But only for an instant, before his resolve reasserted itself. He must be free of her, for she was a Delasaine, when all was said and done, and no passionate, incredible kiss was going to change that.

With grim determination to do what he must and be done, he rose and held out his hand to escort her to the center of the hall, where the tables were rapidly being taken down to clear a space for dancing. Her face expressionless, Anne silently and obediently let him lead her forth and he forced himself to pay no heed to the pleasurable feeling of her warm, slender hand in his.

He was no green youth, after all. When his marriage was ended, he would hold other hands. None might be as graceful, or so fascinating. None might be so easy to imagine brushing over his aroused body—

He must stop this!

As those who were to dance formed a circle, he became acutely conscious of the scrutiny of everyone else in the hall, especially that of the Delasaines and his own companions. Clenching his jaw, he ignored them as his beautiful, serene wife glided around the circle as if she always danced and never walked like mere mortals.

He could and would restrain this wayward, foolish, impossible excitement singing through his body, encouraging him to seek a different, more primitive dance as old as mankind itself.

He would disregard the throbbing drumbeat of the tabor that seemed to set his own heart pounding with passion. He would pay as little heed as possible to Anne.

As the dance required, he clapped and turned, and found the queen his partner for the next few steps. He gave her his very best smile and wondered how she felt when she was betrothed to Henry. Did she know she was not Henry's first choice?

In his youth the king had fallen in love with the sister of the king of the Scots, but that match had been deemed politically unsuitable. Did Eleanor care, since she had gotten him at last? Either way, it was very clear to him that she was determined to rule Henry, if not the entire kingdom. As recent events had so forcefully demonstrated, she had already succeeded to a certain extent.

The barons of the kingdom would not be pleased. They had achieved much because of the weakness of Henry's father, John, and then during Henry's subsequent minority. They would not be anxious to give up their influence, especially to a French woman.

Another hand clap and turn, and he was once more facing Anne—a much pleasanter prospect, although perhaps one no less fraught with political consequences, at least until he could get the annulment.

The dance required them to touch, palms together, as they circled. He couldn't avoid watching her profile as they moved. The straight nose. The full and sensual lips. Her shapely, delicately arched brows that seemed to be always asking a question of him. The curve of her jaw. Her slender neck and the pulse beating there.

This beautiful woman was his wife, to look at but not love.

He realized he was perspiring like a youth dancing with a pretty girl for the first time and like a youth, he hoped she didn't notice.

Ridiculous. Utterly ridiculous.

At last, the music ended. With a relieved sigh, he bowed stiffly to Anne, then turned to bow to the queen.

When he faced Anne again, he discovered Blaidd Morgan standing beside his wife.

"Sit down, boy," Blaidd genially commanded. "You look like you're about to swoon. The side aching, is it?"

"No, my side is not aching." *Much.* Genial or not, Blaidd Morgan had no right to order him about and certainly no right to call him "boy," as if he were ten years old. "I'm fine, *lad.*"

Blaidd grinned and ran a skeptical gaze over him. "Are you, indeed? Well, well, then I shall simply have to confess that I want to dance with the most beautiful woman at court—saving the queen, of course,'' he added as Eleanor and the king strolled past.

Short of ordering his friend not to dance with his wife, there wasn't much Reece could do.

He looked at Anne. Her expression was…well, there wasn't much of an expression on her face at all. There wasn't pleasure, anyway and so, he decided, subduing his completely unnecessary and foolish jealousy, he would go and sit down.

As for what Blaidd was up to, he could guess. It was as he had said. He wanted to dance with the most beautiful woman at court.

He was surprised that Blaidd hadn't already noticed her and tried for more, like following Anne into a secluded corridor. He wondered how Anne would have reacted if Blaidd the merry and charming had followed her instead.

He doubted the Delasaines would have behaved any differently, for Blaidd Morgan's father had been a shepherd before the Welsh-Norman lord Reece was named after had taken him under his wing. While Baron Emryss DeLanyea was well liked and respected, the Delasaines would only care that Hu Morgan was but his foster son, and therefore had no noble blood in his veins. Like his own father, Hu Morgan had achieved his rank by merit, not by birth.

These were the sort of excellent men Reece intended to represent at court, once he rid himself of his unsuitable wife, and this was what should be foremost in his thoughts.

As a disgruntled Reece neared Gervais and the others, they motioned him to join them. He did not want to sit at the high table with the king and queen any more than he had to, and they were talking with other nobility anyway, so he did.

"How do you like *our* plan?" Kynan demanded in a conspiratorial whisper the moment Reece sat on the bench between Gervais and the Welshman.

"What plan is that?" Reece replied, his voice likewise hushed.

"Why, to keep her away from you this evening," Kynan replied. "Or, despite what you said, you away from her."

"Yes," Gervais grimly agreed. "I thought you wanted an annulment."

"I do."

"Didn't look like it to us. You could hardly keep from staring at her during the feast and the dancing."

"I only looked at her once or twice," Reece protested, certain that was so.

"Her face, maybe. Not the rest of her."

Reece silently cursed as he felt the heat of a telltale blush. He was only a mortal man, though. What man wouldn't look at a woman sitting next to him who was as graceful and lovely as Anne, even if she wasn't also that man's wife?

"Not that we're blaming you," Kynan said, his gaze darting between the brothers, obviously trying to defuse the tension. "She's got the finest—"

"That's my wife you're talking about," Reece

growled, not willing to hear Kynan, or anybody else, discuss his wife's personal attributes. "For now, at any rate."

Blaidd danced blithely past, his arm about Anne's slender waist. He was grinning like an idiot and, God help him, she was laughing. A beautiful laugh she had, too, like water tumbling over the rocks of a brook in the spring thaw, merry and welcome after a long, cold winter.

"So we decided you needed some help," Trev offered. "Blaidd and Kynan and Gervais and I are going to take turns dancing with her."

Reece eyed his little brother. "You? I thought you hated dancing."

Looking away, Trev blushed bright red and mumbled something.

"What was that?"

"He said, that was before he got here," Kynan answered. He grinned, the very image of his handsome elder brother. "And saw all the lovely young ladies, and they saw him." The Welshman clouted Trev lightly on the shoulder. "Mind you don't follow any of them out of the hall, my lad. Trouble that is, and no mistake."

"I think we all realize that," Reece muttered. "You don't need to keep harping on the subject like a minstrel who knows only one tune."

The dance ended at last and Gervais got to his feet. "My turn now."

He looked as though he was being led to his death,

and Reece was fiendishly pleased. Anne wouldn't be laughing when she danced with Gervais. He had the feet of an ox.

But then, as Blaidd made his way back to his place on the bench, it seemed the king or his queen had decided a ballad was in order, and thus there was a lull in the dancing.

So now Reece had to watch Gervais sit across the hall beside a panting Anne. As Gervais handed her a goblet of wine, some skinny, spotty-faced youth began to warble a silly song about love everlasting and devotion divine.

"She's some dancer, your bride," Blaidd offered after he had downed a gulp of wine himself. "Graceful as a willow in the breeze."

"Is that why you were grinning like a jester?"

"Aye, and the fact that I had my arm about the prettiest woman in the hall."

"What a pity you weren't the one forced to marry her, then."

"Well, if it were just the woman alone, I could think of worse fates," Blaidd admitted without hesitation.

Reece's hand itched to punch him. Not to damage. No, never that. Merely to make him reconsider his words.

"But unfortunately, there are her half brothers in the mix," Blaidd finished, his words resuscitating their friendship.

"She seemed to find you most amusing," Reece noted, his tone somewhat less sarcastic.

"Easy enough to get a woman to laugh," Blaidd replied with an airy wave of his powerful hand that could knock out teeth. "Tell her you're afraid to talk to her."

"You said that? To Anne? That you were *afraid?*"

Blaidd's grin grew even wider and he shrugged. "Got her to laugh, didn't I?"

"If all you want is a woman to laugh *at* you, I suppose that's good advice," Reece grumbled.

"It's a start," the Welsh expert on female responses sagely noted.

"I don't need to start. She's my wife, remember?"

"And not destined to stay that way, aye, I do." Blaidd grew serious. "But there's no harm in making her a bit happy, is there? You're not the only one suffering, you know."

Reece's breath caught in his throat. Was Anne *suffering?* "No need to look devastated, boy. She's not enduring the torments of hell. But you might spare a thought or two for her. Not easy for a woman after what her idiot relatives claimed."

"You're right," Reece admitted, determined to be kinder to Anne. She was as much a pawn in all this as he was.

No, more, for she had done nothing save attract his attention. She had not enticed him openly in the hall that night, or teased him, or asked him to a clandestine rendezvous, yet she had been forced to marry, too. As she had said, she couldn't help it if she was beautiful. Even now, she had no way of knowing that her clear green eyes, her soft skin and wondrous lips made his heart race, or that the simple brush of his lips across hers inflamed him so much he could scarce draw breath.

The skinny, spotty minstrel finally stopped caterwauling and the other musicians picked up their instruments. Without a word, Kynan jumped up and darted across the hall. In the next few moments, he was leading Anne in a round dance.

Reece sat on a hard wooden bench, telling himself his torment would not last and trying not to scowl.

Chapter Seven

Attempting to calm her racing heart, Anne sat motionless on the stool before the dressing table as Lisette combed her hair. Worries and questions about what was going to happen tonight kept careening about her anxious mind.

She clasped her hands in her lap and tried to enjoy the rasp of the comb, the gentle tug on her scalp, the relief of being free of Damon and the others...

It seemed but moments ago that she had retired from the wedding feast amidst whispers and smirks, knowing smiles and jealous scowls. Before that, it felt as if she had danced for an eternity, although never again with Reece after the first.

She should not have been surprised that he didn't want to dance with her, given his feelings about their marriage, but it was distressing nonetheless, especially after that mind-numbing kiss.

But Reece couldn't very well stay away from her chamber tonight, or the king would hear of it and per-

haps guess what he planned to do. That would anger
the king even more, and since Reece was wisely cautious in that regard, she doubted he would take that
chance.

So, he would come to the chamber…and then what?
Sleep on the floor? If they were alone for any length
of time in the night—or indeed, for more than a few
minutes, she supposed—people would assume the
marriage had been consummated.

Reece would not want that.

What, then, was he going to do to imply to the king
that he was doing his husbandly duty, while leaving
it possible for people to believe that he had not?

"*Mon Dieu,* such a sigh," Lisette said with a giggle. "And no wonder, my lady, with such a husband.
Many young ladies are in despair this day! I tell you,
several of them had hopes that Henry would change
his mind and call off the wedding. I heard more than
one thought of visiting Sir Reece last night for a last
chance with him before he wed."

Although Lisette spoke merrily and surely only in
jest, a sharp stab of jealousy pricked Anne nonetheless.

"But then they did not dare. They did not wish to
ruin their chances with his brothers or his friends."

Anne pushed aside her foolish jealousy. "Despite
the lowly birth of Sir Urien Fitzroy?"

"What is that when his sons are such fine, noble
fellows? I assure you, their looks and their wealth
make up for their father's low birth, do they not? Why,

the Morgans' father was basely born, too, and there is not a woman here who would not consider herself fortunate to catch their handsome eyes.''

Perhaps not, Anne reflected, but whether their families would approve such a marriage was another thing entirely.

Lisette smiled wistfully and Anne studied her reflection in her mirror. ''Would you count yourself fortunate to catch a Fitzroy's eye?''

Lisette giggled and her cheeks reddened as if Anne had boldly offered her husband to her. *''Mon Dieu, non!''*

''But you think they are handsome men, do you not? Does not every woman at court?''

Lisette set down the comb and returned her mistress's steadfast gaze. ''Handsome, yes. But for me, they are too much the warriors, the leaders of men. I want a man to be like clay in my hands, my lady. Soft and yielding. I would have a lover, not a warrior.''

Anne saw the sincerity in the young woman's eyes, and believed her.

Then she thought of Reece's lips on hers. They had been soft and yielding, and Reece might prove to be an even better lover than he was a warrior, if his kisses were anything to go by—but she would not tell Lisette about that.

''That doesn't mean they will not be the perfect lovers for somebody else, my lady,'' Lisette continued. ''Especially for a woman who, I think, wants a warrior in her bed.''

Lisette was, perhaps, a bit too shrewd.

"Now you are ready, my lady."

For bed. Anne flushed and warmed as she imagined Reece in her bed, naked save for the silken coverlet over his body.

Fighting a surge of desire, she stood up and turned in a circle, her long, unbound hair to her waist.

"How do I look?" she asked, trying to sound amused and not quite succeeding as Lisette studied her as if she were a work of art, and she the artist. "Like an angel, my lady."

"Then why are you frowning?"

"Because a man wishes to find a passionate woman in his bed, not an angel."

No doubt Sir Reece would prefer it if she were a preternatural creature. Then he could have the marriage annulled on supernatural grounds.

However, this maid was not to be privy to their plans, for it was a fact that all maids gossiped, and Reece would not want his plan to get to the queen, or the king. "All my shifts are white."

"Your skin is not."

Anne didn't think it was possible to blush more than she already had, but she discovered she was wrong. "I...I cannot be naked," she protested.

"You do not have to reveal all," Lisette said with a cunning smile. "A shoulder will do. Indeed, I have heard that the curve of a shoulder can be more exciting than a breast."

Anne stared at her maidservant. "Where did you hear such a thing?"

"A lady's maid hears many such things." Lisette frowned. "Do I shock you, my lady?"

"Not really. I just never gave such matters much thought."

At the sound of footsteps, Lisette gasped and giggled at the same time, her hazel eyes bright with an excitement that was nothing to Anne's. "The groom—he comes!"

Could one forget how to breathe? How to think? How to walk? It seemed as if her body was totally benumbed, except for a sort of gnawing hunger deep inside.

"To the bed, quick!" Lisette ordered as she frantically began to tidy the dressing table. "And your shoulder, my lady." When Anne didn't move, she gestured wildly, as if trying to shoo a gaggle of geese. "To the bed, my lady! And your shoulder!"

Jolted out of her momentary numbness, Anne scurried to the bed and scrambled under the coverlet. She scooted backward until she was sitting with her back against the headboard. Once there, she swiftly tugged the knot in the drawstring at her neck until it came undone, then shoved the garment off her right shoulder.

"Your hair, my lady!"

She put her hand to her head. "What about it?" she cried, an edge of panic in her voice.

"It should be like a curtain, spread upon the pillows."

Without pausing to ask why, anxious and excited in equal measure, Anne fluffed out her hair. Then, her throat dry, her whole body tense as that of a startled doe when it first hears the beaters in the bush, she swallowed hard and smoothed the coverlet over her lap. She couldn't be more tense and anxious if Reece really was going to make love with her that night.

The door burst open and a horde of men crowded into the room, the king among them. Very conscious of her exposed shoulder only half hidden by her hair, she realized Piers and her half brothers were not with Henry. Thank God. They were the last people she wanted to see tonight.

As the king came to a skittering, laughing halt, he stared as if taken aback, but what else did he expect? He had made her a bride.

Anne suddenly wanted to pull the coverlet up over her breasts, or slouch down beneath them. Instead she sat as still as a stone, unable to do anything except stare herself as Reece came to stand at the foot of the bed.

How handsome he looked in his dark garments, despite his bruised cheek and reddened eye. His intense, enigmatic gaze raked her and her stomach clenched and her body hummed with a primitive response to his burning scrutiny. Despite his plan and the reasons for it, she wanted to sink into the feather bed with his body settled between her hips, her legs and arms holding him tightly to her.

She wet her dry lips and forced the image away as she tried to control the response of her body.

That proved to be impossible.

"We bring the bridegroom, my lady," Henry finally—and unnecessarily—declared.

Still staring at her, Reece bowed with great formality.

Clearly the sight of her, bare shoulder and all, was not affecting him. Or maybe there was something wrong with her, that she felt so much while he felt so little.

Looking like the young man he was, the king chortled drunkenly, snapping her mind to attention.

"God's wounds, man, what are you doing?" he demanded, slapping Reece so hard on the back, Anne winced. "You're standing there like a damn eunuch and I know full well you're not. If she's not a sight to warm a man's blood, I don't know what is!"

Anne pressed her lips together and tried not to take umbrage, even if the king spoke as if she were an inanimate object, like the stool or the table. She was used to that, but that didn't mean she liked it.

Henry frowned at Reece, who could have been made of marble, so still was he. "Are you dead? A corpse? Don't just stand there, man!"

Reece flinched. When he spoke, he stopped staring at her and glanced at the king—with a look a soldier would hate to encounter from an opponent on the battlefield. His voice was very calm and steady, though, despite that swift, acrimonious look that was just as quickly gone. "I assure you, sire, I am very much alive."

The king roared a laugh. "Only stunned by her beauty, eh, like the rest of us? Some men would kill for a woman like that. My God, Reece, you should be down on your knees thanking me."

"Thank you, sire," Reece said with another bow to his king.

"You're most welcome!"

Anne wanted to squirm. Or tell them to go, all except Reece.

Henry's gaze swept over the other men, including Reece's brothers and his Welsh friends, who were studying her as keenly as he had. "But now," he cried, "let us depart and leave the merry couple to their *rest.*"

The king laughed merrily at his own joke as he led the way.

As the men crowded out the door, Reece's gaze flicked from her face to her bare shoulder, which seemed to burn hotter than the rest of her warm body.

What was going to happen now? Would he speak, or should she?

Finally, as the silence stretched taut as a drawn bowstring, Reece cleared his throat and said, "You make a very beautiful bride, my lady. I am the envy of the court today."

She swallowed, wetting her throat as best she could. "So am I."

His gaze seemed to grow even more intense as he regarded her, and his eyes darkened. Her body knew what that meant before her mind did. Her heartbeat thundered in her ears, erratic and wild. Her nipples puckered beneath the silkiness of her shift.

"If only they knew," he muttered.

This was to be expected, yet a silent wail of dismay and disappointment keened inside her nonetheless, until a movement behind him stole her attention.

Lisette, who had been at the back of the mob, sidled toward the door.

"*Bonsoir,* my lady," she whispered when she realized Anne had seen her.

Reece abruptly turned on his heel. "Who the devil are you?"

"M-my lady's maid," Lisette stammered, wringing her hands and more subdued than Anne would have believed it was possible for the vivacious French girl to be. "I will go now—"

"No. You stay. I shall leave."

"B-but sir—"

Reece strode past a flabbergasted Lisette and the door banged shut behind him. Openmouthed, Lisette stared at the closed door, then slowly wheeled around to look at Anne.

"I do not understand, my lady," Lisette said, her eyes wide as a cart wheel. "I was leaving. Why did he not stay?"

The words were barely out of her mouth before Lisette gasped and covered her bow-shaped mouth with her hand. "But of course! He is in pain from his injuries! The poor man! And you, my poor mistress! To have to wait until he is better."

Despite the emotions roiling through her, disappointment most of all, Anne couldn't help but be impressed with Lisette's conclusion. It made sense, and hopefully other people would think that, too. They would not automatically guess what Reece had in mind, and need not assume there was something wrong with *her*.

Lisette grinned, and lascivious mischief danced in her merry eyes. "But when he is better, oh la, my lady! He will be the beast uncaged!"

Merciful God, what images that provoked!

"I thought he was not the sort of man for you," Anne replied, sounding much more calm than she felt.

"To make love with?" Lisette shook her head decisively. "*Non,* he is not to my taste. But that is not to say I cannot appreciate such a man from a distance."

Suddenly very weary, Anne burrowed down beneath her coverlet. "We leave at first light, so I bid you good night, Lisette."

"*Bonsoir,* my lady."

When her maid had gone, Anne closed her eyes and tried to sleep. It had been a busy day, and tomorrow would be even busier.

But as she lay alone beneath the silken coverlet, all

she could think of was a passionately, primitively aroused Reece Fitzroy making love with her. The beast uncaged, indeed!

The next morning, a disgruntled, frustrated Reece watched the last of his wife's baggage being loaded onto the cart.

He might have been in a better humor if he had not had to endure watching his brothers and his friends dance with his wife.

He might have been in a genial frame of mind if he had managed to sleep.

He would certainly have been in a much better mood if his wife were not one of the cursed Delasaines. Then he could have made love to her last night. And dear God, how he would have! With that bare shoulder she seemed at once innocent and yet worldly, and the contrast had struck him like a wild gale in the mountains.

He had tossed and turned thinking about loving her. What he would do. How he would begin. Remembering the taste of her soft mouth on his, the feel of her slender, shapely body in his arms, the astonishing sight of her bare shoulder visible through the drapery of her lovely hair. Looking at Anne in bed, so soft and vulnerable, he had been robbed of every feeling save passionate, incredible desire, and so immobilized he could barely move or think. If the king hadn't spoken, he might be standing there staring at her yet.

More than once since, he had wished he *was* a eunuch, just so he could rid his mind of his wild, impossible desire, and sleep.

"Good morning, Sir Reece."

He started and turned to find Anne close beside him.

In the dim light of dawn, wearing a soft green cloak the color of chestnut leaves, the hood surrounding her lovely face, she looked like a nymph or sylph, some delicate mystical creature from when the world was new. A few wisps of her blond hair hid her forehead and curled about her ears, giving him the incredibly arousing impression that she had just that moment arisen from her bed. A downward glance revealed the white hem of another garment beneath her cloak, and his body instantly responded to the notion that she might be wearing nothing more than that thin shift beneath it.

Swallowing hard, he clenched his jaw, mentally stuck his head in a water trough and raised his eyes to her face.

That was not a particularly wise thing to do, for as he looked into her brilliant eyes, he saw again that fascinating contrast between innocence and worldly wisdom. Despite his powerful yearnings, he forced his voice into some semblance of calm normality. "Good morning, my lady."

"It looks to be a fine day for traveling," she offered.

He glanced up at the eastern sky, where the deep blue of night had already given way to the pink, orange and yellow streaks of morning. There were no clouds, and the breeze was slight. "Yes." He shifted his feet, like a horse refooting—or an awkward lad. "You are attired for the journey?"

She nodded. "I awakened early and finished packing my things. When that was done, I looked out of my window and saw you here. I realized that I had forgotten to ask you some things at the feast yesterday."

"Such as?" he prompted, determined not to betray his bashfulness.

"How far is it to Bridgeford Wells?"

"About five days journey to the north and west."

"Ah. And the roads? Are they good?"

"Yes."

"We will stay at inns, or do you have friends who will offer us hospitality along the way?"

"Inns."

God save him, he must sound like a tongue-tied fool—or rude. "I would prefer not to take a long time to get home, and if we stay with friends, that will add a few days."

"You have many friends between here and your home?"

"A few."

She looked down at the ground, and he once more wished he had Blaidd's glib ease of speaking. "Would you prefer to ride, or would you rather travel in the cart?" he asked.

Her smile blossomed and his heart seemed to twist

in his chest. He would have said it was not possible for her to be more attractive, but that wide and honest smile informed him otherwise.

"I would dearly love to ride," she replied. "When I was a girl, I had a pony I rode all the time, as long as it wasn't lashing rain. My half brothers have not allowed me that pleasure for a very long time, though, so I should have a placid beast."

He could imagine her as a petite blond girl galloping about the countryside on a sturdy pony, her hair streaming behind her.

"Perhaps they fear for your safety."

Skepticism flashed across her face. The look quickly disappeared, but it had already spoken volumes about how her family treated her. That made him even more determined to see that she suffered as little as possible from the unfortunate turn of fate his hasty act had caused.

"I have the perfect mount, a mare named Esmerelda," he continued without waiting for her to answer. "She was supposed to be Trevelyan's mount for the squires' melee, but that was my mother's idea. Before we left, my father took us aside and said Trev was to use my horse, or Gervais's, for no man of pride would ever want to appear in a tournament mounted on poor old Esmerelda."

Anne laughed softly, and he was delighted to think he had caused it. He also wished Blaidd was there to see that a man didn't have to debase himself to make a woman laugh.

"Poor old Esmerelda sounds about right for me, then," she acknowledged, her eyes sparkling like dew on the meadow in the summer's sun.

His gaze drifted to her parted lips. A primitive impulse urged him to cover them with his own and kiss her thoroughly and completely, until neither one of them had breath left in their lungs. Fortunately, he had the strength to ignore it.

"Piers has his own horse," she remarked, nodding toward the stables across the courtyard.

Tearing his attention from her mouth, he followed her gesture and saw a younger, thinner and undeniably better looking version of Damon Delasaine saddling a dark brown horse.

He had nearly forgotten about her petition to the king. "That's good." He slid Anne a glance. "How does he feel about coming with us?"

"He is pleased to have the opportunity to learn from your father."

He caught an undercurrent in her voice and suspected Piers Delasaine was not particularly overjoyed with the opportunity. While she might be free of prejudice against those of lesser birth, her younger brother might not share that view. Well, he would not be the first youth who came to Castle Gervais scornful of his father, only to discover that they had been wrong to harbor such a bias.

Anne glanced around the courtyard. "Where are your brothers? Are they traveling with us, too?"

"Just Trevelyan," he replied. "Gervais will stay at court."

"Ah, to let us know when Henry seems of a more compliant humor."

He hadn't thought of that—not exactly, anyway. "Yes."

"Then where is your younger brother?" She nodded toward the youth still fiddling with his saddle. "Piers is nearly ready."

He realized they were looking at him. Anne gestured for him to join them and he did, ambling across the courtyard in a way that set Reece's teeth on edge.

It seemed a common failing of boys on the edge of manhood, for Trev also ambled as if everyone had all the time in the world.

Piers finally reached them. He came to a halt beside Anne, his attitude wary yet full of protective bravado.

Good for him. It showed he had a proper brotherly regard for Anne that their siblings obviously lacked.

Kynan, Blaidd and Gervais appeared at another door. Kynan and Blaidd seemed surprisingly and astonishingly refreshed, despite their late hours last night. Gervais looked as exhausted as Reece felt.

"So, here they are, the happy couple," Blaidd declared as he joined them. He ran an insolent gaze over Reece that he did not appreciate. "You look like a dog's breakfast."

"So do you," he shot back. It wasn't true, but he didn't care. What a thing to say in front of Anne!

"Well, I've been more rested in my life, I agree,"

Blaidd replied jovially. He winked at Anne in a familiar way that made Reece's blood boil.

Even if she was his wife in name only, that didn't give Blaidd leave to flirt with her.

"Ready to go?" Gervais asked, breaking the sudden tension.

"We will be, if Trevelyan ever deigns to get here."

"Seems there was a young lady-in-waiting he wanted to say farewell to," Blaidd said. "Young love, you know. Tongue-tied he'll be, like all you Fitzroys, so it'll take a while."

"While you would be eloquence itself, I suppose," Reece replied with a hint of exasperation and wounded pride that he could not mute. Neither he nor Gervais were particularly eloquent around women, nor was Trevelyan—but then, compared to Blaidd Morgan, who was?

Blaidd had the audacity to wink at Anne again. "Of course. A Welshman, aren't I?"

She flushed, looking very modest and very pretty, and it was a struggle not to scowl.

Blaidd grinned as if vastly amused, the bastard. "We also came to tell you Henry's still abed, so you can make your retreat before he even knows you're gone."

Reece did not appreciate the word "retreat." He wasn't fleeing. It was simply not practical, possible or prudent to remain at court when he didn't intend to sleep with the wife the king had chosen for him. Besides, they had to wait for Trev and that little French maidservant of Anne's, the one whose presence had proved very necessary last night.

"Oy!" Trevelyan called out from the kitchen door. He waved as he strolled toward them.

"Where have you been?" Reece demanded, crossing his arms.

"A man can't help it if a woman doesn't want him to leave, can he?" he replied, grinning.

"A man can be prompt whatever the circumstances, and not keep his fellows waiting," Reece snapped. "I have no intention of being benighted in the woods and prey to bandits."

Anne's maid came scurrying out another door, carrying a big bundle of what looked like bed linens.

Every head turned to watch her as she hurried across the courtyard.

"Mille pardons!" she cried, panting, as she tossed the bundle into the cart. "I had to fight the laundress for the sheets."

Oh, good God, the sheets! As bloodstained sheets were proof a virgin had been bedded, sheets without them could prove he had not slept with his wife.

Or, he suddenly realized with a sick feeling, that she was not a virgin. Some people at court would surely jump to that conclusion, and Anne's reputation further soiled.

"I brought my own from home," Anne said quietly beside him. "Royal household or not, I prefer to know that they are clean. That is why she had to get them back."

He subdued a relieved sigh and gave her a little smile.

"Since we are all here, we can be on our way."

As those who were leaving prepared to depart, Reece did his best to ignore his wife. Meanwhile, he noticed both Trevelyan and Piers Delasaine surreptitiously eyeing Lisette, then glaring at each other when they caught the other at it.

God's blood, a foolish rivalry over a maid's affections was something he did not need! He already had enough to trouble him and make this journey an ordeal.

"A moment before you go, Reece," Blaidd said, taking his arm and pulling him away from the cortege to a more secluded part of the courtyard.

Reece was disconcerted to see the serious expression on his friend's usually merry face. "What is it?"

"Look you, I know she's a beauty and she seems harmless enough, but you mustn't trust your wife," Blaidd said, his tone as grim as his visage.

"What are you talking about?"

Sympathy shone out of his friend's dark eyes. "I know you think you can resist her, and I hope to God you can, but she's a rare woman, Reece. I realized that after one dance. She could tempt the gods themselves to reveal their secrets with just a look from those eyes. Yet she is a Delasaine, and they're as dangerous as mad dogs. I'm not saying she's evil, Reece, but who knows what she's really like? We don't, that's for certain, and you cannot judge by looks alone.''

Reece took a deep breath. He knew his friend spoke out of concern and compassion. Nevertheless, he was sorry to realize that Blaidd was right. Harsh reality must win out over whatever fancies his heart might conjure.

"I will," he vowed.

Blaidd nodded and clapped his hand on Reece's shoulder. "Give my love to your parents."

"Of course."

"Safe journey, friend."

Reece grinned. "You be safe, too. Keep away from the married ones, Blaidd."

"Don't I always?"

"There's always a first time," Reece replied as he went to join his cortege.

Blaidd gravely watched his friend mount. "Aye, my friend, there is," he murmured. "Like Adam with the apple."

Chapter Eight

Under other circumstances, Anne would have enjoyed riding through the countryside. The day stayed fine and the roads were excellent, neither too muddy or too dusty. Rolling hills gave a comforting sense of protection, and the occasional reaching of a rise provided stunning views.

Unfortunately, she could not forget the circumstances that put her in this placid mare's saddle any more than she could completely ignore the silent, lordly knight riding beside her, the handsome young man who was also her husband. She also remembered well her meeting with Damon, and what he wanted her to do. She was tempted to look over her shoulder every few moments and search for Benedict on the road behind them.

Well, she didn't have to look to be sure he was there somewhere. Damon had said he would be, so he would be, whether Benedict wanted to obey him or not.

It was always so between them, for Damon controlled Benedict as he did her and Piers. She didn't know exactly what hold Damon had over him, but she didn't live in a solitary cell like a holy hermit. She heard things at Montbleu, whispers of violent acts and women hurt, or worse. Both her half brothers had a temper and were so greedy, she could well imagine they would not take a woman's refusal lightly. Damon, however, could control his rage better, although in him it became a cold and twisted thing. Benedict lashed out, just as he had at Sir Reece. No doubt he had gone too far in one of his rages, and Damon used fear of legal punishment or retribution to bend Benedict to his will.

She shivered, for she had felt Benedict's wrath herself. She could too easily picture him taking out his ire on a woman who had refused him.

"Are you cold?"

She started and looked at Reece. "No, my lord."

"Ah."

He went back to staring straight ahead at the road, as enigmatic as before. They were at the front of the cortege; behind them came the baggage cart, where Lisette sat beside the driver. Piers, Trevelyan and the soldiers of their guard rode behind.

Anne sighed and shifted, settling herself more comfortably on Esmerelda, who was indeed a model of placidity. She was so placid, Anne wondered what would happen if she had to gallop. The mare would probably balk, turn her head and give her the same sort of look that had been on Sir Reece's face when the king commanded them to marry.

"Something amuses you?"

Startled, she gave an inadvertent tug on the reins.

Esmerelda's protesting whinny indicated the mare was not impressed with the unexpected yank.

Anne stroked the animal's pale mane as she regarded Reece. "I was thinking that if we have to hurry at any time in our journey, Esmerelda will not be pleased."

He glanced at her. "She can gallop if she has to, but she won't like it. I don't expect she will have to, though. This road is safe enough and we are well guarded."

It occurred to Anne that this was just the sort of opportunity Damon would tell her to exploit. God save her, how she hated being Damon's spy, but he had given her no choice. "My lord, you spoke before of the powerful and influential friends of your family who can help us at court. Who might they be?"

"First among them would be the Baron De-Lanyea."

"I think I've heard of him. He was wounded on Crusade and has only one eye, I believe."

"Yes. He is half Welsh and half Norman, and respected by both, as well as the king. His opinion carries great weight at court, although he rarely attends. He is too old now to travel much."

"How did your father come to make such an important friend?"

"My father was hired by the baron's enemy."

"That hardly seems a basis for friendship."

The tips of Reece's ears reddened, as if he were embarrassed. "My father soon realized the kind of man who had hired him, and went to the baron's aide. He has trained all the baron's sons, too, and his nephew. If one or the other needs help, they have but to ask, and it is gladly given."

Anne thought of her half brothers. They knew men she would call allies, but none she would call friends, certainly not the sort of friends who would help in a crisis. Damon especially would turn anybody's trouble to his own advantage if he could, and the people he associated with would be no different.

"There is also the Baron DeGuerre, Sir Hu Morgan, Sir George de Gramercie and Sir Roger de Montmorency, to name a few. He has either fought beside them, or trained their sons."

Powerful and influential, indeed! These were all famous and notable warriors, all said to hold their honor very dear. They were also completely loyal to the crown. No wonder Damon thought to learn what he could of them, for men like this would be his natural enemies.

If these friends of Sir Urien Fitzroy spoke in favor of an annulment, the king would likely grant it. She sighed wearily as she thought of what would happen to her after that.

"Are you tired? We have come a long way."

Damon would never ask her such a question when

they traveled. He alone decided when to stop, and where, and what they all would eat. "Not particularly. We made the journey from Montbleu to Winchester in only a few days. Damon does not like to stop at inns. He claims the innkeepers are too greedy and the food is terrible. Benedict always argues with him and calls him a penny-pinching miser."

"Is he?"

"I don't know that I could call him a miser, exactly. If it is an expense he can justify to himself, he spends willingly, but if he thinks the price is unjustified or inflated, he complains as if he was being asked to give up his arm along with his coins."

"I can well believe it. Still, some would say he is wise."

"They would not have to listen to the quarrels about it," she replied, enjoying speaking with Reece in this amicable manner about something that was not tied to Damon's plan, even if she would prefer a subject other than her family. "Benedict loves to stay at inns—or at least he enjoys flirting with the serving women there and he pays no heed to the costs. I must confess that Benedict would probably have bankrupted the family by now had Damon's hand on the purse strings not prevented it."

Reece frowned.

"I may not love or even like my half brother," she said, "but I will be honest about him."

Reece slid her a speculative glance. "That's very

just of you. I do not think he would do the same if the situations were reversed.''

She flushed at his compliment and was pleased to think that for once, his eyes had revealed something of his thoughts.

"Probably not," she agreed. "He has always hated me, because he hated my mother. She 'interfered' too much, he says. I believe he would have hated anybody who took our father's attention away from him.''

"Yes, I can believe that, too.''

"What of you and your brothers, Sir Reece? Do they begrudge you your place as eldest son?''

"They might," he admitted, "but I doubt it. Our parents treat us quite equally, all things considered.''

"What sort of things?''

"As the eldest, I am expected to set a good example, in the same way that Henry expects his knights to behave. Obviously, I have recently failed on both counts.''

The companionable mood shifted away from that amicability, and she sighed with regret as they fell into another silence, until Reece put his hand on his side. "Since you have been honest, so shall I. I confess the wound in my side is beginning to ache. I, too, should probably rest awhile.''

With that, and before she could make a response, he held up his hand to halt the cortege. He pointed to a little clearing off to the side of the road, beneath some chestnut and oak trees, and Anne heard a stream babbling nearby. "We will stop here awhile and rest and water the horses."

The driver of the cart, a big, burly fellow, clicked his tongue and turned the wagon. Piers, Trevelyan and the soldiers likewise went to the clearing and dismounted, their chatter adding to the general noise.

She studied Reece's side as he dismounted slowly and with some care. She could see no moisture or other signs of blood, so she hoped his wound had not started to bleed again and that he was simply, and wisely, being cautious instead.

Anne thought again of her half brothers. They would complain of pain the moment they had the slightest twinge and send for the old woman in the village who was learned in such things. Fearing that she would be pressed into service as their nurse if she ever learned, Anne had assiduously avoided being anywhere near the woman. Now, for the first time, she regretted her ignorance.

Reece called out Trevelyan's name and nodded at her, obviously intending that his brother help her dismount, but Piers was there first. "Here, Anne, allow me," he offered, raising his arms.

She put her hands on his shoulders and realized that he wasn't looking at her at all. He was facing her but watching Lisette out of the corner of his eye, and especially her shapely ankles as she lifted her skirt to climb down off the cart.

"Piers," Anne admonished gently. "She's very

pretty, but please pay attention. I don't want to go tumbling in the mud.''

Grinning sheepishly, Piers gave her his full attention and helped her dismount. Meanwhile, Reece went over to the soldiers. One muttered something and grinned. Reece laughed despite his pain, the sound as melodious and pleasant as his voice, and he clapped the fellow on his shoulder. Obviously he was capable of easy camaraderie, just not so much with her.

But then, she was almost a stranger to him, and he to her, even if she was vastly impressed by what she had seen of him so far, and his kind treatment of her.

Trevelyan Fitzroy's voice came drifting across the clearing from the vicinity of the cart, drawing her attention. ''You must allow me to escort you to the stream, Lisette. There could be fierce brigands about.''

Fierce brigands who wouldn't notice a guard of twenty armed men and a knight? Piers glared at the youth, who was leaning against the cart and grinning at Lisette. He really was a good-looking young man, although not as impressive as his older brother, nor was he any better looking than Piers.

Anne glanced back at her husband. He had raised his tunic to study his bandage, and she noted with satisfaction that there was no fresh blood on it.

''Brigands my eye,'' Piers muttered darkly, capturing her attention as he echoed her previous thoughts. ''He just wants to get her alone.''

Lisette and Trevelyan headed toward the stream, and Anne studied the couple as they walked away.

"But look how far away she is from him," she noted. "And he seems to be doing all the talking. That, I assure you, is not natural for Lisette."

Anne knew that Piers's greatest desire was to be a champion of tournaments, so she gave her brother a comforting smile and said, "No need to be jealous, Piers. She told me she wants a lover, not a warrior. I don't think either one of you will stand much chance with her."

Whatever Piers planned for his future, however, it became immediately and unfortunately clear that he wasn't about to let Trevelyan Fitzroy triumph in the matter of Lisette. "She didn't refuse his offer."

"He's the son of her new overlord. She might not want to offend him."

Piers's eyes narrowed. "I don't think they should be going off alone together. I don't trust him. Look what his brother did."

As if she, of all people, needed reminding! Nevertheless, Anne ignored the pang of annoyance as Piers headed off toward the stream looking so purposeful she feared he might do something foolish, like start a fistfight. She began to follow him.

"My lady?"

She halted and turned to see Reece striding toward her. She didn't know what to do—wait for Reece, or continue after Piers.

The speed with which Reece crossed the distance between them decided for her. Short of running, she could never get away from him before he reached her.

"The men have spread a blanket on the grass," he said, nodding toward it.

A few of the soldiers were also fetching baskets and wineskins from the cart, and the delicious smell of fresh bread wafted to her.

"In a moment," she said. "I would like to stretch my legs a bit first."

And if that takes me after Piers, so be it.

"I, too, could use a stretch of the legs."

He held out his arm, and she had no choice but to slip hers through it. Once again, and despite the distraction of a possible tussle between Piers and Trevelyan, the contact of her body with his sent warm thrills along her body. She could scarcely imagine what it would feel like to make love with him.

Yet her vivid imagination was doing a very good job of trying, at that particular moment—so good, in fact, that she felt the heat of a blush color her face.

"Shall we walk by the stream, my lady?" he asked, as calm as a windless day while she struggled to disregard the sensations he created.

"If you like."

He headed the same way Piers, Trevelyan and Lisette had gone. Perhaps he had seen the competition between the two youths and had chosen this route for that very reason.

Should she speak of it, or let it rest? After all, considering what Lisette had said before, there was probably no reason for concern.

On the other hand, Lisette was young, so were they,

and both boys were good-looking and from noble families. If Lisette allowed herself to be swayed by either of their addresses, she would not be the first maid to do so, or the last.

She relaxed when she spied Piers squatting on the riverbank ostensibly to drink, while Trevelyan and Lisette stood talking nearby.

Reece halted and she had to, too. "There was no need for worry. Trevelyan is a gentleman."

So, he had guessed why she had decided to walk toward the river. Perhaps that should not have been unexpected, nor should it be cause for annoyance, but there was something in the tone of his voice she did not like. Pulling her arm from his, she faced him and raised her chin. "So is Piers."

"I'm glad," he murmured as his gaze traveled lower, over her body.

In spite of her indignation only a moment ago, heat seemed to follow in the wake of that gaze.

Suddenly she felt as she had on her wedding night, breathless with anticipation and yet full of trepidation.

She forced herself to concentrate on the problem of the present. "Perhaps you should speak to your brother. I don't want him trying to seduce my maid. I won't have Lisette treated as a woman for him to practice on, as so many young nobles consider the young serving women of their household."

She immediately regretted speaking so firmly. That tone would enrage Damon. Then she realized Reece did not look angry. He looked…impressed.

"Your concern for your maidservant does you credit, my lady," he said quietly, in the sort of soft and intimate tone she could imagine he would use with a woman he had just delightfully bedded. "But as I said, Trevelyan is a gentleman. He would no sooner treat her poorly than he would a lady."

Reece's lips curved upward in a little smile. "Besides, once we reach Castle Gervais and they begin training, they will both be too tired to think about a girl."

The mood between them encouraged her to ask another question that had been troubling her. "I have been wondering how you intend to explain our sleeping arrangements when we stop for the night, for I assume you do not intend to join me in my bed."

"Of course not. There must be no doubt that we never...that we have not...that the marriage has not been consummated," he replied. "We may need witnesses, too."

She recalled what glib Blaidd Morgan had said about the Fitzroys being tongue-tied around women. At the time she had believed that another of his silly, teasing remarks, but now she began to wonder if that was true. That would explain Reece's general silence and short answers.

And what, then, did it mean when he spoke more freely? That he felt comfortable with her, or that he didn't care what she thought of him?

"Lisette assumed that you left me on our wedding

night because of your wounds," she said, giving him an excuse. "Surely no one will question that."

Try as she might to focus only on the immediate problem, she could not, unfortunately, separate the notion of making love with him from what else Lisette had said. *The beast uncaged.*

Even now, simply standing by the stream and with his side no doubt aching, there was an aura of caged vitality in him. And with that thought, as always, came the wonder of what would happen if that constraint were ever to drop away.

"Then let us hope everyone makes that assumption, too, since I have no desire to explain myself to an innkeeper or anyone else, and I am very loath to lie."

She was surprised he would have any compunction about lying to an innkeeper or any underling. Damon and Benedict certainly wouldn't. They would lie to the king if it suited their purposes—as they already had.

She glanced at Reece's side. "Is your wound giving you much pain?"

"No."

"It is not bleeding again, is it?"

"No."

"I regret that I know nothing of the healing arts, so I cannot help you."

"I do not want your help."

His brusque words, unexpected after the way they had talked, hit her like a painful thunderbolt. She abruptly turned to go back to the cortege.

He put his hand on her arm to stop her.

She faced him, doing her best to blink back her tears. She did not want him to know how he had hurt her. She would not give him the sort of power over her Damon possessed.

"I am a gentleman, too, Anne," Reece said, his voice low and husky, as if he were anything but a gentle man. "But God save me, no woman has ever tempted me as you do."

Chapter Nine

As Anne looked up at him with her brilliant, questioning green eyes, his resolution wavered like a sapling in a strong wind. Oh, God, he wanted to kiss her!

And then he could no longer resist the impulses surging and crashing within in. He forgot that Trevelyan, Piers and the lively little maid were nearby. He pulled Anne into his arms and captured her mouth with a fiery kiss.

His wife, his beautiful, utterly desirable wife, the woman whose presence beside him had been a torture, made a little sound of acknowledgment, almost a whimper. It was the sort of sound a woman made when she was in the throes of passion.

The sort of sound he desperately wanted to hear Anne make as she lay in his arms, despite the impossibility of their marriage.

Her head tilted back as if she were thirsty and drinking deep, and her mouth moved upon his with wondrous sensuality. Her hands crept around his waist and

up his back, holding him to her with a strength he had
never imagined she possessed. His kiss softened and
gentled as his lips slid over hers, then his tongue
parted her lips and slipped into the moist warmth of
her mouth.

That was too much, or too soon, or else she recalled
better than he the reason they should not be alone
together, for she broke the kiss. Panting softly, she
stared at him.

Again he cursed himself for a weak-willed fool. It
was as if all caution and reason fled like chaff in the
breeze when he was with Anne.

She didn't speak, but what was there to say? Once
more, the fault for this was his, and his alone. He
glanced swiftly at the boys and Lisette.

They had not seen them there, or the kiss. They
didn't know he and Anne were there at all, hidden by
the shadows of the trees. Thank God.

"I'm sorry, Anne," he said brusquely. "That will
not happen again. Now come. We should get back to
the others."

Before she could answer or question him, he
shouted for Trevelyan and strode back toward the
clearing, leaving her to follow.

He wouldn't even take her hand again. If his plan
was to have any hope of succeeding, he must stay
away from Anne, and she from him. He must not
touch her or kiss her or be alone with her, not ever
again.

Not unless he wanted his family tied to the detestable Delasaines forever, and his future a ruin at his feet.

"So then, the *duc* said, 'But sir, that is my wife!'" Lisette finished with a merry giggle.

She had been regaling Anne with tales of life at the French court ever since they had started on their journey again and Anne had decided to ride in the cart rather than on Esmerelda. She had claimed she was too fatigued and would prefer the softer seat of a cushion in the cart; in truth, she was so confused by her husband's manner and searing kiss that she did not want to ride beside him.

She had been caught totally off guard by his embrace...well, perhaps not totally. She had seen the change come to his eyes, and felt her own heartbeat quicken at the sight. She had waited with breathless anticipation, wondering what he was going to say.

And then his mouth had covered hers, and all she knew was that kissing Reece was like nothing else—exciting, marvelous and wonderful.

Shocked by his unleashed passion and the force of her own response, she had been overwhelmed, while all too aware that Piers was close by. She would not have him confront Reece, too, coming to her unnecessary defense.

Or perhaps it was necessary. Although it no longer seemed likely, it could be that Reece would still blame her if his plan went awry.

Judging by his words, though, this would be the last

time he kissed her, so it would surely be wiser to forget it. Besides, she should be using this time to find out what Lisette thought about Piers and Trevelyan, so she would know better how to deal with her brother. Surely Lisette could not be insensible to their behavior and what it meant. "Lisette?"

"*Oui*, my lady?" the girl asked brightly.

"Lisette, you must have noticed that my brother and my brother-in-law—" It was the first time Anne had said those words, and they struck her as a little strange. "Both my brother and my brother-in-law like you."

The sparkle in Lisette's eyes did not diminish. "Oh, la, of course, my lady. They are boys."

Anne hadn't thought Lisette vain.

"It is the nature of boys that age to notice girls, is it not?" Lisette continued matter-of-factly. "Short, tall, thin, plump, they do not care."

Anne was no expert on boys; she only knew Piers. "Really?"

Lisette laughed again. "Indeed, it is, unless they are very ill. They are like puppy dogs, always chasing after something. So of course they will talk to me and try to get my attention, and they will growl and snap at each other as if I am but a bone to wrangle over."

She, too, knew what it was to feel like an object for men to quarrel over. She hated it, but oddly enough, Lisette seemed amused. "You don't mind?"

"What is there to mind? It is simply in their nature,

like eating and sleeping. If it were not me, they would be quarreling over some other girl, or a horse, or a pair of boots. Have you ever seen two rams butting heads? That is what boys of that age are like.''

Lisette spoke as if young men were a species to be indulged. Still, this rivalry could be a problem, so she had to be clear about Lisette's feelings. ''Do you *like* either of them?''

That sobered Lisette at once. ''Like, as in to take to my bed? *Mon Dieu,* my lady, *non!* I want a man, not a boy. I am sure they are both virgins so they have no experience, no knowledge. I would feel like a teacher, and I assure you, my lady, I do not want to be giving lessons when I am with a man. I do not want him fumbling about, unsure and uncertain, either. I want to be swept away by my lover's passion, lost in his embrace, feeling only need and desire—''

''I understand,'' Anne interrupted, her voice a little strained. Lisette's descriptions were rather too vivid.

Especially because they seemed to describe exactly how Anne felt when Reece kissed her. ''I thought you were not encouraging them, but I wanted to be sure.''

''Well, my lady, you may be *very* sure,'' Lisette retorted with a shake of her head as she crossed her arms.

Anne put her hand lightly on Lisette's arm. ''I didn't mean to upset or offend you, Lisette.''

Although her countenance remained grave, Anne was glad to see the merriment return to Lisette's bright eyes. "Forgive my temper, my lady. I suppose it is a sister's duty to make certain a younger brother is not being seduced by a lovely young Parisian girl."

Anne laughed. "Yes, it is. One of many duties. As you say, boys are like puppies and they need a lot of tending."

"So do men," Lisette noted with another giggle.

Anne's laugh turned into a sigh. "I don't know very much about men."

Only Damon and Benedict, and they are proving to be no better examples to me of how an honorable man behaves than they were for Piers.

This time, it was Lisette who patted Anne's arm companionably. "As long as he desires you, you have plenty of time to learn. And the rewards are great," she said with a wink, "as you will soon find out when your husband's wound is healed."

Anne flushed. She would never know about the rewards being the wife of Reece might offer, but she wanted to. Oh, how she wanted to!

Reece wheeled his horse around to ride toward them.

She swallowed hard, taken aback by his sudden action. Had he heard them talking? Had he heard the last thing Lisette said? Oh, heaven help her, she hoped not!

"We will stop for the night soon," he announced as he reached them.

His gaze did not meet hers before he rode back to

tell the others, and she did not doubt he meant what he had said: he would not touch her again.

Three days later, Benedict slouched into a wayside inn. There had been no other inn between the last one and this. That damn Fitzroy and Anne must have stayed here last night.

After taking off his sodden cloak and tossing it on the nearest bench, he sat and bellowed for ale. Rain had been falling in a steady, demoralizing drizzle all day, making the roads a muddy mess. Water dripped through the louvered opening in the roof onto the fire in the central hearth. A skinny dog lay beside it, sleeping. There were other leaks through the thatch, but none fell on him.

"Curse you, Damon," he muttered under his breath as his gaze wandered over the empty room.

He shouted again, his ire growing. Where was the innkeeper or his woman? He was of half a mind to fetch his own ale and the devil take him if they made him pay, when a woman sauntered into the room. She was tall, in poorly mended garments, but her measuring gaze took in his clothes and his sword, as well as the purse dangling from his belt. Her subsequent slow smile immediately ameliorated the worst of Benedict's rage. He knew at once that she would offer more than food and a bed for the night. "At last, my beauty," he said. "What's a man got to do for some ale?"

She strolled closer. "Pay, same as if he wants anything else around here."

He reached out and hauled her onto his lap. She laughed, low and throaty and knowing.

She wasn't as young as he first thought, and her teeth were far from good, but she was a woman. He patted his purse. "How much for a meal and a night's lodging?"

"Thruppence."

"How much for more?"

She laughed again. "Five pennies."

The sum made him frown and shove her from him. "Too much."

She didn't look at all nonplussed. "If you say so. Others pay it." She gave him a sly, far-from-innocent smile. "I'm worth it."

Benedict had been with enough whores to know the bargaining ploys. "Then let them pay it. I'll settle for the food and bed."

"Well, seeing as how you're such a well-made man, maybe for you, I'll charge less."

He grinned, pleased. And Damon thought he was a spendthrift. "All right. How much less?"

"A penny less."

He nodded. "Food first though, eh?"

"Of course."

While she fetched it, Benedict shook his head to try to dry his hair a bit, then found a better seat, where he could lean against the wall.

Damon could go to the devil if he criticized his spending money on a whore—or he could follow Anne and her husband himself. Let him ride along country roads in all kinds of weather, trailing after them like a whipped dog.

And for what? Not money, not jewels, not pleasure. Information.

If he thought that anything Anne could tell them was so bloody important, Damon should be here, not him.

The woman returned with bread and a beef stew that smelled surprisingly good. For the moment, all his inner grumbling about his brother and his task were forgotten as he ate heartily and downed two mugs of ale.

That appetite sated, he turned his attention to the wench. "What's your name, my beauty?" he asked as she brought him a third mug.

"Radella."

"Well, Radella, since there doesn't seem to be anybody else here, why not join me for an ale?"

What was another penny or two for her goodwill? She'd be all the more eager later, and he liked his women eager.

And maybe she wouldn't mind if he got a little rough. He liked it rough, too.

Radella raised her brows, then nodded and fetched herself a mug and joined him at the table.

"So, Radella," Benedict said, his mouth full of the

last of the bread and gravy from the stew, "not much business today?"

She took a long gulp of ale and wiped her mouth with the back of her hand. "No, not today."

He would also show Damon he was clever. Maybe not as clever as Damon, but he could find out things.

He gestured at the room. "Is it usually so empty?"

Radella shook her head, and her expression suggested she was a little peeved, as if he was insulting her. "No. It's the rain. We had a large party here just yesterday. A knight and his lady and their guard."

Benedict raised an encouraging brow as he swallowed the bread.

"Sir Reece Fitzroy it was," she went on after another swig of ale.

"A fine man, I hear," Benedict said after a belch. "Generous, too."

Radella frowned and shrugged. "That's as may be." She eyed him suspiciously. "Do you know of him?"

"I've heard of him, and his father."

"Ah." She still looked suspicious. "Who are you?"

"A knight traveling home," he lied. Damon wasn't the only one who could lie well, either. "My mother is ill."

He found talk of a sick parent worked well on tenderhearted women, but Radella didn't seem particularly impressed. Apparently she was a hard woman.

He liked that kind. They didn't complain if he hurt them.

"Good-looking fellow, they say," he continued.

Another disgruntled shrug was all the answer Radella made.

Benedict could guess why Radella was so sullen. A canny whore like Radella would have noticed the distance between Reece and Anne, and probably thought to fill it, at least for a night. Reece must have refused her offer.

"He was forced to marry his wife, I heard," Benedict prompted.

Radella's eyes widened with triumph and she leaned forward eagerly. "I *knew* it was more than what he said. He said he was wounded, but I could tell that wasn't all. Why, he hardly spoke two words to her the whole time they was here."

So, Anne wasn't making any progress. Damon wouldn't be pleased.

But whatever the hell was going on between Anne and her husband could wait for the next day. This woman would want to be sure she was still attractive after a man rejected her. A woman in that frame of mind would go out of her way to please another.

He wiped his mouth and smiled greedily. "And now, my beauty," he began, rising. He started to tell her exactly what he expected her to do next.

Radella rose and backed up. "I don't do that sort of thing. Just the regular."

Benedict let no woman dictate to him. He had hated Anne's mother for trying to tell him what he could and could not do. "You're a harlot. You'll do it," he said as he approached her.

Loathing coupled with fear came to Radella's eyes as she sidled away. "My man's out back chopping wood. He'll come in any minute and sooner if I scream."

Benedict lunged for her and got her by the throat. "Then I'll just have to make sure you stay quiet."

Chapter Ten

Reece once more slid a surreptitious glance at Anne as she rode beside him on the placid Esmerelda. Today, as she had been most of the time on this trip, Anne was just as placid as the mare, and as still and silent as if she were a tomb effigy carved from a block of stone. At least it was not raining this afternoon, as it had yesterday. Today the skies were cloudy but not heavy with rain.

Well, Anne was not quite an effigy, for once again she shifted and half turned, looking back at her brother, which she did often.

He wondered if she was still worried about jealous rivalry over Lisette. He wasn't, for it was as he had told Anne. Once they were at Castle Gervais, neither Piers nor Trevelyan would have time or energy to fight over a girl.

He couldn't see what they were so keen to quarrel over himself. Yes, Lisette was pretty and vivacious, but she giggled a great deal and talked quite a bit. In fact, she reminded him of the women at court, who giggled and flirted almost constantly—the ones who were so different from Anne.

In spite of that, he never should have followed her from the king's hall. He never should have gotten within ten feet of her, either that night or since, and God's wounds, he never should have kissed her. After that embrace, the memories of her soft lips against his added to his growing desire—and frustration.

Soon, thank God, they would ride through the gates of Bridgeford Wells. Surely it would be easier to pay little heed to Anne when he was back at home, among familiar people and with more to take his mind off her.

He heard a voice raised in what sounded like a quarrelsome tone, and recognized it as Trevelyan's.

"I tell you, Richard was right to kill them," Piers declared hotly in response. "They were infidels, after all."

"No, he wasn't," Trevelyan retorted. "They were prisoners. I have heard Baron DeLanyea speak of this, for he was there. Richard had them slaughtered like animals, and after Saladin had been nothing but chivalrous toward him. His men deserved the same consideration."

Subduing a sigh, Reece glanced surreptitiously at Anne and noted the slight downturn of her lips.

"But they were infidels all the same," Piers said, "and if he had not killed them, they would have lived to fight against the Holy Cause again."

An old, old argument among soldiers, and one that he did not need to hear. It had been over thirty years since the battle at Acre, and Richard was long dead.

Reece twisted in his saddle and addressed his brother. "The inn is around this next bend. Ride ahead, Trevelyan, and tell them we are coming."

Piers, like a young idiot, shot him a triumphant look.

Reece could guess why he was so pleased. That would mean he would be left near Lisette. "Piers, you go, too."

As triumphant as Piers had been, Trevelyan laughed, then kicked his horse into a gallop. Piers scowled, then spurred his mount, making it a race.

Not the wisest idea he had ever had, Reece realized with a frown as they tore past, their horses' hooves kicking up mud and splattering both him and Anne.

Before he could call out to them to stop acting like dolts, they rounded the bend. Then, up ahead and out of sight, somebody screamed.

Punching his horse's side with his heels, Reece spat out a command for half their guard to remain with the women and the others to come with him.

Anne was not about to be left behind. That cry did not sound like Piers, but she would be certain he had not fallen or otherwise been injured. Miraculously, and in response to Anne's slap on her haunches, Esmerelda broke into a run.

They rounded the bend. The soldiers who had gone

with Reece had come to a halt a short distance from Piers, Trevelyan and her husband, who had all dismounted. The boys were pale to the lips, and Reece knelt beside something.

No, *someone*.

A child was on the ground. As Anne quickly got off her horse and hurried to join them, she saw Reece very carefully and gently help up a boy of about eight years old. The lad stared at his foot. His lip quivered, and Anne knew he was trying very hard not to cry.

Meanwhile, folk who looked like laborers came rushing out of a walled enclosure that was probably the inn.

"It's your ankle, is it?" Reece asked, his voice low and calming as he took the boy's foot in his strong hands and slowly ran his hands over it and up his calf.

The lad nodded as Reece carefully turned his foot, a look of satisfaction coming to his face that relieved Anne, too.

She wondered what Lisette would make of a warrior who had such a calm and soothing voice. So might he sound in bed as he rested after making passionate love.

"Oh, Peter, are you killed?" a woman cried as she shoved her way through the little knot of men and threw herself on her knees beside the boy.

"His ankle isn't broken," Reece said, laying the lad's foot down carefully. "Have no fear, my boy. I've tended many an injury on the tournament field. I'm sure it's just a sprain. I'll bandage it for you and you'll have to be careful for a little while, but no lasting harm has been done."

The lad looked as if the king himself had offered to tend his injury.

Anne thought Reece was far more impressive than the king, and she doubted Henry knew any more about wounds and injuries than she did.

Reece lifted the lad in his strong arms as easily as if he were made of straw. "Where should I take him?" he asked the woman.

"To the inn. He's my son," she replied, more composed now. "I'm Erwina."

"He is not seriously harmed," he assured her again. "You have my word on that, and of course, you'll be compensated for the fright my brother gave you."

Erwina's mouth made an *O*.

Trevelyan, having recovered from the shock, crossed his arms. "Piers was just as—"

Reece silenced him with a look. "Bring my horse."

Peter in his arms, he marched off toward the inn, Erwina scurrying behind him like a subdued hen.

They could hear Reece's friendly words all the way to the gate. "Why, this puts me in mind of the time Lord Rothenbury got knocked off his horse. He was built a lot like you, Peter. Sturdy. But you will be taller, I think."

Anne was sure the lad would be paying little attention to his aching ankle with such a companion.

Meanwhile, Trevelyan grabbed the rein of Reece's horse as well as his own, and stomped after him.

Tempting though it was to follow at once, Anne decided to find out what had happened from Piers.

"We were riding down the road," her brother explained in answer to her query, "when all of a sudden, the boy stepped out from those bushes there."

He pointed to some yews and she saw a basket lying nearby, with chestnuts scattered beside it. The lad must have been gathering them in the wood.

"He stopped dead in his tracks when we called out a warning. When he finally tried to get out of the road, he fell. I suppose that's when he twisted his ankle."

"Then no horse struck him?"

"No."

Her relief that neither Piers nor Trevelyan were directly responsible for the boy's injury gave way to annoyance. "And you both *had* to gallop?"

Staring at the ground, Piers shrugged one reluctant shoulder. "Trevelyan started it."

"No, he didn't. You both went off at a gallop together, like two ninnies. Do you think Sir Reece is going to be impressed with such childishness?"

"I don't care what he thinks of me."

Anne put her knuckle under her brother's chin and raised it so that he had to look at her. "You should."

Defiance gleamed in her little brother's bright blue eyes. "Why? *I'm* not married to him."

Anne's hand fell and she stepped back. "Because there is much he can teach you, too."

"I'm sorry, Anne," Piers said, his defiance dwindling. "I know you didn't have a choice about marrying him, just as I don't have a choice to be here, either. I should try to use this opportunity as best I can. But that Trevelyan, he's a smug, arrogant, spoiled—''

''He's Urien Fitzroy's son, so it would not be wise to cross him.'' She put her hand lightly on Piers's arm. ''Not in anything.'' She glanced meaningfully at Lisette as the cart came creaking round the bend in the road.

Piers colored and shook her hand off. ''You think I should just give up and let him win?''

''What is there to win? A girl's notice? You will have plenty of time for that after you are trained. And horse racing, too. You have more important things to do with your time while you are with the Fitzroys. Come, we should get to the inn.''

''That boy really did just come out of nowhere, like a spirit,'' Piers reiterated as they walked toward the enclosure.

''I'm sure it happened as you said. We shan't say anything more about it.''

Obviously grateful for that, Piers said no more.

The inn was not an impressive place. The yard was dirt, hard packed, and the surrounding wall made of simple, undressed stone. Chickens scratched near the stable and pigs grunted in a sty at the far end, well away from the main building, which was wattle-and-daub and timber, and not very large.

As Piers took charge of Esmerelda, Anne went inside and joined the little group gathered by the injured boy. Straw covered the floor, also likely dirt, and the fire in the central hearth smoked rather badly.

Peter lay on a bench, well cushioned with goose down pillows, while Reece bandaged his ankle. The boy gazed up at his physician with wide-eyed awe, his pain apparently minor or completely forgotten as Reece regaled him with stories of the hapless Lord Rothenbury. Erwina bustled about fetching Reece ale and bread and cheese, each one apparently requiring a separate journey to the kitchen.

Anne felt utterly unnecessary.

Then Peter spotted her, and his eyes widened even more until he resembled a startled owl.

Reece glanced at her over his shoulder. "This is my wife, Lady Anne," he said as if Peter were a high-ranking noble and so worthy of great deference.

"How do you do?" she answered in the same manner.

Peter seemed too stunned to respond. Erwina, however, made up for his silence.

"Welcome! Welcome, my lady!" she cried. "What would you have to eat? Anything you want, my lady, provided we've got it, for you and your excellent husband. I can wring the neck of a few chickens in a trice and have them on the spit in a nonce. Or there's some ham, well cured by own hands and the pride of the shire, if I do say so myself. Or some beef stew? I made some yesterday that should be even better today. A meat pasty? Some cheese? Apples?"

"Roasted chicken would be most welcome," Anne replied. "Enough so that all our party may have some."

"Of course, of course and not a bit of trouble!" the woman cried, hurrying off.

Anne had barely taken a seat on another bench when the sound of squawking told her the woman was making good on her offer. Meanwhile, the rest of their party began to enter the main room, so she had no chance to speak to Reece.

The soldiers were clearly anxious for some ale, and once the chickens were plucked and roasting, Erwina hurried to fetch it.

Meanwhile, Reece tied off the cloth bandage, then straightened, smiling down at his young patient in a way that made Anne's heart lurch in her breast.

So a doting father might regard his own son.

So might Reece look upon a child of theirs, if only he wanted her for his lawful wife.

She stifled a sigh as he sat beside her and reached for the mug of ale Erwina had brought. He silently offered it to Anne first, but she shook her head.

"I didn't realize you could tend injuries," she said after a moment, trying to break the tension caused by his presence so close to her.

He shrugged. "Such knowledge comes in handy. My father insists all his charges learn how to tell if a bone is broken or not, and how to set it if it is. They also learn how to deal with other injuries one might get on a battlefield."

She nodded at his side. "Did your brother look after that?"

Reece made a small, rueful smile. "No. We are not so confident to refuse a physician if one is nearby."

He looked away, then sat up straighter and surveyed the room. "Where are the boys and your maid?"

Concentrating on Reece, she had not realized they were not there. "I don't know."

Reece swiftly got to his feet and marched from the inn, Anne right behind him.

Lisette was retying the canvas over the baggage cart, a small chest containing Anne's toilette articles at her feet. A groom was leading the last of the horses into the commodious stable. The boys were nowhere to be seen.

Reece cocked his head in the direction of the kitchen, and then she heard it, too—the muffled sounds of a fistfight.

With a grunt of exasperation and annoyance, Reece marched toward the back of the kitchen. Anne had to trot to keep up with her husband's long strides as they rounded the corner of the building.

Her stomach knotted with dread, while Reece blurted out a shockingly colorful curse. Piers and Trevelyan were rolling on the ground, pummeling each other.

Reece dashed forward and she was right behind. She had no idea what Reece was going to do, but her first impulse was, as always, to protect Piers.

She skittered to a halt as Reece grabbed the two boys by the back of their mud-covered tunics and hauled them to their feet. He let them go and they stumbled to regain their balance. It was immediately apparent that no serious physical harm had been done.

There was no blood flowing, and they would probably have a few bruises, but that was all.

Evincing a patience she would never have believed a warrior could possess, Reece simply looked at them for a long moment. Panting, they glared at each other, then at him. Slowly they began to calm down.

''Now, what in the name of God do you think you're doing, rolling around like pigs in the mud?'' Reece finally asked when their breathing returned to normal.

She wasn't sure if she should stay or go, but one thing she was sure of: given that Reece was apparently not going to take out his anger physically, it would probably be better if she did not speak. Piers might be more upset by what he would consider a sister's meddling if she did.

''Well, Trevelyan?'' Reece asked, his voice so stern and cold, she was almost sorry for the lad.

''We were settling something,'' Trevelyan declared, swiping at the mud on his cheek with an even muddier hand.

''What have you got to fight about?'' Reece asked with cool deliberation. ''Whose fault it was that you both put that lad's life at risk? As far as I'm concerned, you were equally to blame for that.''

Piers drew himself up. ''I am willing to accept blame for my part in that,'' he said. ''Unlike *some* people, I can admit that I have been mistaken without making other people suffer for it.''

Trevelyan's hands clenched. ''What do you mean by that?''

''Just what I said! Anne had to marry your brother and she was completely innocent.''

She should have guessed Piers would mention this, but she wished he hadn't.

"Be quiet, the pair of you," Reece said.

"But Reece, he's insulting you!" Trevelyan protested.

"Then it is I who should take offense," Reece replied, still just as calm and just as stern. "But I don't. I don't care *what* this lad thinks about me."

Anne was glad Reece wasn't offended, but she winced nonetheless. No young man wanted to hear that his opinion or his intended insult was considered unimportant.

"I do care about fighting," Reece continued, "and I order you never to do it again. While you are in this company or at Castle Gervais, you are allies, not enemies." He pointed at the nearby building. "Now get inside the inn, the both of you, or I'll pick you up and carry you there."

Anne could well believe him capable of doing so. Yet as impressive as his physical strength was, she was more impressed that he was not favoring his brother. He was treating the boys equally.

That reminded her of what he had said about his parents treating their children equally. Given *her* family, she had been somewhat skeptical. Now she could believe it—and envy him for it.

"I only spoke the truth!" Piers cried.

"Piers." She said his name not loudly, but firmly. "Please do as he says."

His face reddening with anger and wounded pride, her brother glared at her for a long moment as if he meant to disobey. Then he took a deep breath, and his hands uncurled. "Very well, Anne. Because *you* ask me."

With that, he stalked back to the inn.

"Trevelyan?" Reece said, one brow raised in query.

Trevelyan hesitated a moment, but he departed without another word, albeit sulking all the while.

Anne sighed and spoke without thinking. "This could be a very long journey."

Reece looked startled, as if she had slapped him, and she chided herself for speaking.

But then he made a wry little smile. "It is obvious that unlike his older brothers, Piers has been taught some self-restraint. That must be your doing, or because of your example."

She flushed at his compliment, and even more because of his approving expression. "I am hopeful your training will likewise prove beneficial."

He took a step closer, his gaze growing more intense in a way that made her heart beat like the rapid flutter of the wings of a bird startled into flight. "Anne, I wish—"

Erwina came bustling around the corner. Anne started as if she'd been struck by an arrow, and Reece looked just as surprised.

"Ah, here you are, Sir Reece and his lady!" Erwina declared. "The meal will not be too long now, and there is bread and soup to begin."

Reece nodded. "We are coming," he said evenly, fortunately sparing Anne having to speak at all.

The woman grinned, a knowing and merry look in her eyes. "There's no hurry. I hear you are newly wedded,'' she said with a wink before she hurried away.

Reece's expression was unreadable. "We had best not linger, or it is likely there will be only carcasses of chicken left. Trevelyan eats enough for three."

"So does Piers."

Emboldened by that moment before Erwina interrupted, she let her gaze travel over his magnificent body. "And I daresay you did not get to be so tall and strong by fasting."

He blushed as red as the trim on her gown as he turned and led the way around the corner of the building.

To think that her compliment had made such a warrior blush! Anne felt the most delightful, girlish urge to giggle as she followed him inside.

Chapter Eleven

The next morning, Reece stifled a yawn, then marched up to Trev and Piers as they stood in the inn's yard. They clutched stout sticks in place of real swords and looked refreshed after a full night's contented sleep. Like them, he was stripped to the waist. Unlike them, he held his broadsword and after yet another restless night that had little to do with bedding down on the earthen floor of the inn, he was exhausted.

Despite his best efforts, and especially at night, he simply could not rid his mind of Anne. The scent of roses that seemed a part of her. The way she would gracefully and absently move back her scarf or veil when it brushed her cheek. The gentle curve of that same cheek, as well as the rosy bloom of her tempting lips. The arch of her brow. The line of her jaw.

The other curves of her shapely figure.

Last night, like every night on their journey, it was all he could do not to march up the wooden steps of the inn and kick open the door to Anne's chamber, then demand...ask...beg for his rights as her husband.

Instead, he had forced himself to think of all the drills his father had ever used from easiest to most difficult, then the names of all the men in the garrison of Castle Gervais, as well as all their horses. Then he started in on the dogs. Finally he dozed off, but it was more like a nap than a night's sleep. This morning, after again waking at dawn, he had decided to begin the training of Piers Delasaine before the women awakened. He hadn't meant to rouse Trev, too, but since he had, he would have them both practice and learn. Surely that would help cleanse his mind of Anne and tire him so that he could rest better tonight. It should also lessen the energy Trev and Piers seemed determined to expend in rivalry and racing.

"Hold your sword up to protect your face," he chided his brother, showing Trev how he wanted him to hold his sword in front of his chest. "And don't just be dancing around for the sake of moving. You should be watching your opponent, too."

Next, he faced Piers. "You must not stand so still. You are like a target on a field."

"I'll get weary jumping around like a flea," Piers muttered.

"What would you rather be, weary or dead?" Reece countered. "You don't have to flitter about like Trev here. Just don't stand there like you're waiting for somebody to make a statue of you. Bob, sway, bend," he commanded, showing Piers what he wanted him to do.

Finished for the moment, he straightened and retreated out of the way of their weapons.

"Keep your eyes open and your wits sharp!" he ordered as a final instruction. "Both of you, *watch* your opponent. Now begin again."

He studied his charges as they started to circle one another. Trev was holding his sword better; Piers was trying to move. Obviously it was difficult for the boy to overcome the notion that simply ringing down blows any and every way possible would lead to victory. However, he was clearly an intelligent lad capable of learning, so Reece had hope he would soon learn to be more mobile.

Piers was also surprisingly strong. He probably should have expected such brute strength from a Delasaine, yet it was surprising nonetheless, given the lad's wiry build.

He wondered how strong Anne was. How muscular her bare arms might be...or her bare legs...as they wrapped around his naked body and held him tight and tighter as he thrust—

A delicate little cough sounded behind him. A ladylike cough.

He whirled around to find Anne standing there, looking as fresh and pretty as the first rosy bud of spring. He felt like a demon of lust to be having such thoughts about a virginal young woman—who was staring at him as if she had never seen a man's bare chest before.

Blushing like a boy caught bathing naked in the river by the village girls, he snatched up his tunic and pulled it over his head. "What are you doing here?"

"I wondered where Piers was."

Not him. Of course not him. She wasn't his mother to keep watch over him, or even a wife, really, either.

"Does this mean we can stop?" Trev demanded, panting. "My arms are nearly dead as it is."

"Is there food yet, Anne?" Piers asked eagerly, and Reece felt a little stab of envy at his easy manner with her.

"Almost. You should wash first." She looked at Reece. "If they are dismissed?"

When Reece nodded, Piers let out a whoop and tossed his stick onto the woodpile where Reece had found them. Trevelyan did likewise, minus the whoop, and then both of them ran into the inn.

They made it another race, and they reached the door simultaneously. Both tried to get through it at the same time. Piers shoved Trevelyan out of the way. Not to be outdone, Trevelyan stuck out his foot and tried to trip Piers, who managed to leap nimbly over the obstacle.

"I hope you're right and this will end when we reach your home," Anne said with a sigh.

He saw the furrow of concern on her brow. He also realized that she looked as weary as he felt. He wondered if she had had trouble sleeping, too, and if for a similar reason.

Then she turned to him with a look of such desperation on her face, he was shocked. ''Sir Reece, what will happen when we reach Castle Gervais? I hardly think your parents will be glad to learn that we are wed.''

She was right, of course, and he had been wondering the same thing.

He slowly let out his breath and leaned back against the wall of the kitchen, giving himself time to think. ''After I introduce you to my parents, I will explain what happened and how the situation will be remedied.''

''You make it sound very simple.''

He did, and he knew far better than she that it was not going to be an easy thing to confess his folly, especially to his father. But there was nothing else to be done. ''There is no need for you to fear, Anne. This was not your fault, and I will make that clear.''

He frowned. ''I should warn you, though, that my father is like a dog whose bark is worse than his bite— except that he doesn't bark. Well, not often. He will stare at you a good deal, though, I expect, and his stares can be…well, they can make you feel as if your whole soul is an open scroll to him and to try to keep a secret rank foolishness.''

Which, if his son was anything to go by, would be bad enough, Anne thought. She was glad to have this opportunity to speak with him about arriving at his family's home—something that was troubling her more and more as they got closer to it—but so far, she was not particularly comforted by anything Reece had said.

"You need have no qualms about my mother. She is a very kind and gentle lady who mothers everybody she meets. She'll be good to you, I'm sure, no matter what."

He sounded so certain of that, she felt a little better.

"And my sisters are from home visiting friends."

"*Sisters?*" She had not heard anything about sisters.

"I suppose Trev's been too busy trying to get Lisette's attention and arguing with Piers to tell you about them."

"*You* might have told me about them."

"I've been distracted. By my wound." He stared at the ground at his feet, and she was suddenly reminded of Piers when she would chastise him for something when he was little, and Piers didn't want to confess.

"What are they like?" she asked, deciding not to chide him more. "I find it difficult to imagine your sisters. You are so…"

Her voice died as he slowly tilted his head and raised his eyes to regard her. "I am so what?"

"Masculine."

She saw the little start he gave and his lack of vanity delighted her, making her glad she had confessed that.

"I have two sisters," he said, choosing not to respond to her compliment. "Roanna was born after me, then Freya after Gervais. They look like my mother, so they do not much resemble me or my brothers. Gervais, Trev and I take after our father."

He studied her some more. "You do not look at all like your brothers."

"I look like my mother."

"Your mother was a beauty, then, too?"

"Yes," she replied, although she did not wish to talk about her mother's unhappy existence married to Rannulf Delasaine, or her death.

"How fortunate."

"Fortunate?" she repeated. "It is the only thing people notice about me, or value me for. Damon and Benedict ignored me until I was twelve. I was a skinny little girl, with eyes and mouth that were too large, and I could do as I pleased when I wasn't looking after Piers. But then there came the day when Damon looked at me as if he suddenly realized he had been overlooking a chest of gold or a piece of fine jewelry. My life has not been the same since. It's as though I have been imprisoned and will never be free again."

"Piers clearly values you for more than your looks," he noted after a moment's silence.

"I am the closest thing to a mother he has known."

"And you have done a fine job raising him. It's obvious that he has been taught better than your half brothers, and I assume it's your influence that's responsible for the difference."

His words thrilled her as no compliment to her face or form ever had. "I hope your father's training will likewise prove beneficial."

His gray eyes flickered with a fleeting emotion that looked surprisingly like wistfulness, if a knight like him could be wistful. "We should go inside. We have been too long here already."

"Yes," she agreed.

Neither moved, as motionless as one of the stones in the wall behind them.

He leaned forward. Thrilled beyond measure, hoping he was going to kiss her again, she held her breath as he gently took hold of her shoulders. Then he pulled her close and brushed his lips over hers.

Desire, penned up like an animal in a cage, burst into vibrant, undeniable life. She was helpless to fight it. She didn't want to fight it.

He responded as quickly as fire to dry thatch. In spite of all his talk about an annulment, he wanted her as much as she craved him. His powerful arms encircled her and held her against his warrior's body as if he, too, had been waiting days for just this moment, this privacy, this intimacy. He deepened the kiss and thrust his tongue into her willing mouth.

He might take her here and now, and she would let him. By the saints, she would—and it would not have anything to do with what Damon demanded of her.

Tasting, savoring, her hips grinding with slow deliberation against him, she ran her hands through his long hair and along the breadth of his shoulders. Gasping for breath, she arched as his mouth slid with devastating leisure along the curve of her neck, then lower.

His hand gently kneaded her breast, the simple action arousing her to new heights of dizzying need. She gripped his shoulders tight as her whole body felt heavy with yearning, the pulse of desire throbbing through her body.

She pressed her hips against him again, reveling in his arousal, an answering moistness blossoming between her thighs.

Leaning forward, she slid her mouth down the strong column of his neck. A low groan rolled deep in his throat, the primitive sound inspiring her heated exploration.

His hand found her breasts again. She whimpered, her lips against the soft hair of his chest, as he brushed her hardened nipple with his thumb.

Then suddenly he went still. "Anne!"

Her name was a word of warning and condemnation combined, as if this was somehow her fault.

"I did not ask you to kiss me!" she cried, anger and despair mixing in equal measure within her. "I never invited your embrace."

He ran his hand through his long hair. "I know. Forgive me. I am…it is my fault. Only mine."

With that, he turned on his heel and marched toward the inn, leaving her alone in the yard.

"So you think I am right, then?" Gervais demanded. "Damon Delasaine *is* conspiring against Henry."

He was seated across the table from Blaidd and Kynan Morgan in a dark and secluded corner, in one of the taverns in the village of Winchester near the river. This place was outside the palace, and Gervais felt better having a confidential conversation away from the court, and curious courtiers.

The wick of the oil lamp on the table spluttered and flickered, and reeked of sheep tallow. There were a few other customers, merchants and tradesmen who had finished the day's toil, but they were wary of men like Fitzroy and the Morgans, for everything about them proclaimed that they were knights.

The only person who approached was the serving wench, a buxom, plump woman no longer young but clearly appreciative of noble custom, and comely young men. She stared at Blaidd, and even when she was busy with her other customers, her gaze strayed their way.

"Aye, I think you've hit the target, although sorry I am to say it," Blaidd answered in a confidential whisper and with a mournful nod.

His hands wrapped around his cup of ale, Kynan also nodded. "He's up to *something,* that one."

"He's up to seducing the queen," Blaidd quietly and firmly said, with obvious disgust. "About as subtly as a battering ram, too. A boy barely out of his nursemaid's arms could do better."

"You don't think he'll succeed then?" Gervais demanded.

"God save you, no!" Blaidd replied. "She's playing it careful, is all, neither encouraging nor discouraging." He shook his head and frowned. "I think she finds his antics amusing, or flattering, or it gives her something to do while the king's away. Once Henry has returned, Delasaine will find a cooler climate in the court."

"Unless Henry decides what Damon's been up to is treasonous," Gervais said.

Blaidd grinned at that. "He won't, for then he'd have to accuse Eleanor, too, and he won't want to do that. Nor should he. I tell you, she's enjoying the man's attention, but no more."

"I wish I could be as certain as you!"

Kynan chuckled. "If Blaidd says there's nothing serious between them, I think you can take his word. An expert on women is my brother."

Gervais did not smile. "Aye, I suppose you are. But even if Damon Delasaine thought he was winning the queen's affection, that doesn't explain why he seems so damnably smug every time he looks at me at court or in the hall. I mean, does he really think he's as good as in the queen's bed already?"

Blaidd slid his mug across the table and back again, leaving a trail of moisture. "He might. He's a vain, arrogant fool."

Kynan's expression grew thoughtful. "I think Gervais is right, Blaidd. I've seen that look he gives Gervais, and he is like a teasing child. *I know something you don't know.* There's more to this than just thinking he's going to get a crown by bedding a queen, bad as that is. He was mad as a hornet when the king announced that Reece was to marry his half sister, yet now it's as if he thinks he's done something clever.''

Blaidd's brow furrowed as he lifted his mug and took a drink. "Aye, now I see what you mean. What sort of thing would he find clever?"

"Maybe the fact that he didn't have to pay a dowry for her," Kynan suggested hopefully.

Gervais sucked in his breath as an idea came to him. "Maybe that he got what he wanted all along. Maybe he *planned* to get Anne married to Reece."

The Morgan brothers eyed him warily as he went on, the words tumbling out of his mouth in a hushed hurry. "Suppose they *wanted* Reece to follow Anne. Maybe Anne enticed him from the hall. Maybe they planned to come upon them when they were together, then claim Reece had acted improperly so that he would be forced to marry her. After all, they were saying he tried to rape her. That would affect their sister's reputation, too, and not in a good way. I wondered about that before, because it made no sense."

"It was the king's decision to make them marry," Kynan pointed out. "Are you saying the king was involved in Damon's scheme?"

"No. Damon could well believe a man like Reece would feel obligated to marry her if there was a scandal. He may not be an honorable man himself, but he could guess what an honorable man might do if he thinks he's sullied an innocent woman's reputation. Henry simply aided his plan without knowing it.''

"Reece didn't think she enticed him,'' Kynan noted. "He thought she was innocence itself, to hear him tell it.''

"You know Reece. He would take the blame if he thought it was warranted at all.'' Gervais looked at the other Morgan. "He's not as experienced with women as you, Blaidd. Unless she was blatant, he might not recognize the entrapment.''

"That may be, but why would they want Reece married to Anne?'' Blaidd protested. "They hate anybody who doesn't have at least a few generations of noble blood flowing through their veins, although what good that's done them, I don't know.''

"Because of Father,'' Gervais answered, the whole scheme becoming sickeningly clear to him. "Because of who he knows and their loyalty to the king. Because he holds Castle Gervais, one of the strongest fortresses in England.'' He leaned closer. "If you wanted to usurp a kingdom, you would want to know who your enemies are, and anything you could about them, wouldn't you? By marrying Anne to Reece, Damon has put a *spy* in our parents' household.''

Kynan paled, and Blaidd let out his breath slowly. "It's possible,'' Kynan muttered. "It would explain those looks.''

Gervais looked at Blaidd. "Well?''

Blaidd pushed his ale away and didn't answer right

away. "I cannot disagree, for it would explain that smugness and yet…"

"And yet?"

"And yet Anne Delasaine doesn't strike me as a sly or deceitful woman." Blaidd shrugged his broad shoulders. "Look you, I'm not saying it's impossible. I'm just saying she doesn't seem the devious sort."

"You hardly know her," Gervais replied. "A few dances hardly makes you an expert on what she might be capable of."

Blaidd made a knowing little grin. "You'd be surprised what you can discover about a woman during a dance." Then, seeing Gervais's expression, he sobered. "But as you say, I don't know her, so I certainly think it's worth warning Reece to take care."

Kynan glanced from one companion to the other. "What about Reece and the annulment plan? Do you think he's managed to keep away from her?"

"Aye," Gervais said firmly. "He's got too much to lose otherwise, and when he hears what we've realized, he'll have even more reason to avoid her as though she carried the plague."

"What will you do, send a message?" Blaidd asked.

"Or go myself in a few more days. Henry returns from hunting in the New Forest soon. He should be in a better humor. I'll try to get an audience with him before I go and see if he seems amenable to an annulment, especially after I tell him what we suspect of Anne's possible involvement. Meanwhile, since you will be here anyway, keep an eye on Damon, and if he seems about to do anything that could lead to even more trouble, send a message at once to Castle Gervais.''

Chapter Twelve

Even more determined in his resolution to keep away from his wife, and not having said one word to Anne that day, Reece led their cortege over the drawbridge, beneath the grille of the portcullis, through the massive studded oaken gates and into the courtyard of Castle Gervais two days after leaving Erwina's inn. Behind him he could hear Trevelyan calling greetings to the people who hurried out to meet them like bees pouring from a hive.

Donald and Seldon, two knights who had been among the first trained by his father, trotted from the barracks where the garrison and squires were housed. Fast friends, they had distinguished themselves in tournaments, then returned to swear their oath of loyalty to Sir Urien. Both had land on the estate, but since neither was married, they preferred to live at the castle and assist Sir Urien in his instruction.

Trev was a great favorite of theirs—and in truth rather shamefully indulged by them. Donald, still deceptively thin, and Seldon, brawny and stout, hurried toward him, but they came to a dead halt when they noticed Anne and Lisette.

Reece realized Anne was looking about as if she'd never been inside a castle before. He felt a moment's pride, for Castle Gervais *was* impressive, and even more so considering the man who commanded it was born a peasant and a bastard.

After greeting Trev, Donald and Seldon marched up to Reece.

"What the damned devil happened to you?" Seldon demanded, eyeing Reece's bruised face as he dismounted. "And who the hell are those women?"

Seldon had never been known for his eloquence, or his manners. He probably should have warned Anne about him, too. A swift glance revealed that while she was maintaining an aloof dignity, the red spots on her cheeks told him she was embarrassed by the blunt question, and no doubt the language, too.

"Where's Gervais?" Donald asked before he could answer. Although Donald ostensibly addressed Reece, his gaze was on a blushing Lisette.

Reece ground his teeth to keep from telling Donald to stop staring. "I'll explain—"

Reece fell silent as his father came striding from the hall, his mother right behind. When they saw him, their pleased expressions died on their faces, and Lady Fritha gave a little cry of dismay.

Well, he had better get the worst over with.

He hurried toward his parents. "Father, Mother, I

am not seriously hurt, and Gervais stayed behind at court.''

His mother was obviously relieved, as well as confused. His father was relieved, too, but less obviously. He was likely just as confused, but he hid it better.

Buying himself some time—although delaying tactics had never been particularly effective with his father—and to avoid his father's steady gaze, Reece went to help Anne dismount. It meant touching her and caused some pain from the wound in his side, but he saw no alternative. And perhaps at that moment, the comforting contact with warm flesh was necessary.

At least he need not be ashamed of his wife's looks, he thought as he set her down on the cobblestones of the courtyard.

No matter what she was feeling or thinking, Anne appeared as serene and lovely as always, if a bit pale and with the hint of shadow beneath her bright eyes. Her bountiful hair was simply braided and coiled about her head beneath her green silk scarf, as thin as a moth's wing, and that seemed to highlight its natural beauty.

She was finely dressed, too, in her fur-lined cloak and emerald-green damask gown. When she had first appeared in the gown that morning, he had been tempted to chastise her for her choice of dress, since it was not practical for travel. His reluctance to speak to her had kept him silent. Now he was glad he had not said anything, for she looked like a princess, something that might lessen the shock of her family connections when he told his parents who she was.

He faced his parents again and subdued the urge to take a deep breath. "Allow me to present Lady Anne. My wife."

He had never seen his mother so flabbergasted. As he had expected, his father simply stared.

Not for the first time he wished his father was hot-headed. That he would curse, shout, or even just raise his voice. His stern calm was as unnerving as waiting to have a tooth pulled.

"Let us go inside and I shall explain," he continued.

His father's left brow rose majestically. "Yes, you will."

Reece glanced at Anne to see how she took this reception.

Her face expressionless, Anne stood as straight as a knight presented to the king.

Sir Urien's voice seemed to reanimate his wife, for his mother suddenly bounded forward as if she were a girl and not the mother of five and chatelaine of a vast castle. "Welcome, my dear."

Then Lady Fritha took Anne by the shoulders and heartily bussed her cheek.

Anne didn't speak, but her look of stunned surprise said enough. His mother could be rather effusive, as she next proved by embracing Reece so tightly he almost muttered an expletive. He was not a little boy anymore.

"Anne," he said as his mother stopped hugging, "this is my mother, Lady Fritha, and this is my father, Sir Urien Fitzroy."

"It is an honor to meet you, Sir Urien," Anne said with a polite bow. She smiled at his mother. "Lady Fritha, I thank you for your kind greeting."

He had never seen Anne smile like that, not even at her brother. When she smiled at Piers, there was something of the indulgent parent about it, as if the youth were still three years old. This smile was more open and honest, unencumbered by responsibility perhaps, and all the more beautifully natural.

This was the woman who had caught his eye at the feast, feeding tender morsels to the hound.

Surely now his impetuous act would make some sense to his father, at least; it certainly did to him.

More soldiers and servants who had got wind of their arrival continued to enter the courtyard. Some youths had obviously interrupted their training, judging by their perspiration. Several of the young kitchen maids huddled by the well, giggling and eyeing both Trevelyan and Piers as they dismounted. A few of the older guards at the entrance leaned on their spears, watching, as did the serving women who came out of the door to the hall.

Anne ignored the onlookers and gestured for her brother to come forward. "My brother has come with me to be trained by Sir Urien, whose reputation is so deservedly well-known."

The compliment was a fine way to begin. His

mother's smile grew even more, and his father displayed a small but significant softening at the corners of his firmly shut mouth.

"Sir Urien, this is my brother." Anne hesitated for the briefest of moments before a resolute glint came to her eyes. "Piers Delasaine."

Oh, God help him! She did not have to declare their name in the courtyard, in front of everybody. She should have waited for him to explain, to soften the blow of her identity, to cushion the ground. She did not have to announce the very worst thing about his marriage to everyone in Castle Gervais.

As the murmurs of surprise and dismay went up from the crowd, the softness at the corners of his father's lips disappeared, replaced by a stern frown.

"As I said, Father, I will explain inside."

"Yes, you will."

With that, Sir Urien turned on his heel and marched toward the hall.

Mentally girding his loins for the ordeal ahead, and inwardly rehearsing his explanation one more time, Reece hurried after his father, leaving his mother to follow with Anne.

The gaping servants parted for them as Reece matched his father's long strides. Not surprisingly, Sir Urien did not stop in the hall but continued to his solar in the southern tower attached to the hall, where they would be alone.

His feet planted, arms crossed and interrogation burning in his dark eyes, his father stood in front of the window shuttered with linen to keep out the autumn breeze. He didn't say a word. He didn't even raise that interrogative eyebrow. He just…waited.

Suddenly, in that comfortable and familiar room, warmed by a brazier of coals, the cold stone walls hidden by colorful tapestries depicting medieval gardens and domestic life, Reece was six years old again trying to explain why he had cut off his sister's hair. *She said it was a bother, so I helped.*

Reece cleared his throat, ready to begin.

Then his mother and Anne entered the room. "Please, my dear, sit," his mother said to his wife.

Oh, God help him, why had they come? It would have been difficult enough explaining to his father alone.

Anne sat, as calm as if she were simply a visitor enjoying their hospitality, while he stood in the center of the room like a miscreant child.

After likewise sitting, Lady Fritha regarded her son quizzically. "How did you get hurt? Was it in the tournament?"

"No, I didn't participate in the tournament."

His father's eyes widened ever so slightly at that.

"I think I should begin at the start."

Nobody made any objection, and he took the moment's silence to collect his thoughts and prepare to relate the events that had brought him so unexpectedly home. "I was at the king's feast celebrating the day of Saint Edmund the Confessor when I noticed Lady Anne sitting in the king's hall. I found her intriguing and wanted to know who she was. I followed her when she retired from the hall.''

By the saints, how foolish and feeble that sounded, as if he were the same age as Trev—but thus he had behaved.

''I detained her in the corridor,'' he resolutely continued, determined to have the worst over with, or so he hoped. ''We talked a little. Unfortunately, her older half brothers, of whom you have heard…''

His father slowly nodded, once.

''They took exception to my speaking with Anne and reacted as men of their ilk react. They attacked me.''

Anne's lips pressed tightly together and her cheeks reddened, but she did not speak. His mother, meanwhile, covered her mouth with her hand as if to keep from crying out in alarm.

''Both of them?'' his father demanded.

Reece nodded. He did not bother to mention that Damon had attacked him from behind. It was enough that they had viciously set upon him for so trivial a reason, and by doing so, had made the situation infinitely worse. ''Fortunately, the king's guards were alerted by Anne's scream. They came before any real harm could be done. However, while I was recovering, they told everyone that I had…''

He hesitated. Then, because Anne and his mother were there, he chose the lesser charge. ''They said that I had been accosting Anne.''

''Accosting, like some drunken lout?''

"Father, I assure you I was not drunk, any more than I was accosting Anne the way they implied."

"We raised you better than that," Sir Urien grimly confirmed.

"When the king heard what happened and the Delasaines' charge, he summoned Anne and me to his hall. Unfortunately, the Delasaines are related to the queen. Although it is a distant relationship, it is enough for them to have her support and those of the French nobles who have come with her to England. Henry wants a peaceful court, so to prevent further enmity, he decreed that Anne and I must marry. As you can imagine, neither she nor I favored the idea."

His father grunted and his mother frowned, but mercifully, neither one spoke. Reece wanted to get through this without a lot of interruptions, as a physician would lance a wound and let the poison run out all at once. "Unfortunately, the king was adamant. I realized there was nothing to do but obey Henry.

"However, since neither Anne nor I wanted to be wed, we are resolved to seek an annulment, once the king's temper has cooled, and other, more important, business take precedence in his mind."

His parents' gaze flicked to Anne, then back to him. Whatever emotions Anne was feeling as he spoke, she hid them well, for only the two small pink spots on her cheeks betrayed that she was involved in this situation at all.

"What grounds will you give for an annulment?" his mother asked.

He flushed, this time feeling like an adolescent forced to talk about his first amorous experience. "We are not completely legally married," he said, hoping it would be enough.

It was. He could tell by his mother's blush and the look in his father's eyes.

After a moment, his mother rose, breaking the tense silence. "Whatever is to be done, I had best see that Lady Anne is made comfortable. You both look exhausted from your journey." She turned to Anne with a warm smile. "Come with me, my dear, and we will see to the baggage and some refreshments."

At the solar door, his mother paused and looked back at her son. "Anne will have your chamber, Reece. Until this matter is resolved, you will share Donald and Seldon's quarters. Move your things when you are finished speaking with your father. As for what we shall tell the servants about these unusual arrangements, I suppose the truth would be best."

She sounded very matter-of-fact, and not nearly as upset as he had feared she would be.

"There would be little use trying to keep the situation secret anyway," she continued. "The whole cortege knows you haven't been sleeping with your wife, do they not?"

He blushed like a little boy caught in a lie. "Yes, they know."

With a nod, Lady Fritha pivoted on her heel and marched from the room. Anne followed her out without so much as a backward glance at him.

What had he expected she would do? Kiss him goodbye?

"By Jove's thunder, Reece," his father muttered as he rubbed his chin with his strong, sinewy hand and sank back down into his chair. He gestured for Reece to sit, too. "This is a mire. And not what I expected from you. To follow an unknown woman like that— it sounds like Dylan DeLanyea's sort of caper, or Blaidd Morgan's."

A nephew of Baron DeLanyea, Dylan's roguish reputation had led to a forced marriage. It had turned out well, though, for Dylan had come to love his wife. She, however, had not come from a family like the Delasaines.

"What in the name of the saints came over you?" his father asked. "Granted she's a beauty, but you are usually the most levelheaded of my sons." His father's eyes narrowed, and his scrutiny deepened. "It wasn't just because of her hair, was it?"

"Partly," Reece confessed. "And her beauty. More importantly, I had no idea she was a Delasaine."

"You had never seen her with her brothers?"

This was not going well at all. "She was seated beside her half brothers at the feast, but she looks nothing like them, so I assumed she belonged to the older man sitting on her other side."

His father's brow lowered ominously. "Assumed?"

"I well remember what you have taught us about the foolishness of making assumptions. Clearly I forgot, or did not apply it to a woman. It was a mistake."

"Obviously."

"I did not mean to cause any trouble, and I certainly did not foresee being forced to marry her."

His father grunted again. "Did you voice no objections at all to Henry?"

Reece folded his hands in his lap. "I did, but Henry said that if I did not marry Anne, he would let the accusations the Delasaines were making be judged in a court of law." Reece leaned forward. "I didn't want to say this in front of Mother, but they were telling people I was trying to rape Anne."

His father shot to his feet as if the seat of his chair had burst into flame. *"What?"* he bellowed. "They would accuse my son of *that?*"

Shocked, Reece fell back. His father was clearly, unforgettably, incredibly enraged. He had never seen such a fierce expression on his father's face, or the burning look of anger in his eyes; he had not even imagined it was possible.

Reece rose and spread his hands placatingly. "None of the English nobles believed it," he said, keeping his own tone calm, as if his father were a snorting, stamping stallion he was trying to gentle. "The Delasaines had to say something like that to justify what they did to me. I don't think Henry believed the charge, but the queen spoke in favor of the Delasaines, and Henry does not want to openly disagree with Eleanor. However, he told Anne that if her relatives objected, he would have them charged with attempted murder for their attack upon me."

His father slowly let out his breath. "I have heard he defers to Eleanor more than he should, or at least more than the nobles like to see. He must be very serious about wanting peace in his court if he would threaten any of Eleanor's relatives, however distant kin."

Reece nodded. "It would be better if all her relations could be banished from the court completely. They are like poison."

"I trust you didn't say such an imprudent thing while you were in Winchester."

Reece flushed with new shame. Before he made the impetuous mistake of following Anne, his father would never have suggested he would do such a foolish thing. "No."

"Good. Henry cares too much about his wife's opinion to tell her relatives to go, like it or not as we will."

"I didn't realize you knew so much about the court," Reece admitted. "You never go, or seem interested."

"Just because I do not endlessly discuss politics doesn't mean I am ignorant, or pay no heed. What goes on there affects everyone in the realm." His father sat again. "That is why I sent you, my most level-headed son, to be my eyes and ears."

Worse and worse.

His father meditatively rubbed his strong jaw again. "The marriage may lead more people to believe the

Delasaines' accusation, thinking the marriage is intended to restore the lady's lost honor.''

As remorse for how he had compromised Anne's reputation stabbed at him again, Reece said, ''That charge will taint Anne, too, but apparently her half brothers didn't think of that, or care, before they made their accusations.''

''From all I've heard, all they think about is their own hides,'' his father agreed. He gave his son a pointed look. ''Which is why they should have been avoided at all costs, except on the tournament field, and their sister, too.''

''I'm sorry, Father. I have disgraced our family and caused us to be linked to that brood of vipers. I promise you I shall do all I can to repair my mistake, as much as possible, but I know I have betrayed your trust, and your faith in me.''

His father's intense eyes softened a bit. ''I regret that you did not show more sense, Reece, but the Delasaines had no right to attack you, and Henry had even less right to make you marry. Fortunately, I believe your plan has merit. I shall also contact my friends and see if they can suggest anything more. In the meantime, you intend to stay away from your wife?''

''Yes!''

His father raised a brow as he studied him. ''You sound determined.''

''I am.''

''Good.'' Unexpectedly, his father shifted as if he

was embarrassed about what he was going to say. "A bastard who has raised himself up in the world is regarded with envy and suspicion, Reece, and so are his children. We must be above reproach. Being tied to the Delasaines gives our enemies more arrows in their quiver to aim at us." He sighed. "Still, it is a pity that this must end this way. In some ways, she reminds me of your mother."

Reece stared at his father. "But she scarcely said a word!"

Sir Urien regarded his son with the merest hint of a wry smile. "Have I ever told you to take the measure of your opponent by the way he speaks? Courage and determination are in the eyes, my son, of women as well as men."

Chapter Thirteen

Reece hesitated on the threshold of his bedchamber. He hadn't expected anyone to be there. Anne was still being shown about the castle by his mother, and he had seen Lisette in the hall not long ago.

Unfortunately, here was Lisette arranging what looked like Anne's toilette articles—combs, ribbons and the like—on a small dressing table that his mother must have found in one of the storerooms.

Behind him, Donald waited to help him carry his belongings from this room to the chamber Donald and Seldon shared. Reece had refused Donald's offer at first, for that was a servant's task, but Donald had insisted.

Now Reece suspected he knew why. He had never seen Donald stare at a woman as he had Lisette. Trev and Piers were obviously about to have more competition there, which was not a pleasing thought.

At least it had been easier to explain the situation regarding Anne to Donald and Seldon than it had been to his brothers and the Morgans, or his parents. They believed Sir Urien the most remarkable of men, and some of that deferential respect extended to his sons. That meant they were, mercifully, less inclined to ask questions or cast doubt on his plan to have his marriage ended.

Indeed, Donald had asked more questions about Lisette, making his interest in the young woman even more obvious. Seldon had been a lot more curious about the knights at court, their battle prowess and how his old friends and foes had fared in recent years.

Donald coughed, startling Reece into motion.

"Oh, Sir Reece," Lisette cried in greeting as he entered the room. Straightening, she gave him a bright smile.

No, not him—Donald standing behind him, and it was a far more friendly smile than she had ever given either Piers or Trev.

Apparently, the competition was already over, and Donald—who really ought to have a woman in his life—had won in record time.

"I have come to get that chest in the corner," Reece explained when he realized Lisette was waiting.

"That will give us more room," she agreed.

She didn't sound at all surprised by his statement. Anne must have told her that he would not be sharing her bed here, either.

His chamber *was* rather crowded, what with the large bed that he had inherited from Lord Gervais, his chest for his clothes and the other for his armor,

Anne's baggage and the table and stool. Lisette smiled at Donald again, and his face turned as red as an apple's peel in autumn.

"I'm helping," he said brusquely, and quite unnecessarily as he strode toward the chest containing Reece's clothes.

"It'll take the two of us to carry the other," Reece said.

"Then wait here. Won't be a moment," Donald said as he bent down. His arms stretched as far as they could go as he grasped the leather handles on either end of Reece's clothes chest.

Reece suspected Donald would curse him, albeit silently, if he offered to help. He clearly wanted to impress the girl, and since it was the first time Reece had ever seen his friend act this way, he decided not to interfere, especially when Lisette kept staring at Donald as if he was the finest specimen of manhood in England. And although the chest was awkward for one man to carry, it wasn't heavy.

Reece shrugged his acquiescence and sat on the bed. "If you're sure, Donald."

"I am."

Lisette looked at Reece quizzically. "Do you not want to remove some clothing?"

Donald staggered and his burden hit the floor with a thump as Reece stared, aghast. Had he been completely wrong about the girl?

"From the chest," Lisette clarified with a giggle when she saw the look on Reece's face. "You will need your clothes, will you not? Do you not intend to move them to my lady's chest?''

God's holy heart, she didn't know. Obviously Lisette had thought their lack of nuptial intimacy temporary.

It was up to him to explain things to her, too.

This girl was a servant. She did not require a long explanation. ''I will not be sleeping here.''

Lisette's brow furrowed.

It didn't matter what she thought, or what anybody else in Bridgeford Wells thought, either.

He turned his attention to Donald. ''Need some help after all?''

Donald again picked up Reece's chest. ''No,'' he declared, the tendons in his neck straining.

''If you're finished here, Lisette, you may go,'' Reece said, looking at the befuddled maidservant.

''Very well, Sir Reece,'' Lisette said, hurrying after Donald.

When she was gone, Reece wandered toward the window and looked out into the courtyard. Lisette wasn't the only one who wouldn't understand his relationship—or lack of it—with his wife.

''Sir Reece?''

He wheeled at the sound of Anne's voice and found her on the threshold of the chamber, regarding him curiously with her sparkling green eyes.

His first impulse was to flee the room, but Donald would surely be back at any moment, and how would it look if he came tearing down the steps like a coward? He could surely stay a few moments.

Anne moved gracefully into the room and raised an inquisitive brow. "I understood this was to be my chamber, and since we are not to live as husband and wife—?"

"I came to collect my things."

She frowned but said nothing.

He must both look and sound ridiculous. He had been standing there staring out the window as if he had nothing better to do. "The chest containing my armor is too heavy for one man to carry. I'm waiting for Donald to return to help me with it."

Understanding dawned on Anne's face and he felt somewhat less foolish. "And Donald is...?" she asked as she went to her dressing table and pulled the silken scarf from her head.

"A knight, one of my father's liege men. He was the thin fellow who came out to meet the cortege when we arrived."

"Who was the other fellow, the stout one?"

"That's Seldon," he replied, shoving away his desire. "Like Donald, he has sworn allegiance to my father and has been given an estate here."

She sat on the stool and began to take out the combs that had been holding her hair coiled smoothly around her head, as easy and cozy as if they were any other husband and wife talking of the people in their household.

His father had seen courage and determination in

her brilliant green eyes. So had he. He had also seen desire there, or so he thought. He wished he could be sure of his interpretations, but he knew so little of women, and trusted his opinions even less where they were concerned.

Anne untied the ribbons holding the ends of the braids. He could scarcely breathe when her hair fell loose about her slender shoulders. As she ran a wide-tooth ivory comb through the thick mass, all he could think about was burying first his hands and then his face in the golden waves.

"They are visiting?" she inquired, drawing him back to their conversation.

He got his wayward thoughts under control and ventured a little closer. "They live here and help my father. Meanwhile, their bailiffs run their estates."

Determined to keep both his thoughts and emotions under control, he cleared his throat and said, "Anne, I doubt we'll see very much of each other except for the evening meal while you are here. I will be busy helping my father and you will be…"

She set down the comb and swiveled to regard him, her green eyes steady. "What shall I be doing, Sir Reece?"

He suddenly realized he had no idea how she would be spending her days.

"May I help your mother, do you think?" Anne asked after a moment, while he stood there like a mute.

"Yes, you could do that," he replied, relieved by

her suggestion. "I'm sure she'll welcome your assistance, especially since my sisters are from home."

"I thought she would not mind. She is very nice, your mother."

The force of Anne's smile struck him like the swat of a strong man's fist and her eyes sparkled like the jewels on the queen's fingers.

He backed away. "Yes, she is."

"Was your father very harsh with you after I left?" Anne inquired evenly, her cool tone making a mockery of his struggle to be calm.

"No."

"He agrees with your assessment of the situation?"

"Yes."

God save him, why must he always sound like a stern soldier or a tongue-tied fool when he was with her?

Perhaps, his mind replied, it was because no woman had ever looked at him with that combination of curiosity and interest, and certainly no woman had ever been so near his own bed. He was no virgin, but he had always sought his sport away from home.

He must and would talk to her as he would to any other acquaintance. "You need not worry about my father's treatment of you, Anne. He knows you are not responsible."

Her expression softened, to a winsome one that smote his heart anew. "Your father seems a very fine man. I already feel more comfortable in his presence than I ever did in that of my own father."

"I do not suppose he was a kind man, to have such sons," he said, his gentle tone encouraging her confidence.

Her smile drifted away. "No, he was not," she said quietly as she toyed with her comb. "He did not want daughters."

She sighed so quietly that if he hadn't been focused on her, he might have missed it. "He took out his disappointment at my birth upon my mother."

"But then she bore him a son."

"After seven years of worry and torment, and died doing so." Anne raised her eyes to regard him, her gaze as firm and resolute as it had been wistful before. "Because she had been so afraid of the consequences of birthing another daughter, she could not eat or sleep properly during the whole of the time she was with child."

Her expression hardened even more, to one he recognized from the battlefield when an opponent refused to yield. "He killed her as surely as if he plunged a dagger in her breast."

"I'm sorry, Anne." His words sounded weak and useless, but he could think of no more to say.

"No, *I'm* sorry," she said, turning away and putting the comb on the table. "I do not need to burden you with such things. They are not your troubles."

"No, but they are yours." He took her gently by the hands and raised her so that they were face-to-face. "If I cannot be your husband, I would still be your friend."

To his surprise, she twisted out of his grasp and turned her back to him. "But I am still a Delasaine."

He went to her, took her gently by the shoulders and turned her so that she faced him. Looking intently into her eyes, hoping she would understand, he explained, and reasserted to himself the reasons he must stay away from her and never let his burning desire free. "Anne, ever since I first realized that some men are noble by virtue of their deeds and honor, and some solely because of their birth, I have wanted to speak for those who have earned their titles and land. I want to be a voice for those who can be all too often and easily overlooked. But if I stay married to a Delasaine, Henry and those men he trusts may not be able to trust me. They will never let me into their inner circle. I will have failed to attain the thing that is the most important to me."

"I see," she murmured, moving away.

"Do you, Anne?" he said.

Did *he?*

As she stood there, her back to him, his resolute goal, the future he had planned for so long, suddenly seemed to waver and diminish.

Someone standing in the doorway coughed loudly.

Reece swiftly turned to find Donald standing on the threshold.

"Do you want to take that chest now, or leave it?" he asked, his cheeks flushed either from the effort of coming back up the stairs, or with embarrassment at having interrupted them.

"Now," Reece replied, crossing the room and grabbing one of the leather handles. Donald wordlessly joined him at the other side. Together they lifted it and left the room.

Erwina bustled toward the large man limned by the evening sunlight in the doorway of her inn. "Good day, sir!" she cried, gesturing a welcome. "Come in, come in. Plenty of room and clean beds here, I assure you."

The man strolled inside, surveying both Erwina and the main room as he did. Peter, seated near the hearth, didn't like the look of him—mean and vicious, with his dark hair and narrow eyes and scornful expression.

Erwina got a better look at the newcomer in the hearth light and seemed to reconsider her invitation, especially when the man ran a measuring gaze over her again. "You alone here?"

"No," she replied at once.

"I mean except for the boy."

Before she could answer, a group of farmers who had been to the market in the nearby town came boisterously inside, talking loudly about the juggler they had seen there.

Erwina stifled a sigh of relief and bustled about getting their drinks, and the ale and food the stranger demanded.

Another man who did not live in these parts came to the door, but Peter knew who he was. Arwen traveled from town to town, an entertainer like a minstrel or those jugglers, but he made his money playing games with his dice. Peter thought that would be a pleasant way to make a living, just throwing dice, and he didn't understand why his mother always looked a little annoyed when he suggested it.

"Ah, Master Peter!" Arwen cried, strolling inside and casting a glance at the men gathered there. "How fare you?"

"I twisted my ankle, but a *knight* fixed it," he eagerly answered.

"You don't say? A knight?"

Arwen took a seat on the bench nearest Peter.

"Aye! It was—"

Arwen held up his hand to silence the boy. "Later, Peter, later I will hear about this knight who has obviously made such an impression on you. First, though, I must earn enough for one of your mother's fine meals."

Arwen took out a leather cup and the small pouch that contained his dice and smiled at the burly stranger. "How about you, my friend? Care to play a friendly game?"

Benedict Delasaine appeared to struggle with an answer.

"Oh, come, come!" Arwen cried. "We shall play for only a few pennies. Hardly a risk to a nobleman like yourself."

"How do you know I'm noble?" Benedict growled suspiciously.

"Why, everything about you proclaims it! Your

clothes, your weapons, your very visage! And surely that magnificent horse in the stable is yours.''

If Benedict had been wiser, he might have noted that the man seemed to be mentally tallying the value of everything Benedict owned.

But Benedict was not wise. Instead, his eyes lighted with a proud and greedy gleam. ''All right.''

Arwen smiled and put the dice in the cup.

''Hold still,'' Lady Fritha admonished as she held her son's head to study his eye in the morning light a few days after their return to Castle Gervais.

''You've got a better grip than some of the lads,'' Reece muttered. He had to mutter because his mother was squeezing his chin.

''If you wouldn't wiggle, I wouldn't have to hold you so firmly,'' she replied. ''Of all my sons, I never thought you would have to be told to sit still, especially at your age.''

Lady Fritha studied her son some more. ''The bruises are nearly gone, and your eye looks much better.''

''Good.''

''They could have blinded you,'' she murmured, shaking her head. ''They could have killed you, too, if the guards hadn't come running.''

Reece shifted back on his cot. ''Yes, it's a good thing Anne screamed. It was like a banshee's screech.''

Lady Fritha went to Donald's bed, where she

straightened the blankets. There was no reason for her to tidy the chamber. However, she had been practically a servant when his father had first come to Bridgeford Wells, despite her title, and her maternal nature made it hard for her to stop fussing sometimes. Or so he told himself. He hoped she wasn't lingering on purpose to talk to him.

Or if she was, maybe her purpose had nothing to do with him, and everything to do with Donald and Lisette. During the day, Donald stared at Lisette like a man seeing heavenly visions, and it was very clear that the girl welcomed his somewhat stunned attention.

"Donald seems very happy," he said, hoping to head off any criticism of his friend's liaison. "And so does Lisette. I confess I was concerned because Trev and Anne's brother were competing for her notice, but they seem to have realized they've lost that contest. I have never seen a man more smitten."

"Haven't you?"

"No, not even Blaidd Morgan pursuing his latest conquest."

His mother stopped fussing with Donald's blanket to regard him steadily. It was quite clear she had something to say, after all, and he knew she wasn't going to leave until she had said it.

"I have no wish to discuss Donald's romantic attachments," she began. "He is a grown man and Lisette is a grown woman, and you're right, they both seem quite happy. It is not for me to pass judgment, unless Lisette fails to attend to her duties. Your father feels the same about Donald. I want to talk to you about Anne.''

Reece had no desire to discuss anything about Anne. He half rose, determined to leave.

''Reece, sit down,'' his mother commanded, as stern and compelling as his father ever was.

Shocked, he automatically obeyed.

''Reece, I know this may be hard for you to believe, but sometimes it's difficult for your father to forget that he's not still a bastard peasant boy fighting to survive in a world that has no use for him. He was alone for a long, long time before we met and he had no friends. But he is not that peasant boy. He is an admired, respected knight, with many friends who would gladly fight for him if he asked—and even if he didn't. Things are not nearly so precarious at court for our family as he believes.

''You are an honorable knight whose loyalty to Henry is without question. You did not seek out an alliance with the Delasaines. It was forced upon you. Many of those same nobles had arranged marriages, too, so if you decide to make it fully legal I doubt they would fault you, especially given Anne's obvious beauty. Indeed, if they knew you hadn't consummated your marriage yet, they might even think there was something wrong with your head.''

His mother came to him and sat beside him, then put a maternal arm around his shoulders. ''My son, I have met many a noble young lady in my time, and there is not a one of them I would have considered a suitable bride for you, until now. Anne is an uncommon woman, Reece. She is not vain, or bitter, or hateful. She does all that I ask without even a hint of complaint, and with a cheerful mien. The servants like her—and you and I both know that is saying a great deal, especially since they have heard of the Delasaines, too. And the only thing you and your father can say against Anne is that she is their half sister.''

Reece got to his feet. ''But that is a great deal. If we stay wedded, our family will be linked to the Delasaines by a legal bond.''

''The king and the rest of the court know where the Fitzroys stand. There cannot be a man in England who doubts your loyalty to the crown. If the Delasaines do something despicable, nobody will believe you were willingly involved.''

''You know the plans I had for my future, Mother. If I am married into an untrustworthy family, I will never be admitted to the king's inner circle, because Henry and his advisors will not trust me, either.''

''You may have a difficult time achieving what you want,'' she agreed without a hint of sympathy, ''but some things, like love, make a struggle worthwhile.''

Was she right? Was it possible that he could be married to a Delasaine and make that *meaningless?*

His eyes narrowed as hope contended with ambition. ''Then you think this marriage is a good thing?''

''I think it could be. I certainly do not think it is

the great disaster you and your father make it out to be.''

''Anne herself believes this is but temporary.''

''Reece, remember what I said about knowing when someone is smitten? I was referring to both you and your wife.''

That had to be a mother's love speaking. He was no charmer, like Blaidd. ''If Anne were smitten with me as you suggest, she would not have agreed to the annulment.''

''I suspect my stubborn, single-minded son did not give her any choice.''

Oh, God. He had not. He had not asked her what she thought or how she felt. He had not supposed her feelings had altered from the first, although his had. He had always—and only—assumed that she did not want him for a husband because they had been ordered to wed.

''Has she given you no sign that she wants to be your wife in the full sense of the word? Or perhaps the better question is, are you certain she does not, for I assure you, if a woman like Anne was not interested, there would be absolutely no doubt in your mind.''

She rose and caressed his cheek. ''Talk to her, Reece. Find out how she feels. Give her a chance to be a part of your life. Do not throw away a chance for happiness because of ambition.''

His thoughts and feelings a tumultuous jumble, Reece did not want to discuss Anne further, or listen to any more advice, no matter how well meaning. "I'll think about what you've said, Mother."

She took the hint and, with a brief farewell, left him to contemplate his feelings, Anne's, and all that he had planned.

Chapter Fourteen

Hidden by a wagon pulled up in the outer ward, Anne peered around it to watch the squires being put through their paces by Sir Urien, Donald and Seldon. Reece was not there, and although she wondered why, she assumed he must have business elsewhere. Meanwhile, Lady Fritha was busy embroidering a new cuff for a gown and she had given leave to Anne to do what she would.

Anne would not leave the castle, though, because she had no doubt that Benedict was lurking in the village. She would delay that meeting for as long as she possibly could.

Anne had never been in a more pleasant household. Lady Fritha was friendly and greeted with affection wherever they went, and she also commanded the respect of all there. As for Lady Fritha's treatment of her unexpected daughter-in-law, Anne could not have anticipated better, and certainly would not have been surprised at much worse. Lady Fritha made her feel like an honored guest, not an unwelcome intruder into their home. It was also clear by her manner that she expected everyone in the household to treat Anne the same way.

She didn't want to leave here and go back to Montbleu and the fate that awaited her. She wanted to stay and be the true wife of Reece Fitzroy. Every moment that passed she wanted it more. Unfortunately, he had his plans for a future at court, a plan he was right to fear a relationship with the Delasaines would destroy. Damon and Benedict were untrustworthy, greedy, vicious men who were sure to come to a bad end one day.

But Reece should be at court. He would be a fine advisor to the king, for he was shrewd, and patient, and kept his temper. His notion of representing the minor nobles who had earned their rank was an excellent and worthy one. It would be far better for Reece to be in the king's counsel than Damon.

So she would not help Damon more than she must, and not until she must. Instead, because she had seen so little of Piers since their arrival, she had decided to watch him train. She didn't want him to know she was doing that, though, lest she embarrass him.

Trying to subdue her unhappy musings, she concentrated on the youths training. The young men held wooden broadswords. Placed about the open space between the inner and outer curtain walls were quintains, dummies with two straight arms. One had a small shield where the hand would be. The youths were to strike the shield with their wooden broadswords and jump quickly out of the way, for from the other "hand," a pig's bladder filled with sawdust hung suspended, ready to hit the swordsman who didn't move fast enough.

The lads had been practicing for most of the afternoon. Several of them were sweating profusely and growing weary, their arms heavy from swinging their wooden swords.

Sir Urien didn't seem to care. He marched through their ranks calling out advice or criticism as if they had begun moments ago. Seldon clumped about like a confused ox. Perhaps getting struck on the head a few times with the bladder because of the overzealous actions of his charges accounted for that. Even Sir Urien got hit once. Donald kept glancing at the wall walk, and after the third time, she noticed Lisette's pert head bobbing past the merlons.

Obviously she was not the only one who wanted to watch the instruction.

Anne looked again at Piers, whose arm clearly ached from the effort he was expending. Damon had little patience for drills, Benedict even less, so this sort of thing was all new to her younger brother. Judging by the way his shoulders slumped, he was winded, too, but struggling not to show how tired he was, especially when Trevelyan Fitzroy, on the other side of the inner ward, looked as if he could keep swinging the sword until the sun went down.

She wondered what Piers thought about Lisette's

obvious liaison with Sir Donald. She had not been alone with her brother since they had arrived, so she hadn't had a chance to talk to him about anything. Given that Trevelyan Fitzroy had also lost that particular race, she was hopeful that he was not much grieved.

Anne did not begrudge Lisette her romance, although she wished she had more hope that it would end well. Donald was a knight, and Lisette was but a serving maid, so marriage was out of the question. On the other hand, judging by the stories Lisette told of the French court and the relish with which she recited them, affairs of the heart seemed only mild and amusing diversions to her.

Her gaze drifted away from the young men practicing to the main gate of Castle Gervais, where servants and villagers came and went in a friendly bustle. Everyone seemed happy and busily content; there was no sign of strife there, either, or in the village, or anywhere else in the castle.

That was certainly different from Montbleu. Damon's guards were fierce mercenaries hired from Saxony because, he said, he could count on them to fight. If they didn't, they wouldn't get paid. The villagers would sooner lie down like dogs than defend Montbleu.

She had not suggested that since he treated them like dogs, what else should he expect?

Sir Urien called out for the boys to halt their practice. He bellowed at his charges to wash before going to the hall to dine because they stank worse than the pigs. On the other hand, he added, he was much prouder of their efforts than anything his pigs did. Panting, the lads chuckled and talked among themselves as they made their way toward the massive inner gate.

She was glad to see that some of the boys joined Piers and walked with him. Like her, Piers had never really had friends his own age, and it warmed her heart to see that he had made some here. If she could stay, she might be able to make some friends, too.

But she could not stay, and surely she would be wise to cease such speculation entirely, for it only added to her unhappiness.

"Here you are, Anne."

She gasped and jumped, then whirled around to find herself looking up into Reece's handsome face. "What do you want?" she said, blurting out the first words that came into her head.

"As a matter of fact, I wish to speak to you."

She swallowed and tried to compose herself. There was, after all, no reason he should *not* speak to her, and they were in a public place. "Of course."

"But not now and not here. It is too close to the evening meal, and I would have more privacy."

His tone was so low and intimate, and his gaze so very intense, she nearly forgot to breathe.

"Will you allow me to come to your chamber later?"

"My chamber?" she repeated, as if she didn't know

what a chamber was. She fought to at least appear calm and composed. "What about your plan? What if somebody sees you?"

"There are secret passageways in Castle Gervais, and one opens out onto the stairwell near your chamber. No one will see me."

A secret passage and a secret rendezvous. With Reece.

"So do I have your permission to visit you later, after you retire?"

Her heart was hammering so fast she thought it might burst right out of her chest. "Yes." She cleared her throat. "Yes," she said more firmly.

"Good." His lips curved up into a devastatingly attractive little smile. "You will see that Lisette is not nearby?"

"She spends most of the evening with Donald," she assured him.

"I thought so, but I wanted to be sure." His smile grew a little more, and his eyes seemed to gleam with a look that sent unbridled, heated desire spinning through her. "Then adieu, Anne. Until tonight."

"Until tonight," she replied in a whisper, for she was not capable of speaking much louder at that moment.

Her tall, broad-shouldered husband strode away, while Anne slumped against the side of the wagon, tried to catch her breath and wondered what this meant.

*   *   *

Anne surveyed the bedchamber once more. She had closed the bed curtains and lit every candle. She didn't want him to think she had any...ideas.

But how could she not have ideas, or at least imaginings, when Reece would be alone with her, and despite the necessary nature of their relationship?

She opened the linen shutter to glance outside at the night sky. Stars twinkled in the chilly air, and the breeze made her feel even more awake than she already was. She took a deep breath and tried to calm herself, although every sense felt more acute and more alive waiting for a knock on the chamber door.

He didn't knock.

She turned and there he was, standing just inside the room, the door already closed behind him. His shadow from the candlelight danced upon the door.

''The hinges must be well oiled,'' she said, fighting the sudden sense that he wasn't really a mortal man at all, but some kind of spirit with supernatural powers.

''My mother keeps things in excellent condition,'' he replied, not moving, either.

She went to the table and poured wine into the single goblet.

''I am glad to have a chance to talk about my brother,'' she said as she offered the goblet to Reece. ''Piers is not used to long hours of practice. Damon had little patience for drills, Benedict even less.''

Reece took a sip of the wine, then nodded. ''That's fairly obvious.''

He set the goblet down on the table beside her. "But to dismiss him early or excuse him would be to point out his weakness. He would not appreciate that. He's proud. He wants to succeed, or at least do as well as Trev. If my father sent him from the field, he would be humiliated. He would rather stay until he dropped."

"Yes, he is proud, but I don't want to think that makes him a fool."

"He is no more a fool than any other young, proud fellow who doesn't want to fail. In that he is like a hundred other youths who have come here to train."

She heard something else in his voice, something that made his advice easier to accept. "And you were just the same."

He smiled a devastating smile, one that seemed completely unguarded—an observation that surprised and pleased her. "How did you guess?"

If she reached out, she could touch him. How much she wanted to touch him! How much she wanted to be his true wife! "You are a proud man yet."

"But not young?" he asked with a quirk of his eyebrow.

"Well, you are older than Piers," she pointed out, trying to be patient and not stare at his face, his lips, his eyes.

"Yes, I certainly am."

She waited for him to say more as he looked at her with his amazing light-gray eyes. "Piers is really doing very well, all things considered."

"What do you mean, all things considered?"

Reece shrugged his shoulders. "He is woefully unprepared for combat, even in a tournament. That's why you asked Henry to send him here, isn't it?"

She nodded her agreement, and forced away the jab of wounded pride that her brother was not better prepared. "But he is doing well?"

"Better than some who have been here for much longer," Reece admitted as he ran his hand along the table, toward her, then away. "He's got a fire in the belly, your brother. He wants to succeed and is willing to do what it takes. No training can give a man that kind of will."

"Really?" she asked, her heart expanding to hear such praise, and from such a man. Her delight took her attention from his long, strong fingers moving across the smooth surface of the table.

"Really. That's why he would not take kindly to a sister's interference, either."

He went to the window, looking out just as she had, then turned and leaned back against the sill. "Are you happy here, Anne?"

Taken aback by his question, she nevertheless nodded. "Very much." She managed a smile. "Your parents are just as you described them."

"My mother is very impressed with you. She told me so herself."

Anne flushed with pleasure.

Then Reece hoisted himself up to sit on the wide sill, as if he intended to stay for some time.

Her throat dried, but she told herself not to be ridiculous. He was simply being companionable.

She, too, sat, on the stool in front of the dressing table. "Your parents seem very happy together. How did they meet?"

"My father was hired to train Lord Gervais's men, and she was Lord Gervais's foster daughter. The first day my father was here, she threw a honeycomb at him."

Anne's eyes widened. "Really?"

He smiled with undisguised amusement. "Really. It hit him in the face."

She could imagine a youthful and more tempestuous Lady Fritha throwing something, if she were upset enough. But to throw anything at Sir Urien... "Why did she do that?"

"He said something insolent and she took exception. He maintains that, given that she was attired like a serving wench, his mistake was only natural. She says he shouldn't have said that to a serving wench, either."

"What exactly did he say?"

Reece chuckled, a low, deep and very pleasant sound. "They've never actually told me."

"It sounds a little like the way we met, except for the honeycomb," she noted. "I might have thrown one at you when you approached me in the king's corridor, had I had one handy."

"I'm glad you didn't."

He rose and came toward her. His expression

shifted. His eyes darkened and his gaze intensified in a way that sent spirals of desire furling through her. "I am happy here, too, Anne, in this room. With you. I am happy having you in my home," he said, his low, husky voice adding to her excitement.

Rising, she could scarcely draw breath. All the reasons for wanting him—a better future for her and Piers, safety from Damon and his threats—melted away, except one. She wanted him because he was Reece, and he made her feel as no man ever had, or probably would again. No man had ever stirred her desire, and her heart, as he did.

"Anne," he murmured, his voice a husky purr of query as she laid her hands on his broad, firm chest, the muscles hard beneath her palms. "I would have you here always. I would have you for my wife. In every way."

Her gaze anxiously searched his serious face, only to realize, without doubt, that he was absolutely sincere.

Even then, she could scarcely believe it. "You want me for your wife? What of Damon and Benedict and your plans for court?"

As he looked down into her eyes, his own blazed with desire and more, a look of such need and such longing, her own seemed a paltry portion compared to what he felt.

"You are not a Delasaine anymore, Anne. You are a Fitzroy. The king and our vows before God have made it so in one way, and tonight I would confirm it, if you are willing.''

"Willing?'' she cried, all her fears and doubts and worries shattered by his words, becoming rubble out of which her hope leapt into vibrant life. "I have never been more willing for anything in my life!''

To confirm her words, she raised herself on her toes, pressed her body against his and captured his mouth in a fervent kiss.

He swept her up into his arms and carried her to the bed. "I will have you for my wife, by God, and I will let no fears for the future stop me.''

He joined her on the bed and gathered her into his arms. Again his mouth met hers and she moved against him as excitement and happiness swamped every other feeling. He wanted her! She could be his wife! She could stay here and be happy and—

His hand caressed her breast, the unexpected stroke taking her by surprise. But only for an instant, for the surprise soon altered to one of aroused bliss as his hands continued to seek and touch, and his tongue slipped inside her mouth to tease and twine about hers.

Nothing had ever made her feel so desired. Nothing had ever inspired such desire within her. It was as if she had waited her whole life to feel this way, over-powered by the sensations and excitement that built with each light touch and brush of his fingertips.

He laid her on her back. Still kissing her, his fingers fumbled with the lacing of her bodice behind her neck. He wanted to get her dress off.

Of course. And she would have him naked, too. At once, she struggled to untie the lacing of his tunic. She succeeded before he did. "Take it off," she commanded, pushing him back so that she could sit up.

He stared at her a moment, his eyes dark with desire, and dumbfounded. "Take off your tunic," she ordered, "and I shall rid myself of my gown."

His smile was devilment itself.

His tunic was off in an instant and his shirt landed on the floor. Before she had finished lifting her gown over her head, his breeches and stockings and boots had joined the pile.

He grabbed her gown and yanked it off, then tossed it on the floor, too.

She held her breath as he studied her in the candlelight. All she wore was the thinnest white silk shift. He wore nothing at all, and as he looked at her, she reveled in the sight of his powerful warrior's body displayed before her.

"I have imagined this a thousand times," he whispered, raising his eyes to her face.

"As have I," she confessed.

With another smile that quickly gave way to blatant desire, he lay beside her on the bed and put his hand flat upon her collarbone, then, with agonizing leisure, moved it lower over her silk shift. "Very nice."

"My body or the shift?" she murmured, doing her best not to squirm, because she didn't want him to stop.

"Both, your body more, though."

Hooking one arm around him to steady herself, she copied his action, letting her palm glide over his naked shoulders, chest and hip. "You have lovely muscles."

"What you have are lovely, too." He leaned down and kissed her breast through the thin fabric. He found her nipple and lightly flicked his tongue across it. That felt even better than his hand.

Would it feel so for him, too?

She raised herself more and pressed her lips to his chest. With slow deliberation, she slid her mouth across his muscles until she felt the dark hairs around his nipple. Then she lightly stroked it with her tongue.

His sharp intake of breath told her it was as good for him.

A rush of satisfaction swept over her and she continued her exploration with her lips and tongue as he continued to stroke and caress.

His fingers trailed along her leg, lifting her shift, and new tendrils of desire furled and stretched and reached. Instinctively she parted her legs, and when his fingers went still higher, she did not resist. She eagerly moved her hand lower and touched the evidence that he was as ready and willing as she.

She lay back, pulling him with her. Her mouth claimed his again, more demanding now, and fervent.

If she had known the feelings and sensations he was asking her to forgo when he had suggested his plan, if she had possessed a better understanding of what making love with Reece would be like, she would never have agreed.

His hand pressed upon her where she was moist and swollen with anticipation. His gaze locked on to hers, powerful and certain. "You are ready for me, Anne but it may hurt a little."

"I don't care. I want you within me."

His eyes flared in the candlelight and his lips curved up slowly as he positioned himself. "I want to be there, too. I want to be your husband."

Husband. Never had the word sounded better.

That was her last thought as he leaned down to kiss her and gently pushed inside. There was a moment's resistance, a fleeting pain, dispelled by the sheer pleasure of holding him within her as they became united beyond the bonds of law, flesh of one flesh, forever.

As the excitement built, she threw her arms around him and pulled him close, telling him the pain was nothing. Unimportant. Forgotten.

He rocked forward, thrusting a little deeper, the sensation making her moan, her lips against his chest. Then deeper still, and deeper, each thrust more powerful than the one before.

Carried along on the waves of desire, she held tight to him, her hips instinctively bucking.

With one swift yank he tore her shift so that her breasts were exposed. She didn't care as he licked and kissed and pleasured, and the tension built still more.

Suddenly it erupted, shattered and splintered as a groan rumbled from his throat. Incredible waves of sensation rocked her, then drifted away as his thrusts gentled and eventually ceased.

Panting, he pulled away and lay beside her. As he slipped his arm beneath her, she rolled so that she was nestled against his shoulder.

He gently brushed a lock of hair from her face. "I have been a fool, Anne. Can you forgive me?"

Still enveloped in the bliss of their passion, she gave him a warm, lazy smile. "After that, I believe I could forgive you anything."

His eyes lit up with delightful merriment. "Ah, be careful, wife! You may be telling me more than you should. If I displease you, all I will have to do to avoid a scolding is this," he murmured, proceeding to demonstrate, "and this…and this…"

She cupped and raised his face from her breasts, which still tingled from his attentions. "That may work, I grant you. But I believe that what works for the mistress may also work for the master. For instance, if I want you to agree to some household expense you do not consider necessary, all I may have to do is this…and this…and this…"

He moaned, then grabbed her hand. "By the saints, you could be right."

"Could be? I would say, definitely."

He chuckled. "We could spend a great deal of time trying to outmaneuver one another."

"I can think of less interesting ways to spend my time."

He rolled so that he was on top of her, his arms braced beside her head so that his weight was not upon her. "I had no idea you thought this way."

She giggled, happy as she had never been in all her life. "Neither did I, but I quite enjoy it. Had you not better blow out the candles? We may set the room alight."

"I believe we already have," he purred, caressing her cheek. Warmed by his words and his touch, she watched while he did as she suggested. The flickering light make his taut, naked flesh glow, and she delighted in the smooth ripple of his muscles as he moved. He was, quite simply, as magnificent a man as God had ever made.

Not just for his face and form, though. He was a good, honest, honorable man.

When he finished, they were cloaked by the intimate darkness.

"Now, my wife," he said softly as he got back into bed. "I can think of a few more things you might discover you enjoy."

"Already?"

"*Different* things."

"There are several?"

"Yes, and we have already wasted a good deal of time."

"Then you had better start showing me."

And so he did.

Chapter Fifteen

Anne stirred when she felt the draft of cool air as Reece lifted the sheet. Still half-asleep, she rolled and groped for him. "What are you doing? It's still dark."

He cursed as he tripped over something. "I think I've torn your shift some more."

"Then come back to bed before you hurt yourself."

"I can't. It's nearly dawn."

Her eyes adjusting to the dimness, she winced as he banged his hip into her dressing table.

He found his breeches and pulled them on. "I do not regret what we have done for a moment, but my father thinks as I did, that our marriage is a serious error. It would be best if I could explain what has happened to him myself. Nobody likes being blindsided. I don't want him hearing that we spent the night together from Lisette or one of the other servants. Seldon might make some comment about being alone in his chamber, too."

He cursed again.

"What's wrong?"

"Father wants to do lances today. He's always surly when we do lances. It's the hardest thing to learn, so the lads make a lot of mistakes and sometimes hurt themselves. Maybe I should wait until tomorrow."

She wasn't pleased by the delay. "I have already waited too long for you, my love. I want to be with you tonight, too."

"I don't see any reason I can't be with you again if I use the secret passage," he said as he pressed a light kiss on her brow. "I owe it to my father to tell him first, and I really think it would be best to wait until an auspicious moment to let him know my excellent plan has fallen by the wayside."

"As long as it won't be more than a day or two, Reece. I want all the world to know how I feel about you."

He brushed his lips across hers again. "And I, you. I don't want to have to pretend anymore, either, so I will tell him tomorrow at the latest, whatever mood he is in."

Another kiss, and he left the room.

As the door closed, Anne nestled down under the covers and sighed. Although she wished Reece would tell his father about the change in their relationship immediately, he knew Sir Urien best, so she would accept the wisdom of his decision. Besides, he had promised not to wait beyond tomorrow. Surely she could endure keeping her love for her husband hidden for one more day.

Her love. For her husband.

She was Reece's wife, safe and secure and loved. Damon had no more hold over her, for Reece would keep Piers safe, too.

She sat up and hugged her knees as she thought of what *she* must do this day. She had to go into the village, find Benedict and tell him she would no longer be Damon's spy.

She contemplated telling Reece of Damon's plan and Benedict's likely presence in the village, then decided against it. There was already enough enmity between them and Reece knew full well that he must beware of Damon. Once Benedict knew that she would not obey, he would not linger, but surely go running back to Damon without delay.

She was finally free of her half brothers, and so was Piers.

She got out of bed and picked up her torn shift, then examined the rip. It could be easily mended.

She laid it on the bed and had to laugh aloud as she imagined Lisette's eyes widening and her giggle if she knew who had made that tear, and how, and when.

The beast uncaged. At last!

"Father, they're doing their best," Reece said as Sir Urien scowled at the line of young men mounted on their horses, their lances dipping and swaying as they tried to keep them straight.

"Tighter under the arm. Hold it against your body

when you are at rest!'' his father called before he turned toward his son. ''I have had enough of this for today.''

He glared again at the lads. ''You're dismissed.''

Like the boys, Reece glanced overhead to check the position of the sun, then regarded his father with a wary expression. ''So early?''

''Yes. Go on! Go!'' Sir Urien waved his hand as if he were shooing a flock of birds. ''Do what you will until the evening meal. And don't you dare be late for it!''

Letting the squires finish early was so unusual Reece's heart plummeted to his boots. Today his father was in an even more foul humor than lance practice generally inspired—hardly a propitious time to tell him what had happened last night. Although he was not the least bit sorry he had finally, passionately, blissfully made love to his wife, it was not going to be easy explaining to his father, his brothers and the Morgans that it was no longer necessary that he seek an annulment. As for the potential trouble that might come from being related to Damon and Benedict Delasaine...he would make certain that his loyalty to Henry was without question, and that he wanted nothing whatsoever to do with them. Considering how they had treated Anne, he doubted she wanted any dealings with them, either. Her loyalty was to her husband now, as his would be to her.

When the last of the young men and their horses had disappeared through the gate, Reece glanced at his father to try to gauge his mood. Perhaps his foul temper would not last long.

Then his jaw dropped with shock. His father was actually smiling. Such evidence of good humor under any circumstances was rare with his father, let alone after a lance practice, and Reece felt dazed. "I thought you were angry!"

Sir Urien shook his head and laughed under his breath. "They're better with a lance than any lot I've had yet."

"What?"

"No need to gape as if I've said I was the king's sire in disguise," his father chided as he started walking toward the gate. "Everybody claims I'm a tyrant when it comes to the lance, so the boys expect it. They've heard all the stories, and I don't doubt Seldon's been going on again about the time he tried to run me through and I simply stood there until he sheered off. I think he likes to act out the part where I stand there waiting, stern of mien. At any rate, who am I to ruin my reputation?"

Reece hurried to catch up to him, then matched his father's long strides. Good God, there might never be a better time to tell him what had happened last night. Well, the basics, anyway. Under the shadow of the wall, he laid a hand on his father's arm to halt him and faced him. "Father, I would speak to you a moment."

Sir Urien raised an inquisitive brow. "Of course, my son." Before Reece could even begin, something behind Reece caught Sir Urien's attention. "Donald!" he bellowed, "where were you? I needed your help with the lances."

Sir Urien started to move toward the gate again, then checked his step. "Can it wait, Reece?"

He would rather not wait, but his father was obviously preoccupied with Donald. While his father might be in a genial humor, this no longer seemed the best time for a vital revelation. Just as long as he spoke to his father before he retired to Anne's... *their*...bedchamber. "Go ahead. I'll speak with you after the evening meal."

His father nodded and hurried onward, calling a greeting to Lady Fritha and Anne. They were leaving the castle, baskets over their arms, probably filled with food for the poor of the village.

Anne caught sight of him and smiled gloriously. As he waved and approached them, images and memories from the previous night came and went. The glow of her flesh in the candlelight. Her soft lips upon his skin. Her hair spread out upon the pillow. Her thin white shift bunched up about her waist. The desire in her eyes as they made love. The little whimpers of encouragement when he touched her.

"What are you doing here?" his mother asked when he reached them.

He glanced at Anne, so demure and quiet. He didn't doubt that he alone of all the world knew how passionate and primitive she could be, which was a very stimulating thought. "Father let the boys go early."

His mother's eyes widened.

"Aye, a shock, I know, but he was quite pleased with them."

"Pleased?" his mother repeated. "I thought he was starting the lances today."

"He did. They managed so well he is actually in a pleasant frame of mind." Out of the corner of his eye, he saw Anne flush slightly, and her eyes sparkled. He wished he could say that he had told his father what had happened and that all was well.

Soon, though, he assured himself. Very soon.

"Well, he always barks more than he has to during a lance lesson," his mother said. "He claims they expect it of him, but I daresay they wouldn't mind if he didn't."

"Aye, that's what he said to me, too. I think he intends this to be a reward, although they surely do not think that is the case." He lowered his voice to a conspiratorial whisper. "I also thinks he likes growling and looking fearsome."

Lady Fritha laughed, the sound as warm and maternal as the woman. "I think you've hit the target there, my son."

"Unfortunately, time on their hands means I'll probably have a few arguments to deal with later, and I wouldn't be surprised if I have to round up a few of them from the taverns before the evening meal."

"And until then?" Anne asked, her tone and gaze presumably all innocence unless one had seen her desire unmasked.

If his mother were not there, he would have responded very differently from the way he did. "I thought I would come with you until it's time to check the taverns for miscreant youths."

"Excellent!" Lady Fritha cried. "Mary's cow's hoof is infected and I could use a strong pair of arms to hold the beast while I apply the salve."

As she turned and headed off along the main road that skirted the market, Reece looked at Anne and pulled a face.

"If you do not wish to act as a laborer, you could return to the castle, I suppose. We can find another pair of manly arms to hold the cow," Anne remarked, her brilliant eyes twinkling with merriment.

He took her arm and gave her a surreptitious caress as they started after his mother. "Am I so easily dismissed?"

She slid him a sidelong glance. "When your mother is with us, yes."

Drawing her close, he laughed softly.

"You are in a very fine humor, husband. Does this mean your father was not upset that our marriage cannot be annulled?"

Reece sobered. "I haven't had the chance to tell him."

"I thought you said he was pleased with the boys," Anne said, frowning. "Surely it was a good time to tell him."

"It was, until he saw Donald, who should have been helping with the instruction. I thought I could wait until after the meal." He dropped his voice to a seductive whisper. "I will tell him before it is time to retire."

She bit her lip and the little wrinkle of worry appeared between her brows. "I shouldn't be so impatient. If he was angry with Donald, you might be wiser to wait, as you said before."

"I don't think he was angry so much as curious. He can guess as well as I where Donald was, and he probably wants to know how serious things are between Donald and Lisette. Lisette is a servant in his household now, and he takes our servants' welfare seriously, because he was a hired man a long time.

"Nor does he have the right to chastise Donald for not being at the practice. Donald's service does not include instruction. He helps because he wants to, not because he is obligated to."

"Do you think your father disapproves of his relationship with Lisette?"

"I doubt it. Donald would never force his attentions on a woman, and Lisette obviously likes him. He probably wanted to insure that Donald will treat her well, if things between them come to an end."

"Do you have any doubts about that?"

Reece shrugged and raised his voice as they neared the smithy, for the blacksmith's hammer rang upon his anvil like the bell of a cathedral. "He will see that she has no regrets, whatever happens, but Donald is a good man. Lisette should have no cause to rue her time with him."

He saw relief in Anne's eyes. "I'm glad to hear that."

He was not surprised to learn that she cared what happened to her servants.

"Then you think you can tell your father today?" she asked after a moment.

"Yes. All things considered, he should be in an amenable frame of mind after the evening meal."

"Since he will be well fed and well wined?"

"My father does not drink to excess."

"I didn't mean that." She frowned. "Well, perhaps I did, a little. Still, you cannot deny a fine meal with excellent wine is very good for settling one's humors."

"I can think of something even better."

"Can you?" she asked, eyeing him with the incredible combination of seduction and innocence that played havoc with his heated longings. He had never met a woman who could be both vixen and angel at the same time.

He drew her back into the alley between the smithy and the chandlers, a space necessary so that the heat of the forge wouldn't melt the chandler's candles and thus ruin his wares.

"I certainly can and so, my lady, can you," he murmured.

He intended to kiss her just once or twice, yet the instant he had his arms about her and felt her mouth against his, one kiss seemed a pittance. His kiss deepened and became more ardent, and his hand began a leisurely, exciting exploration of his wife's slender body, albeit through her clothes.

"I think I've dropped the basket," she whispered a few moments later, her lips trailing along his jaw.

"Nothing spilled."

"Your mother will be wondering where we are."

"She'll want to chat with Mary first anyway."

"But we shouldn't be long."

"We won't." He took her face between his palms and kissed her fervently.

Anne drew back, panting. "We cannot. Not here."

He struggled to calm his own breathing and to take heed of her cautions. He might have, had she not looked at him that way. "Do you really want me to stop, Anne?" he asked, his voice a deep, seductive purr.

"No," she admitted, her hands making their own explorations.

"I don't want to, either."

"One more kiss, Reece, and then we should go."

"Aye, one more."

It was a very long kiss.

When Anne and Reece finally stepped back into the road that circled the market, he held her hand.

He chuckled softly. He could hold her hand like this every single day for the rest of his life.

Anne's grip suddenly tightened and she sucked in her breath. "Ouch! What's the matter?" he asked.

"People are looking at us. I think we should stop holding hands."

A swift glance along the road and around the market proved that her observation was, regrettably, correct. The people buying and selling turned away quickly and suddenly became intent upon their bargaining.

He sighed with resignation and did as she suggested. "Aye, you're right. The way rumor and gossip fly about the village, my father might hear of our hand-holding before we even get to Mary's. But after I've told him, and Mother, too, I'm going to hold your hand every chance I get."

Anne blushed, and she still looked worried.

"Have no fears or concerns, Anne. Everything will be fine."

"I hope so."

She spoke so softly her husband didn't hear.

Trying not to make it look obvious that she was searching for someone, Anne walked slowly through the village. She had waited until Reece had gone from Mary's to round up any of the youths who had come to the village before she left Lady Fritha, saying that she wanted to return to the castle to mend a shift.

Her shift did need mending, but more importantly, she needed to speak to Benedict.

She had spotted him in the alley near the tavern on the green. Her first reaction was a flinch of fear, but that quickly gave way to triumphant exaltation. She would tell him to go back to Damon and inform her half brother that she would not be spying for him. If he did not like that, let him try to take her, and Piers, away from Castle Gervais. Her beloved husband would surely never allow that to happen, and so Damon's threats would be meaningless.

Benedict's familiar bulk slouched in the shade of the smithy as if he was half in his cups. She slowed her steps until she was sure he had seen her, then she gave him a pointed look and headed toward the alley between the smith's and the chandler's. The chandler's shop was shuttered now and the smithy's business concluded for the day.

Benedict appeared at the alley's entrance, swaying like a sot. "Well, aren't you the lovey-dovey little woman?" he sneered, his words slurred. "Have you managed to get that eunuch to bed you at last?"

He wasn't half-drunk. He was nearly insensible. She could smell the ale on him from here.

She had to be careful. A drunk Benedict was a mean Benedict. She made sure her back was to the wall and noted how far it was to the end of the alley as she calculated how to get past him.

Thank God a drunk Benedict was also a slow Benedict.

"Keep your voice down!" she commanded in a harsh whisper as he came to a swaying halt. The last thing she wanted was for somebody to discover her with him.

He flushed and came closer still. "Shut your mouth!" he snarled.

"You have no right to order me. Neither does Damon. I am the wife of Sir Reece Fitzroy—in every sense of the word, as you guessed—so Damon has no power and no rights over me. Therefore, you will leave this place and when you return to him, you will tell him that there will be no information about the Fitzroys and their friends coming from *me*."

Benedict's bleary eyes narrowed as he stumbled closer. She tried to move to the side to get away, but he caught her, bracing his two hands on either side of her head. He leaned forward, so that his foul breath was full in her face. "Who do you think you are, girl?"

Despite his bravado, she saw dread and dismay in his narrow, ugly eyes.

Emboldened, she straightened her shoulders and curled her lip with disdain as she faced a man who had tormented her for so long. "I am the wife of Sir Reece Fitzroy. The king himself has made me free of Damon, and you, and if you have the sense of a flea, you will run to Damon and tell him that he threatens me, and my husband, at his peril."

Benedict blinked stupidly, as if he couldn't take in what she was saying.

She shoved his right arm down and stepped away. "I am not afraid of you, or Damon, anymore."

"Then we will take Piers."

"If Damon is such a fool as to move against the wife of Sir Reece Fitzroy, let him try."

"If you want me gone, get me some money to buy a horse."

"What happened to yours?"

"I lost it."

Lost? No doubt he had done so gambling.

Although she didn't want to give him even so much as a ha'penny, she had little choice unless she wanted him to try to steal a mount. He would surely get caught, and then explanations would have to be made. Better he should leave here, and take her message to Damon. "I shall have to give you something to sell."

He shrugged. "All right."

"I will meet you here tomorrow."

"Good."

She hesitated. "Whatever you do, Benedict, be careful not to reveal who you are."

"Do I look like a fool?" he demanded.

Anne didn't answer as she marched away.

Chapter Sixteen

The main room of the inn far on the outskirts of
Bridgeford Wells was not large, and it stank of cheap
ale and even cheaper wine, filthy rushes on the floors
surely infested with fleas, and bones and spills from
several meals. Although the sun still shone, the windows let in little light and allowed almost none of the
smoke from the hearth to dissipate. Near the entrance,
a noisy game of dice was in progress. Several youths
from Castle Gervais were involved, and wagers were
being made.

Piers Delasaine had come because he was flattered
that the other boys asked him. As much as he loved
his sister, he was discovering the pleasure of friendship among comrades-in-arms.

He had not been happy that Anne had asked the
king to send him with her, thinking his lack of skill
would prove humiliating. Instead, he had found that
he was better than many here, and with the instruction
of Sir Urien, Reece, Donald and Seldon, he could be-

come better still, and probably even a champion of tournaments someday.

Then he would show his half brothers that they had been wrong to treat him like an unnecessary nuisance, and very wrong to treat Anne as they had.

He sat in the farthest, darkest corner, nursing his sour and overpriced wine that had taken far too much of the meager funds he had been hoarding for months, since he had first heard Damon's plan to take them to the king's court.

Trevelyan Fitzroy, who was likewise not making wagers but who had been quipping about the progress of the game, detached himself from the huddle and sauntered closer.

"What do you want?" Piers asked without making any attempt to sound polite, or even interested.

Trevelyan Fitzroy had everything he wanted: a loving father and mother, brothers worthy of admiration and emulation, several friends, a handsome face and a charming manner. It still struck Piers as nothing short of miraculous that Lisette had not responded to Trevelyan's overtures. However, it had made her lack of attention to *him* much easier to take.

If he had known Trevelyan was going to be in the group, he would have stayed in the barracks and polished his armor.

To his surprise, Trevelyan grinned and sat on the bench opposite him. "I've come to sue for peace."

Piers's eyes narrowed with suspicion. "Why? I'm a Delasaine, you're a Fitzroy. My brothers attacks yours. And defeated him, too,'' he couldn't resist adding.

Trevelyan's cheeks reddened. "Aye, they beat him—shamefully—and it took both of them to do it.''

As Piers half rose, Trevelyan grabbed his arm and held it.

"Sit and listen. I'm willing to overlook what happened. My father always says that while you should pay heed to the company a man keeps, it is the man himself you should measure. You don't give up, you fight hard but fair, and if I were in a battle, I'd feel better knowing you were by my side. If you don't want to be my friend, that's fine. But I don't want you to be an enemy.''

There could be no mistaking his sincerity, and Piers could not help feeling pleased, and flattered. His envy might never disappear, but he could not refuse this offer of friendship. In his heart he knew he would be a fool to let pride rob him of this chance. "If we are ever to battle, I would want you by my side, too.''

They both sensed the import of this pact and sat in solemn silence for a moment.

Then, because he was happy, Piers sought to lighten the mood. "And Lisette doesn't want you, either.''

Trevelyan's laugh rumbled up from his chest. The merry sound drew the attention of the gamesters for a brief moment, but soon enough their attention was once more on the game. "No, she doesn't. She's got Donald—and talk about dead gone! He's practically daft when he's anywhere near her.''

The door burst open as if blown by a great gust of wind. The gamesters cried out in protest until they saw Reece Fitzroy silhouetted in the doorway.

"What the devil are you young louts doing here?" he asked, his hands on his hips.

"Quick, follow me," Trevelyan whispered, slipping around the table. "Out the back. Careful. Keep low or he'll see us."

Piers made no argument as he obeyed. Clearly Trevelyan had made a clandestine escape from this tavern before. He led Piers out through the kitchen, past the chicken coup and pigsty, and over the fence to the trees behind.

Laughing with relief, Trevelyan threw himself on the ground. "Oh, God's wounds, that was close! There'll be hell to pay when they get back."

"I suppose they'll be punished?"

"Oh, a little extra duty, maybe. My father let us go early today, so they had to know some of us would make a beeline here."

Piers clambered to his feet. "And you came anyway?"

Trevelyan rose and brushed off his clothes. "Aye. They expect it, you see. Why should I spoil Reece's fun?"

"So long as *you're* not caught, eh?"

Trevelyan chuckled ruefully. "Oh, I have, plenty of times when I've been too slow, and they're a lot harder on me than the others. To set an example, you see. Even then, it's not that bad.'' He regarded Piers gravely. ''Not used to having fun, are you?''

He didn't wait for Piers to answer. ''Come on, we'd best head back. I'll go to the east, you to the west, and I'll see you in the hall.''

With a nod, Piers left his brother-in-law. Then, as he hurried through the village, he saw a sight that brought him to a shocked halt. Anne came marching out of the alley beside the smithy as if she were on an important mission for the king.

That was surprising enough. But then Benedict lumbered into view, heading toward the tavern like a bad omen made flesh.

Humming the tune to a ballad about a bold knight and his faithful lady love, Reece entered the hall. He had marched the errant youths to the barracks, given them a good tongue-lashing, and left them sitting on their cots with orders to polish every speck of armor they owned by tomorrow morning. They could start in the short time before the evening meal and finish afterward.

All things considered, though, they hadn't gotten into too much mischief. None had been drunk, and not much money had been lost on their youthful wagers. He had made certain of that, and the owner of the tavern knew better than to lead the boys training with Sir Urien too far astray. Sir Urien himself had made that point very clear soon after the man had opened his establishment in Bridgeford Wells.

He wondered again where Trevelyan and Piers Delasaine had got to, hoping they weren't fighting again, or getting into trouble of another sort.

Then his gaze moved to the dais. His father was there, and so was—

"Gervais!" Reece called out, hurrying forward.

Even as he did, his heart hammered in his chest. What news did his brother bring? From the look on Gervais's face, it did not appear to be good. He also looked exhausted, as if he had rushed to Bridgeford Wells as fast as he could.

They embraced in greeting. "What news from court?" Reece asked.

"I bring a summons from Henry. You are to appear before him immediately," Gervais replied.

Reece could think of only one reason Henry would summon him back to court—the annulment that he no longer wanted.

Gervais and his father studied him, so singular in their expression, they were like mirror images.

"To the solar," Sir Urien brusquely ordered after a sweeping glance around the hall. "We need not discuss all our business in the hall. Your mother is from home, but she can come to us there when she returns."

He turned and led the way. Reece followed with Gervais, who glanced at him uncertainly.

Was his change of heart obvious? Reece wondered. Could Gervais see how unwelcome his news was, news that days ago would have been cause for relief?

After they entered the solar, Sir Urien closed the

door behind them and took his seat at his table. He gestured for his sons to sit. "Now, Gervais, begin at the beginning."

Gervais nodded, but first he methodically drew off his gauntlet gloves. He unbuckled his cloak and let it fall behind him on the chair. His preparations, so characteristic of him, threatened to make Reece scream with impatience.

There was nothing new in that, either.

"I finally got an audience with Henry, after he returned from hunting in the New Forest. As I had hoped, he was in a genial frame of mind, and I was able to convince him that an annulment of the marriage between Anne and Reece would be the best thing for all concerned. He agreed and that is why Reece and Anne are to return to court."

Oh, God. His plan had worked. His stupid, unnecessary plan had worked.

"He was not angry at the implied criticism?" his father asked.

"No." Gervais cleared his throat and spoke without looking at Reece. "Damon Delasaine has not been acting wisely, and I think Henry understands why a man loyal to the king would not wish to be allied with that particular family."

"You are not at court now, my son," Sir Urien rumbled. "Speak plainly."

"As bad as we already knew the Delasaines to be, they are even worse. Their crimes are more extensive than we thought."

Reece leaned forward. ''What crimes?''

''There are stories of rape, possibly murder. Even on my way here, a serving wench in a tavern was found dead, and the man seen riding away sounded like Benedict Delasaine.''

''Was he not at court?'' Reece asked.

''No. He has not been at court since shortly after you left. As if all this is not bad enough, Damon Delasaine is apparently trying to seduce the queen.''

Surely Gervais was wrong, interpreting rumour and gossip in the worst possible light because the Delasaines were their enemy.

''How do you know what Damon Delasaine plans?'' Reece demanded. ''I don't imagine he discusses such things with you.''

''He's a vain, arrogant fool who makes his goal plain. Everybody at court can see what he is trying to do.''

''If everybody at court can see it, why isn't he charged with treason?''

''Because then the queen will be implicated, too. Henry cares for Eleanor, and thus far, she is blameless. She has not encouraged the man. She hasn't sent him away, either,'' Gervais added grimly, ''but she has done nothing criminal so far, and neither, exactly, has he. But Blaidd says—''

''Oh, and what the *expert* on women says must be true?'' Reece charged. ''He can read Eleanor's mind and heart?''

''Not Eleanor's—Damon's,'' Gervais retorted.

Reece's hands balled into fists as he fought to control the rage and dismay building within him. "I point out that so far, there is no proof of any crime on the part of the Delasaines. I agree they seem quite capable of violence and murder and even treason but—"

"But?" Gervais cried, staring at him. "*But?* What more do you want? You had less evidence of the man's evil ambition when you made the wise decision to annul your marriage to his sister. The Morgans agree with me that Delasaine would probably be willing to assassinate Henry if he succeeded in becoming Eleanor's lover."

"Even he could not be such a fool," Reece declared. "For one thing, he does not have royal blood, so he could never be king."

"Unfortunately, he does," his father said. "Only about a drop, but for him, that may be enough to believe he can succeed. Or a man may rule without a crown."

"If the risk to Henry is so grave, have the man arrested and charged."

"You do not want to believe this, do you?" Gervais demanded.

"Of course not. Delasaine is my brother-in-law."

"For now," his father said sternly. "What Gervais has learned makes it even more imperative that you free yourself from this liaison. Damon Delasaine has no more sense than a mad dog, and he will take others down with him in his ambition."

Reece could not disagree that any tie to a convicted

traitor to the crown meant danger for the traitor's family.

"What about these other crimes—the rapes and murders?" he asked. "Why has he not been charged with them? If he were in prison, or executed, he could not assassinate the king."

"So far, there is not enough proof for a jury of nobles to convict a knight in a court of law."

Reece crossed his arms. "But there is enough for me to annul my marriage?"

His father studied him with a searching intensity that would have made him flinch two days ago. "What are you saying, Reece? That you no longer want the annulment?" he asked incredulously.

"Our loyalty is without question."

"A man in power can be very suspicious if he thinks that power is in jeopardy," Sir Urien answered sternly. "Former loyalty may count for nothing if he feels threatened. You should not tarry, but go to court before Damon does something traitorous, especially given that Henry sounds amenable to reconsidering the marriage. I've known men like Damon before, and patience is not one of their virtues. When he moves, you do not want to be tied to him."

In his mind, Reece knew his father spoke the truth about Damon Delasaine. Men like him would over-reach themselves, and like Icarus flying to the sun, destroy themselves. Unlike Icarus, Damon would take others with him.

His father's expression thawed a tiny bit. "I was afraid of this. You have started to care for her."

"Yes, I have. She is my wife, after all." He looked at Gervais. "If what you say is true, what will happen to Anne if she is not my wife? The whole family could have their money and land stripped from them."

"Reece," Gervais began, "I did not want to have to tell you this, but now it seems I must."

A shadow seemed to fall across Reece's heart as he watched his brother warily.

"Whenever I encountered Damon after you had gone," Gervais said, his tone grim but certain, "he regarded me with smug satisfaction, like a peddler who's sold something at twice its value. It was strange, and raised my suspicions. If he were upset about the marriage as he seemed to be at first, he would not act so. Why should he now be pleased after opposing it before?"

"He realized there was nothing he could do, and he had no dowry to pay," Reece replied.

Gervais's expression grew even sadder. "Or he realized there was some benefit to be had by this marriage."

"It ties him to a better family," Reece suggested.

"Yes, it does. But where has Benedict Delasaine gone? I had news of a man fitting his description at all the inns I stopped at on the way here, yet nobody in the castle knows of him. He has not come to visit his sister—at least, not openly."

Reece felt a leaden ball forming in his stomach.

"What are you getting at, Gervais? As our father says, speak plainly—or do not speak at all."

"I am saying that we are the natural enemies of men like the Delasaines. A wife learns many things, and information can be a weapon. It could well be that Damon Delasaine is pleased because he has someone in our household who can pass such information on to him."

Reece leapt to his feet. "You accuse Anne?"

Gervais nodded.

Reece turned to his father. "Anne is not a spy!"

"Do you know that with absolute certainty?" his father asked, his voice quiet but cold as a blizzard's wind.

Anne could not be a spy. She would never betray him.

Yet even as his heart shouted denials, his mind recalled her questions about their friends and other things that had seemed unimportant on the journey. He realized the many things a woman helping the chatelaine would learn, of stores that could be used if they were besieged, or weaknesses in the buildings needing repairs. He remembered the way she had surveyed Castle Gervais and that he had told her of at least one secret passage. He would willingly have told her where it was, if she had asked.

But she had not asked.

She must be innocent. She could not have been insincere when they were alone together.

"I know this situation has not been easy for you,

but annulment is for the best after all,'' his father said, interrupting his tormented reflections. "The Delasaines are the worst sort of men and any links to them must be severed."

But Anne? What of Anne? Beautiful, loving Anne, the Anne he had come to love, in every way.

This had to be wrong. "Father, Gervais, I cannot—"

A fist pounded on the door. "Sir Urien!" Piers Delasaine shouted, his voice desperate. "Sir Urien, I have to talk to you!"

Reece started to protest the interruption, but his father held up his hand. "See what he wants that brings him in such alarm."

Gervais strode to the door and pulled it open.

Piers stood on the threshold, his face pale and his body trembling with suppressed emotion. He appeared as upset as Reece felt.

"What is it? What's happened?" Sir Urien demanded.

"I have to talk to you," Piers said as he looked past Reece and Gervais to Sir Urien.

Sir Urien gestured for the boy to enter.

"I have come to warn you," Piers said, his expression grimly resolute, giving them a glimpse of the stern warrior he might become. "I saw my brother Benedict. He was talking to Anne in an alley in the village."

Oh, God. Reece felt for a chair and sat heavily.

"Are you certain?" his father demanded.

Piers nodded. "I would know Benedict anywhere."

"You came here at once?" Sir Urien asked.

"Yes." Piers swallowed hard and his gaze faltered, but he spoke out nonetheless. "If Anne is deceiving you, I want you to know I had no part in it." He raised his eyes to regard Sir Urien steadily. "I want to be a good and honorable man, like you."

Reece jumped to his feet and strode to the door.

"Where are you going?" his father demanded.

"To find my brother-in-law," Reece growled as he marched out of the room.

Chapter Seventeen

Anne looked up from mending her shift as Lisette hurried into the room.

"Oh, la, my lady! Here you are!" She frowned as Anne put her shift down, as if wondering what she was doing, but did not puzzle over that for long.

"What is it?" Anne asked. "Does Lady Fritha need me?"

"*Non, non!* Your husband's brother has come from court."

Anne swiftly sucked in her breath. She put her trembling hands on the arm of her chair and rose. "When did he arrive?"

"Not long ago. He is in the solar with your husband and Sir Urien. Or they were there. Your husband passed by me in the hall and…" She hesitated, blushing. "And perhaps I should be silent."

This was such an unusual thing for Lisette to say, more trepidation filled Anne. "What about my husband?"

Lisette reached for the basket. "I will finish this if you like, my lady."

Anne kicked it out of the way, paying no heed to her garment tumbling onto the floor. *"What about my husband?"*

The girl didn't meet her gaze. "He was angry, my lady. More angry than I have ever seen him. And I have heard…that is, I overheard Sir Gervais say that your husband has been summoned back to court."

Anne went to the window and looked out unseeing. Gervais could have come to tell them Henry was amenable to an annulment. Perhaps Reece had told his brother, and his father, that the plan was no longer to be followed. Maybe they had quarreled over that alteration, and were angry at Reece for what they had done.

No matter what had happened between the members of her husband's family—and now hers—they would have to go to court because it was the king's command. Once there, Reece would have to tell the king that there was, after all, no cause for an annulment.

And then what? If his father was angry because the marriage could not be annulled, if Sir Urien still thought her a serious liability, she and Reece would have to…what? Leave here, perhaps.

She didn't really care where she went, as long as she was with Reece. But then they would not be so safe from Damon. She could well believe her half brother would try to exact vengeance if he thought them vulnerable.

And what of Piers? Would Sir Urien let him stay to complete his training? Would Piers want to?

"My lady?"

She had forgotten Lisette was there. "Yes?" she asked, glancing over her shoulder.

Lisette held up the shift. "Would you like me to finish mending this?"

"Yes, please, Lisette."

The girl sat in the chair and Anne went back to looking out the window. Where had Reece gone in his rage? When would he come back?

She would keep watch, and when he returned, she would speak with him at once. Lady Fritha would likely be too preoccupied with her other son's return, or the possible rancor in her household, to miss her daughter-in-law.

Who was the cause of that rancor.

Anne sighed and leaned her head against the window frame. She did not want to be the cause of dissension in this happy household.

"I should not have told you," Lisette murmured, and with a sniffle.

Anne turned toward her and saw a tear sliding down her cheek. She hurried to Lisette and patted her shoulder. "It's all right. I would have found out eventually, and I would rather have such news from a friend."

Lisette made a tremulous smile. "I am your friend, my lady?"

"Indeed, you are. I hope you will always be my friend."

Lisette started to sob, hunching over the bundled shift in her hands.

Before Anne could say anything to comfort her, a shout caught her attention and drew her again to the window, for she instantly recognized Reece's voice.

The guards opened the wicket in the inner gate and she waited anxiously to see her husband.

But it was not Reece who came through first.

It was Benedict.

She watched in horror as Reece frog-marched her half brother across the courtyard and into the hall.

Fear's cold fingers squeezed her heart. She had not foreseen this. She should have. Benedict was a fool. He had probably said something when he was deep in his cups that revealed his identity.

Yet the greater fault was hers. She should have told Reece Benedict was in Bridgeford Wells. She should have told him everything last night, of Damon's plans and her decision to foil them. She should have confided in her husband—because now what would he think?

This was the worst thing that could have happened, far worse than Reece's delay in telling his father of their union, for if Benedict was trapped, he would say anything to free himself—implicate anyone, tell any lie.

She must confess all now. At once. Reece must hear it from her own lips.

With firm resolution strengthening her, she ran from the room. As she rushed to the hall, she dared to hope all would soon be well, and her dishonorable covenant with Damon would have no serious consequences. She had erred by not being truthful from the start, but she would make things right.

She must.

And because he cared for her, Reece would believe her, and trust her.

He must.

Reece and Benedict were not in the hall. The solar, then.

She was panting by the time she reached it. Trying to catch her breath, she knocked.

Sir Urien himself opened the door. Reece had a grip on Benedict's arm, and Gervais stood beside the large table, glaring at her half brother. Even more surprisingly, Piers was there.

But not for long. When he caught sight of her as she stood on the threshold, he marched out of the room, pushing his way past her without a word.

What was he doing here? Why did he ignore her?

Worse and worse, puzzling and confusing and frightening.

Her resolution wavered for a moment, but only a moment. She lifted her chin and entered the room. Sir Urien went to sit behind his table, as stern as a judge in the king's eyre. Reece let go of Benedict and stood on the opposite side of the table facing them. Anne searched for some hopeful sign, and saw it in his eyes.

Whatever was going on, he was not against her.

And yet…and yet his intense gaze scrutinized her cautiously, as if he doubted.

Dear God, how could he doubt her after last night?

"As you see, we have an unexpected visitor," Sir Urien began.

She glanced at Benedict, who was trembling and as cowed as a half-drowned dog. He smelled of ale and mud, his clothes mute witness that he had not come willingly, and his whole attitude proclaiming him for the coward he was. Here at Castle Gervais, he did not have mercenaries or Damon to support him. Here he was all alone, to stand or fall on his own merits.

"My lord," she said, looking at her father-in-law, "he was not unexpected to me, and I deeply regret that I did not inform you of my other half brother's plan before this."

Benedict sucked in his breath. "You'd betray us all, would you?" he snarled under his breath. "You did just what you were told. *Everything* you were told to get him to keep you. You got him to—"

"Be quiet," Anne snapped, her words like the crack of a whip. She had loved her husband because it was her desire, and only that; she would not have Benedict say otherwise, even if he believed it otherwise. "Reece, don't listen to him. You know the kind of man he is."

"Yes, I do."

But what kind of woman are you? What do I really know of you, after all? The questions tore through Reece's heart, for there could be no mistaking what

Benedict was implying to one who knew what had transpired last night. She had been told to do anything to get him to keep her. She had been ordered to...

Surely it couldn't be. Please God, her desire and her affection could not have been feigned, even if they had known one another for such a short time. His feelings were sincere enough, and he had known her just as briefly.

Who do you think you are, boy? Blaidd Morgan?

He had feared what being tied to her half brothers would mean to his future; he had not stopped to think that Anne herself might be cause for worry. But the memory of Anne's impassioned, heated kisses—the way her kisses had been from the very start—shattered him now.

Suddenly, every moment he had shared with Anne twisted and took a different, terrible shape. What if everything he had done, from the first moment he had spoken to Anne in the corridor, had played into Damon's hands?

Anne had claimed to find his attention in the corridor unwelcome and impertinent, but she had not left. If she truly had not welcomed his company, why had she not told him so in no uncertain terms and gone on her way?

Damon and Benedict had attacked him with far more violence than his actions warranted, then spread the word of attempted rape. He had thought that was only to justify their attack, but perhaps they had foreseen that marriage might be the result, a necessary end to preserve their sister's honor.

All Anne's questions on the journey took on a sinister cast. God save him, was it possible she herself had given him a clue to her deceptive abilities when she feigned swooning in the king's hall? Had he been blinded by temptation and desire and the demands of his flesh?

The pieces of his shattered heart gathered and reassembled into something wounded and broken, hard and sharp as the ends of quarried stone. He faced his wife resolute, inexorable. "Anne, is there any truth to anything this man says?"

Anne's impassioned eyes shone with sincerity as she fervently clasped her hands—a sincerity that might be feigned by a clever woman, and Anne was no fool.

"Damon did want me to be a spy here," she said, "to tell him what I could learn of your allies and your fortress. Benedict followed us here because I was to give the information to him, and he was to take it to Damon at court. At first, I was willing to go along with Damon's demand because of his threats, but then I refused."

"When did you refuse?" Reece asked, his deep voice as dead as his trust.

"Today."

After they had made love.

Again the shattered pieces of his heart shivered and

regrouped, stirred by the faint hope that he was wrong to doubt her.

And yet, *what did he really know of her?*

At first he had believed himself a fool to follow her and start the boulder of disaster rolling down the slope, threatening to ruin the plans he had for his future. Had he been a greater fool to make love with her, joining them forever as man and wife?

"What happened to change your mind?" Sir Urien asked.

Anne glanced at Reece and saw the doubt in his eyes, his very stance.

He believed Benedict and not her?

If he loved her, would he not trust her? She had erred by not revealing Damon's plan sooner, but otherwise she was innocent.

Yet if all he felt for her was but lust, the sort of earthy passion that could be destroyed with a rumor or a hint of impropriety...if all he wanted was to share her bed because she was beautiful...

A wail of despair began within her, until her pride forced it back.

"I ask you again, my lady," Sir Urien said, his voice firm. "What happened to change your mind?"

"Ask your son."

"I am asking you."

She tossed her head. If Reece would not intervene, if he would not put a stop to this interrogation, or confess what they had done—for clearly his father and brother were ignorant of that—she would stand alone, as she had always done. "I decided I would rather live in Castle Gervais than Montbleu. Nor did I wish to marry another man of Damon's choosing. Your son, my lord, is young and handsome, and I could not be certain Damon's choice would be."

She didn't care if her words wounded Reece. His mistrust had been like a stake through her body.

"A very convenient tale, my lady," Gervais observed, his glare like a knife flaying her flesh. "But if you were unwilling to do as Damon ordered, why did you say nothing to Reece or my father?"

"Because I thought it was not necessary for you to know. I told Benedict to return to Damon and tell him I would not spy for him."

"So you say now," Gervais noted, while her husband still said nothing. He neither spoke nor moved. He might be dead and propped against the table.

"She did," Benedict affirmed. "I don't know anything. I've done nothing wrong. It isn't a crime to talk to your—"

"Hold your tongue!" Sir Urien ordered, his tone so imperious Benedict cringed and seemed to shrink before them as he fell silent.

"If you are as innocent as you claim," Gervais continued, "why did we have to learn of your meeting with Benedict from another?"

That had to be Piers, Anne thought, her despair increasing. That was why he had been in the solar. He must have been in the village that afternoon and seen them together.

And then he had gone to Reece instead of coming to her, the woman who had devoted her life to him.

How could he not come to her first and give her the chance to explain? How could he not give her that opportunity? Did he not trust her, either?

Were men's affections so shallow, their love so easily overcome? Was this to be the repayment for her love, her passion and her devotion? That her husband and her brother would both so quickly leap to the conclusion that she was untrustworthy and dishonorable?

If so, she had wasted her entire life, and her dreams had truly been delusions.

But who was more at fault? She, because she loved with all her heart?

No, them, because they did not.

Anger, resolution and pride stanched the wound in her soul and gave her strength. Thus strengthened—or hardened—she faced them resolutely.

"As I have already explained, I decided I did not want to be a spy, and that Damon's threat to take Piers away and insure I never saw him again was meaningless. Piers was here, and you would help me keep him here. Or so I thought."

Reece straightened and his eyes flared with another emotion, but it was too late. She glared at him, her hopes and dreams and love for him like so much ash at her feet.

"Of course Damon threatened me, through the one person I love. Why else would I ever agree to such a thing? I have my honor, too, Reece, although you thought little of that when you followed me from the king's hall, or were so quick to accuse me of base deception. But I thought...hoped...deluded myself into believing that you would support me against my half brother. Obviously, I was wrong.''

He believed her duplicitous; would he prove *himself* otherwise, and admit that the grounds to destroy their union no longer existed? ''How soon can we have our marriage annulled?'' she demanded, her words a challenge. Would he admit the grounds no longer existed, or would he grab the chance to be rid of her, even though it meant deceiving his family?

''We are summoned to court at once,'' he replied flatly.

So, after all his talk of love and honor, he would choose deception and be rid of her. ''If you will all excuse me, I believe this discussion is ended.''

With that, she turned on her heel and marched to the door. Then, her stern resolution faltered, for the one thing that had been the center of her life could not be easily forgotten or denied. She halted at the door and turned back, looking only at Sir Urien. ''And Piers?''

Sir Urien's expression was as unreadable as his son's. ''If he wishes to stay, he may. But it shall be as you choose.''

''No, my lord,'' she replied as she opened the door. ''He will stay because he has already chosen.''

Numb, Reece stared at the door after Anne slammed it shut. Only this morning, his future had been bright as the sun on a summer's day; now it was as dark and bleak as midnight in the northern mountains.

Daggers of self-doubt ripped at him. After Benedict's words and her own confession, how could he be sure that anything she had ever said or done was true, even to loving him in return?

Especially loving him.

The sullen Benedict shifted, drawing Reece's attention and breaking the tense silence. "You heard her. I never did anything wrong. She never told me anything."

"Innocent of helping Damon you may ultimately be," Gervais said, "but there is the matter of the dead woman found in an inn on the way here."

Benedict's jaw dropped, then his mouth snapped shut. "I don't know what you're talking about."

"That will be for the court to decide, Delasaine," Gervais replied. "Somebody who looked a lot like you was seen riding from the inn before her body was found, and you must know this is not the first time such an accusation has been muttered about you. We shall take you back to that shire, where you can await the king's justice. Now come."

"But I am innocent," he protested. With a look of panic, he turned to Reece. "We are related by marriage now, Fitzroy. You must help me!"

Disgust and anger overwhelmed Reece's dismay. "Yes, I am your brother-in-law, for the present. Because I am, I will see that you have counsel before the court, but if you are guilty, you will have to pay the penalty of law.''

Benedict stared at him, wide-eyed with disbelief and fear. Then, with a roar, he dove at Gervais, who was closest to the door, knocking him down.

As his father hurried to Gervais, Reece tackled Benedict before he could get to the door, bringing him down as a hound does a stag. Straddling the struggling man, full of rage over what the Delasaines had done to him and to Anne, knowing that they had robbed him of his chance for true happiness with her, Reece raised his hand, ready to strike.

Benedict's eyes filled with tears and, with a cry like a terrified child, he threw his arms over his flushed face to ward off the blow.

Panting hard, Reece slowly lowered his fist. ''I will be content to let the king's justice deal with you, Benedict Delasaine, and may God have mercy on you despite all that you have done.''

With that, he climbed off the fallen man and walked to the farthest corner of the solar, as if the man's very breath could taint him.

His sword drawn, Gervais went to Benedict and hauled him to his feet. ''Come with me, and don't try anything. Reece might not be willing to hurt you, but I am. In fact, I'd welcome the chance.''

As Gervais pulled him from the room, Sir Urien went to stand beside his son. ''What do you want us to do?'' he asked after a moment.

''Take him to London for judgment.''

"I meant about Anne."

Reece turned to his father, no longer a boy facing his father, but as one man to another. "We return to court, as the king commands."

Sir Urien put his hand on his son's shoulder. "I'm sorry, Reece. Let me help—"

"No," Reece said firmly. "She is my wife, and this is for me to deal with."

Unsure what he was going to do, Reece left the solar. He shook his head to clear it as he continued through the hall and out into courtyard, not really caring where he went until he reached the cool, quiet little chapel that would be deserted this time of day. He ducked inside and leaned back against the closed door, inhaling the familiar scent of incense and candle wax.

He slowly slid down until he was sitting on the frigid flagstones.

Then he wrapped his arms about his knees and hid his face. *Oh, God,* he silently cried, the words a cross between a prayer and a plea. *What am I going to do?*

The memory of making love with Anne arose. Had she been lying to him when she gave herself to him in that wondrous intimacy?

Although he had felt not an inkling of a doubt of the sincerity of her emotions last night, all his past insecurities made him wonder if he had seen merely his own love mirrored back, because he wished it so.

Yet as he sat, alone and despairing, hope and love refused to die. Deep in the core of his heart, his love for her still lived and urged him to believe her version of events.

He remembered her as she faced them in the solar just a short time ago—determined, resolute, alone.

Alone. Aye, alone, one woman bravely facing three knights who stood accusing her of a terrible crime. She was as alone as she had been when Damon had threatened her back at court and ordered her to do his bidding. What else could she do but agree, or lose her brother? Then she did not love her husband, or he her. Then it was different.

She had always been alone, in many ways. And if he had been alone all his life, making decisions with no help, no succor, might he not be loath to ask for assistance, or tell anyone his troubles? Might he not come to believe he must and would deal with those troubles on his own?

Oh, sweet Jesu, what had he done?

Chapter Eighteen

Suddenly certain of what he must do, Reece rose and threw open the door to the chapel. He ran across the courtyard and tore through the hall, ignoring his mother, his father, Gervais, Lisette, Donald, Seldon and everyone else assembled there once a quick survey told him Anne was not.

He took the steps to their chamber two at a time and grabbed the latch. When he pushed down, he discovered the door was locked.

He pounded on the oaken door so hard it rattled. "Anne! Anne! I must speak with you! Anne, please!"

For a long moment, as he held his breath and listened, he feared she wasn't going to answer.

Then the door flew open. Anne stood there, as still and cold and hard as a granite statue in the dead of winter. "Go away, Reece," she said, her voice even colder. "You have nothing to say that I wish to hear."

"But Anne—"

"No!" she cried, glaring at him, all the cold suddenly turned to heat, her whole body quivering with the rage of years of being treated as if she were unimportant or unworthy heating her blood. "You have already shown me what you think of me! There is nothing you can say to make me forget that as I tried to explain what I had done, you would not believe me."

"Anne, please, I love you—"

"Love!" she cried, stepping back as if the word had been a blow. "Is it love that is so quick to render harsh judgment? Is it love that makes you listen to a man you know to be a liar before your own wife? I thought that you were different, that you saw me as more than a body to take to your bed. I thought there was something better, stronger, truer, between us. But I know now I was wrong. I was a fool to think you loved me."

"But I did! I do! I was shocked and—"

"And so, despite this love you profess, in spite of what we shared last night, you leapt to the conclusion that I would still betray you." Her eyes seemed to fairly shoot with flames of indignation and anger. "If that is your idea of love, I do not want it! I do not want to be your wife!"

With that, she grabbed the door and threw it shut.

Anne would not speak to Reece during the whole of the journey back to court, either. Even Esmerelda seemed to feel the tension, barely lifting her feet as they traveled along the muddy road, for the fine autumn weather had given way to a gray winter's chilling rain.

But Anne had meant what she said, and she believed it still: if Reece truly loved her, he would not have been so quick to assume the worst of her. He was no different from any other man, and she had been a fool to believe otherwise.

She tried not to remember taking solemn leave of Piers. What she had always feared had come to pass. Piers was being taken from her, and while he would be better off with Sir Urien, her heart had been more broken all the same.

It had been difficult to leave Lisette, too. When she had bluntly told her maid that the marriage to Sir Reece was to be annulled, Lisette had stared in shock at first, then burst into tears and begged to stay in Bridgeford Wells. She loved Donald and wanted to be with him. He had even asked her to be his wife.

Anne had been surprised, for Donald was a knight and Lisette but a serving maid, but Lisette's impassioned words quickly told her that she had heard aright. Donald was going to marry a maidservant because, Lisette explained, he didn't care what people thought of him. He never had—unlike Reece.

Anne had assured Lisette that she could stay if she wanted, and although she had not said so to Lisette, she thought it would be some small comfort to have at least one of them happy.

Benedict had been taken away to face the charge of murdering the tavern wench, that grim cortege headed by Sir Gervais. Lady Fritha had stayed behind at Bridgeford Wells.

That leave-taking had been difficult, too. Lady Fritha had been sympathetic, and yet her first care must be to her son, so she kept a certain cool distance. Anne understood why, but it was painful nonetheless.

Sir Urien had come with them, his stern presence adding to the gloomy atmosphere. As for Reece, she utterly and completely ignored him, even when they arrived at court at last. Damon came to her chamber nearly as soon as she had been escorted there by the queen's servants, but she refused to see him, too. She would be back under his control soon enough; until then, she would not speak with him or explain anything. Let him find out what had happened to Benedict on his own. All her energy must be concentrated on getting through the audience with the king, when Reece would ask for the annulment.

When they would both stand before the king and lie.

Soon enough, the summons came. She refused to walk into the hall with her husband and his father. She was alone in the world, and she would be alone there, too. She gave them time to get there first before she slowly made her way to the great hall.

As before, the crowd parted for her. She ignored the whispers and curious stares, and kept her gaze focused on the king and queen seated on their thrones. They were as richly dressed as always, and Eleanor's eyes gleamed with a crude nosiness that turned Anne's

stomach. This was her life on display, her future to be
decided, and Eleanor looked like a scullery maid over-
hearing a choice bit of gossip.

His father to his right, Reece stood in front of the
throne, watching her approach. She steeled herself to
feel nothing, to notice nothing—not how magnificent
he looked in the king's hall and as if he belonged
there, not the hungry look in his eyes or the tension
in his shoulders. She would not look at him at all, if
she could help it.

Out of the corner of her eye she spotted Damon
who, not surprisingly, looked far from pleased to see
her there. She would not glance his way again.

The Fitzroys' Welsh friends stood on the other side
of the throne. She paid no heed to them, either, as she
came to a halt and made her obeisance to the king and
his queen.

"Welcome back to my court, Lady Anne," the king
began. "How fare you, my lady? Feeling faint?
Should we adjourn to my solar?"

She flushed hotly but held her head high. "If you
wish, sire."

"No, I do not wish to meet in private this time,"
Henry replied, surprising her with his stern manner as
much as his words. "I wish to have this matter settled
once and for all, and I will do so in public, where
there is less chance for rumor and gossip to twist the
truth."

If it had to be in public, there was nothing she
could do.

Henry turned and addressed Reece. "I have heard that you have come to ask my permission for something."

Reece stepped forward. "Yes, sire. That is why my brother Gervais sought this audience."

"Your brother informs me you wish to have your marriage annulled."

Before Reece could answer and follow through with what he had planned all along despite the intimacy they had shared, Damon pushed his way forward. "That's impossible!"

A sharp look from the king brought Damon to a halt a few feet from the dais.

"I beg your pardon, sire," Damon declared, "but this is outrageous! An annulment? Ridiculous! Why, you yourself ordered their marriage and—"

"I know full well what I ordered," the king interrupted.

"On what grounds, sire?" Damon demanded, glaring at Reece.

"Nonconsummation," Henry supplied.

A murmur of scandalized surprise rose from the crowd, but Anne still held her head high. She was innocent in all of this and she would not act guilty or ashamed.

Not now, and not ever.

"That's impossible!" Damon repeated.

Reece raised a brow and quietly inquired, "How do you know it is impossible? You have been here at court."

Anne waited with bated breath for Reece to announce to the whole court that he had never made love to her.

To destroy their marriage.

It was what she wanted, too.

Wasn't it?

It was as she had expected.

Wasn't it?

It was what she had demanded of him. What she still believed must be.

Wasn't it?

The king addressed Anne. "Well, my lady, is there, in fact, a basis for an annulment?"

Yes, but not the one he meant. The annulment should be because Reece did not truly love her and did not trust her. To say yes for any other reason would be to lie to the king, her sovereign. To agree to the lie that they had not made love would be to dishonor herself and make herself the liar Reece believed her to be.

Reece turned toward her, no doubt waiting for her to tell the falsehood that would separate them forever, just as he had originally planned.

Then, there came to his face a look of such regret and longing she could scarcely believe the evidence of her eyes, and in plain view of the whole court of King Henry, Sir Reece Fitzroy went down on his knee before her and bowed his head in humble contrition.

"Anne," he began in a loud, steady voice that all the court could hear, "I am a proud, stubborn, pig-headed fool. I should have realized at once that all your experience has taught you to be secretive for your own protection. That for most of your life you have had no one to rely on except yourself. That you learned to keep truths hidden if that would prevent conflict. When you did not tell me about Benedict, you were only trying to protect me from knowledge that you believed would do no harm.

"And how did I repay you for that protection? I showed you that love does not mean trust or faith or gratitude. I acted as if love is easily cast aside at the first hint of trouble."

He reached out and took her hands in his, then looked up into her incredulous face with pleading eyes. "I should have listened to you and trusted you. I should have understood how difficult it was for you, and how love for a brother could make even a person as strong as you go against the dictates of honor when it came to protecting him.

"So now I would have all here for my witnesses. I love you with all my heart, Anne. I do not want an annulment. I want to be your husband for the rest of my life."

Sir Urien stepped forward.

Reece glanced at him sharply. "Father, I understand your concerns, but they are not nearly so important to me as regaining Anne's trust and, I hope, her love."

Then Reece forgot his father, the king, and the court, all his attention focused on the woman he loved, the woman *he* had betrayed with his mistrust, and without whom his life would be incomplete. "Anne," he pleaded softly, "can you forgive me? Can we begin again?"

"But you do not trust me…"

"I did not trust my own heart. I did not have faith in my own love. And I was wrong. Terribly, horribly wrong. I would put my life in your hands without a second thought, and I promise I will never doubt you again."

"What of my family and your worthy ambition?"

"I will either succeed with you by my side, or fail and have you to comfort me—I hope."

As Anne looked into his pleading eyes, all the love she had been trying to deny after the horrible confrontation at Castle Gervais burst free, unconstrained, and happiness filled her. Then, like the first rays of sunlight after a black night of despair, Anne's eyes sparkled with new and vibrant life, and her lips curved up in a glorious smile. "After such eloquence, how can I deny you a second chance?"

Reece gathered her into his arms and his mouth found hers. Anne returned his kiss with all the passion she had ever felt, and as their kiss deepened, another murmur went up from the court, as if all the ladies present exhaled as one.

"I have loved you from the first," she whispered, "and despite all that I said and all my anguish, I could not stop."

King Henry cleared his throat, reminding them that

they were not alone. "Well, it seems this problem has found its own solution."

"Sire, a moment," Gervais said.

He came up to Reece, who reluctantly stopped kissing Anne but kept his arms around her.

"Are you mad, Reece?" he demanded in a low voice.

"I am in love." With a little smile of apology, he said, "I am sorry for your wasted time and effort, but we can't annul the marriage anyway. It's too late."

"What?"

"You heard me. It's too late. The marriage was consummated before we left home, because I love her."

There were more sighs, and some muffled laughter, as well as murmurs of approval from several of the male courtiers.

Gervais spun on his heel. "Father, how could he—!"

"The usual way, I expect," Sir Urien Fitzroy calmly interrupted. "Leave it, Gervais. They are in love, and they are husband and wife."

He raised his voice and addressed the brooding Damon Delasaine whom Reece had forgotten. "She is under our protection now, so you approach her at your peril. Aye, and Piers, too, who has the makings of a much better knight than you will ever be."

Reece let go of Anne and staunchly faced the king. "Sire, I would have a word with you, if I may. Or rather, a few. Of warning."

"Reece—"

"No, Father. Damon is my brother-in-law. Let me deal with this."

"Sire," Damon protested, fear gleaming in his dark eyes, "as you know, there is bad blood between Reece Fitzroy and my family—"

"Between you and Benedict and my family," Reece clarified, his hand finding Anne's, his warm touch thrilling as always, if not more so now.

Damon scowled at them, then smiled at the king. "This man speaks with malicious intent to do me harm in any way he can."

"Are you questioning my honesty and my honor?" Reece demanded. "Do you think I will tell lies about you? Or is it that the truth will damn you?"

"Eleanor," Damon cried, turning to the queen, "are you going to let him insult your relative?"

The queen's eyes glittered like hard little stones. "I think that if you are a wise man, Sir Damon, you will take yourself home at once and come rarely, if ever, to this court. Then Sir Reece will not be forced to defend his honor in a fair competition, which my royal husband may decide is the best way to decide who is in the right. In fact, I think he most certainly would."

Reece put his hand on the hilt of his sword. "I am willing to meet Damon on the field of combat, my liege, since I have my own score to settle with him."

"I will not taint my sword with the blood of a bastard's son!" Damon snarled.

"I fear you overestimate your skill in many

things,'' Henry said. ''It is rather more likely that Reece's sword would be tainted with yours. A wise man, Damon, ought to know when to quit the field. You, alas, are not a wise man, as so many of my loyal subjects have been anxious to point out.''

''Sire, I—''

Henry rose in fierce, indignant majesty. ''We also understand your brother is about to face trial for a most heinous murder. You are both a disgrace to your family, this court and your country. I strip you of your title and Montbleu.'' Henry signaled to his guards. ''Take him to join his brother in the Tower.''

Damon fell to his knees sobbing and held out his hands to Anne. ''Anne, help me! Don't let them do this! I took care of you!''

Anne looked down at him. Completely humbled, groveling at her feet, he was more terrified than she had ever been at his hands, and for the first time in her life, she pitied him. She looked to the king. ''Sire, perhaps banishment—?''

Henry frowned with irritation as the guards hauled Damon to his feet. ''The courts will decide his fate,'' he declared with absolute finality, and Anne knew there was nothing more she could do for him.

Damon sobbed and pleaded for mercy and forgiveness as the guards dragged him away past the solemn courtiers. The sounds of his cries disappearing in the distance made her want to weep, in spite of all that he had done.

''As for Montbleu, my lady,'' the king said, breaking the hushed silence, "I give that to your brother, Piers."

Anne blinked back her tears and made a tremulous smile of thanks, happy for Piers's sake.

"I trust he will rule it better than his half brothers."

"He will, sire. I promise you, he will."

"Well, I daresay he could hardly do worse," Henry muttered. His expression remained stern, but the expression in his eyes lightened. "Now I trust we shall have no more complaints from you, Lady Anne, or your husband, or your younger brother?"

"You shall have none from me, sire," she assured him as Reece put his arm around her and held her close.

"Or from me, Your Majesty," he seconded. "Where my brother-in-law is concerned, however, I regret I can make no promises. I have learned the folly of making assumptions about people."

Henry rolled his eyes, but there was merriment in his tone when he spoke. "God save me from Piers Delasaine, then, if he is anything like his sister. I don't think I've ever met such a bold—"

Eleanor cleared her throat, and the king fell silent. Then he blushed like a little boy about to be scolded as his wife smiled blandly at Reece. "Sir Reece, I suggest you take your lady wife somewhere private and ask her again for forgiveness." She smiled as if nothing of serious import had just transpired. "Your very charming apology should serve as an inspiration to all young men. Now you and your family have our leave to go, so that the courtiers can gossip with more freedom. Do you not agree, Henry?''

Eleanor laid her hand lightly on the king's arm and leaned close, brushing her breasts against him. She whispered something in his ear that made the tips of his ears redden.

''Yes, of course, they may go,'' he said, looking at her with an expression Anne recognized. Politically, a king in love with his wife might not be the best of things, but Henry was not a baby or a child. He was a grown man, and had to take responsibility for his own choices, whether Eleanor expressed an opinion or not.

However, the state of the king's marriage was far less important to her at that moment than her own, so when Reece took her arm to escort her from the hall, she went eagerly and he had to ask her to slow down. ''Or what will they think, my lady?'' he whispered.

''I do not care,'' she replied, marching briskly past a group of gaping courtiers.

Unfortunately, they could not be alone just yet, for Gervais came hot on their heels. ''You might have told a body!'' he declared, catching up to them.

Anne halted, partly to catch her breath, and so did Reece.

''There will be plenty of time to discuss what has happened,'' Sir Urien declared as he, too, joined them in the hall, the Welshmen right behind. ''Let Reece and Anne go and make—'' He fell silent.

Then, to Anne's delight, the stern, formidable Sir

Urien blushed like a boy. "Make up," he finished in an embarrassed mutter.

"Aye, Gervais, don't keep them two standing in the corridor all day," Blaidd said with a good-natured smile and a very lascivious wink.

"Not Welsh, are they?" Kynan remarked in an aside to his brother.

"My son has some dignity," Sir Urien retorted with a stern majesty that would have intimidated Anne before, but did no longer.

"Poor sod." Blaidd sighed, his eyes twinkling.

With a laugh, Reece swept Anne up into his arms. "I'll leave you all discussing my dignity or lack thereof, for you heard the queen. I must apologize some more to my wife."

"Interesting way to put it," Anne observed in an amused yet sultry voice as she wrapped her arms about her husband's neck.

"I intend to be very thorough about it," Reece vowed as he carried her away. "Just as I will love you for the rest of my life."

"And I, you, my husband," Anne whispered as she nestled in his arms, safe and free and beloved at last.

*   *   *   *   *

MARGARET MOORE

Award-winning author Margaret Moore actually began her career at the age of eight, when she and a friend concocted stories featuring a lovely damsel and a handsome, misunderstood thief nicknamed "The Red Sheik." She's had a soft spot for dashing rogues ever since.

Unknowingly pursuing her destiny, Margaret graduated with distinction from the University of Toronto with a Bachelor of Arts degree in English literature. Margaret was a Leading Wren with the Royal Canadian Naval Reserve, where she learned many new skills, including how to spit-shine shoes and the joy of marching for no discernible reason.

Since selling her first book to Harlequin in 1991, Margaret has written more than twenty historical romance novels and novellas for Harlequin Historicals® and Avon Books. Margaret lives in Toronto, Ontario, with her husband, two teenagers and two cats. You can write to her c/o Harlequin Historicals, 300 East 42nd Street, New York, NY 10017, or visit her Web site at www.geocities.com/margaretmoorewilkins.

ENJOY THE SPLENDOR OF
Merry Old England

with these spirited stories
from Harlequin Historicals

On Sale November 2002

GIFTS OF THE SEASON
by Miranda Jarrett
Lyn Stone
Anne Gracie

*Three beloved authors come together in this
Regency Christmas collection!*

THE DUMONT BRIDE
by Terri Brisbin

*Will a marriage of convenience between a lovely
English heiress and a dashing French count
blossom into everlasting love?*

On Sale December 2002

NORWYCK'S LADY
by Margo Maguire

*Passion and adventure unfold when an injured
Scottish woman washes up on shore and is
rescued by an embittered lord!*

LORD SEBASTIAN'S WIFE
by Katy Cooper

*Watch the sparks fly when a world-weary nobleman
discovers that his adolescent betrothal to a deceptive
lady from his youth is legal and binding!*

 Harlequin Historicals®
Historical Romantic Adventure!

HHMED27

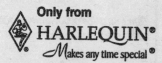

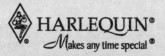

Princes...Princesses...
London Castles...New York Mansions...
To live the life of a royal!

In 2002, Harlequin Books lets you escape to a
world of royalty with these royally themed titles:

Temptation:
January 2002—*A Prince of a Guy* (#861)
February 2002—*A Noble Pursuit* (#865)

American Romance:
The Carradignes: American Royalty (Editorially linked series)
March 2002—*The Improperly Pregnant Princess* (#913)
April 2002—*The Unlawfully Wedded Princess* (#917)
May 2002—*The Simply Scandalous Princess* (#921)
November 2002—*The Inconveniently Engaged Prince* (#945)

Intrigue:
The Carradignes: A Royal Mystery (Editorially linked series)
June 2002—*The Duke's Covert Mission* (#666)

Chicago Confidential
September 2002—*Prince Under Cover* (#678)

The Crown Affair
October 2002—*Royal Target* (#682)
November 2002—*Royal Ransom* (#686)
December 2002—*Royal Pursuit* (#690)

Harlequin Romance:
June 2002—*His Majesty's Marriage* (#3703)
July 2002—*The Prince's Proposal* (#3709)

Harlequin Presents:
August 2002—*Society Weddings* (#2268)
September 2002—*The Prince's Pleasure* (#2274)

Duets:
September 2002—*Once Upon a Tiara/Henry Ever After* (#83)
October 2002—*Natalia's Story/Andrea's Story* (#85)

 **Celebrate a year of royalty with
Harlequin Books!**

Available at your favorite retail outlet.

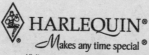

HARLEQUIN®
Makes any time special ®

Visit us at www.eHarlequin.com

HSROY02

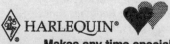